Past Praise for author Mindy

For *Hindsight*

"Tarquini charms her audience with heady wit and laugh-out-loud humor
... This is a fast-reading, enjoyable journey through past and present that
many readers will enjoy."

—*Booklist*

"*Hindsight* is an evocative and inventive reincarnation tale. Drawing on
snippets of wisdom from long-gone literary giants, including Chaucer,
Dante, Goethe, and Kipling, Tarquini illustrates the eternal universality
of human behavior ... the narrative emphasizes the importance of acting
in the here and now: saying what should be said, forgiving what needs to
be forgiven, embracing opportunities to deepen connections with others,
and seizing moments of happiness when they're presented. Consequently,
Hindsight is a sustaining and deeply personal reading experience."

—*Foreword Reviews*, FIVE STARS,
Book of the Day Selection

"Tarquini's innovative concept is paired with realistic characters and
sparkling wit, making this enjoyable novel a keeper."

—*Publishers Weekly*, Starred Review

"This contemporary jewel is a literary parade that reminds us to live life
fully in the now."

—*Working Mother*, "21 New Books to Fall for This Autumn"

"Witty and thought-provoking, Mindy Tarquini's debut is a must-read for
lovers of Chaucer, magical realism and literary ingenuity."

—Buzzfeed

"Funny and irreverent, this modern fable is a good reminder to love the
life you have."

—*Real Simple*

"This charming contemporary fable marks a fabulous debut for author
Mindy Tarquini."

—SheKnows, "The best books written by women
you need to read this fall"

The INFINITE NOW

The INFINITE NOW

MINDY TARQUINI

spark
press

Published by SparkPress, a BookSparks imprint,
A division of SparkPoint Studio, LLC
Tempe, Arizona, USA, 85281
www.gosparkpress.com

Published 2017
Printed in the United States of America
ISBN: 978-1-943006-34-2 (pbk)
ISBN: 978-1-943006-35-9 (e-bk)
Library of Congress Control Number: 2017945547

For Rosie,
who is always very brave.

The Scourge

A long time ago, and a very long time after, historians told us the disease started as a tiny outbreak in a remote farming community. A farming community in a far-off place called Kansas. A place where tornadoes swept in without warning, strong enough to carry a house over the rainbow, and land it in a magical world.

The community's doctor treated the stricken with the strongest medications he had—antitoxins, against diphtheria, maybe tetanus—confounded by a disease which looked like influenza, but killed faster than plague. A disease which targeted the young, the healthy, the hope for the future.

The disease might have stayed in that far-flung farming community chained by isolation and weather, but for a more powerful pestilence. Flagrant and fulminant and indiscriminately destructive.

War.

Virulent enough to infect with patriotic fervor, overwhelm patriotic dissent, redraw our boundaries, redefine our limits, and sweep other news to the sidebars.

We saw the shadow descending. We scurried for cover. We cowered, constrained by a wall of ignorance.

The shadow, when it landed, crushed us all.

Exposure

One

September 25, 1918
Philadelphia

I was deposited at the old man's door, wet, cold, and hungry, my possessions clutched in a blanket-wrapped bundle and my dignity in tatters. Brought there by the tailor's wife, who worried about contagion.

"I can't take her." She put a hand on my shoulder and pushed me into the room. "I have to protect my children. What if she gets sick?"

Eyes downcast, all I saw were the old man's shoes, every crevice clean and the leather over the toes reflecting the floor's speckled linoleum. The laces were new.

The old man tapped his heel. Three times. "It'd be better for her to go with a woman. The Widow Frezza, perhaps. She is lame. This young lady could be useful." His voice, deep and gravelly, trailed off.

Useful. Like an ugly scarf. Unwanted, but serviceable.

"Impossible. This is Rosina Vicente's daughter." The tailor's wife said my mother's name in a rush, as if she feared letting it land too solidly on her tongue. "There is nobody else. No place for her to go. Her parents are dead. The landlord turned her out. Was I supposed to leave her on the street? What if she got angry?" She gave me another nudge. "You've lived your life. If you die . . . What I mean is, no one depends on you."

Fear makes the wise foolish, and the tailor's wife was not wise. Even so, all these many years later, I remember her words and my breath still catches, my cheeks still burn. Like I was the one who said it.

The old man made a clicking noise, tongue against the roof of his mouth, faster, then slower, the way I do sometimes when I'm trying to think. "There are no relatives?"

The tailor's wife crossed her arms. "I heard maybe a cousin."

He touched my elbow. "Is there a cousin?"

There was, a fat man who used to sit at my parents' table and eat all they had, wine trailing a spittle-filled path down his chin. "He stayed with us when he first arrived. But he went west. To Pittsburgh. To work in the steel mills."

The old man put out a finger. He lifted my chin, raising my gaze past shins covered in brown felt spats, shoe coverings which buttoned to the knee. The spats ended at the bottom of well-creased tweed knickerbockers, the short pants of the time, into which was tucked a tailored linen shirt, its every seam and pocket reinforced by a double row of expert stitching. "Then what are we to do with you?"

I looked him in the eyes, tried to take his measure in their smoky depths, so close in color to Poppa's. All that returned was a cold neutrality, blue-gray and grim and incisive as shears.

I looked past him. A kettle heated on an enameled gas stove; a loaf lay on a cutting board beside. The scene was a warm spot in a world gone cold, and my mind filled with images of hot tea and toast and frozen toes thawing while I waited.

My stomach grumbled. "You don't have to do anything about me. Nothing about me needs doing. I've already written to my brothers. They are fighting in the war. Soon they will return."

"Tomorrow we will write to your brothers again. Let them know that you are here." The old man pointed to a hook by the entrance. "In the meantime, hang your coat there."

I did so. The tailor's wife took me by the arm. "I am two floors down. If you need anything. Do you understand? Not the first door. That one goes to the shop. The one next to it, closest to the stairs."

"With the big iron ring." I pointed to a similar knocker hanging from the old man's door.

She touched fingers to forehead and heart, then flicked them to either side in a miniature sign of the cross, put the tips to her lips, and kissed them, nose scrunched like she'd stepped in something impolite to mention.

Perhaps she hadn't expected me to be so observant.

She set her gaze on the old man. "I'll check in tomorrow, maybe the day after. With all the preparations for the parade, we are working day and night. Banners. And streamers for the Sons of Italy." She jutted her chin. "All she has is in her hands. She says the landlord kept the rest. I don't know if she has any money. I didn't ask. With so many sick, I'd suggest she look for a job, but considering what's happened, who would hire her?"

Heat rushed across my forehead, fire across my chest. My hands jerked. My fingers twitched. I was sick, also, sick of it all—the sideways glances, the whispered prayers, averted eyes, and subtle gestures.

Superstitions. Silly, backward, soul-stymieing superstitions. Stitched into the fabric of our society. Shaken out in times of crisis. Shrouding our struggling-to-be-modern world.

I dropped my bundle to the floor, bent, turned up the hem of the tailor's wife's skirt, and waggled it at her. "You know who'll hire me? Somebody who doesn't like stitches long enough to strangle a cat."

The tailor's wife backed up a step, shaking her skirt to dislodge my grip. I held on, wishing I had a pin to puncture her insufferable presumption.

The old man wrapped a firm hand over mine and pried the fabric from between my fingers. "I don't need the young lady's money."

"I didn't mean it that way, Don Sebastiano. I meant—"

"It is fine, Signora Lattanzi. I know what you meant." He moved with her onto the landing, closing the door behind him.

Don. A title of deference, of distinction, reserved for those held in highest esteem. Men of great knowledge. And breeding. I glanced at a collection of buttonhooks hanging beneath a drugstore calendar advertising the benefits of castor oil.

Not a title for shoemakers.

Maybe he owned the building.

I pressed my ear to the door, fingertips splayed across the wood, but all I got was muffles, his stalwart and steady, hers strident, then meek. Her descending steps followed, and I had the impression that whatever their argument, the old man had won.

The handle turned. I stumbled back, all innocence. He entered the room. "So tell me, Rosina Vicente's daughter, do you have a name?"

I drew myself to my full height, near standing on tippy-toes. "Fiora. I am seventeen years old."

The old man eyed me.

I settled back onto my heels. "Almost seventeen. Another six months." My stance slumped. "Or more."

He waved my comments to the side. "Sixteen. Seventeen. What's it matter? Have no worries. We will be fine."

We. For five days it'd been only me after sixteen years with a mamma and a poppa and two brothers who used to tug on my braid before they went to fight the Kaiser, or maybe it was the Turks, in a place called the Isonzo.

I dug deep into a pocket and pulled out an envelope. I gave it to the old man. "Six dollars and fifty-two cents. What Mamma had hidden in the sugar bowl. That should be enough for a week, maybe two. Maybe more if you let me do some chores to make up the difference." The old man didn't need to know about the other money, twisted into a handkerchief I'd pinned between my breasts. "What I mean is, when my brothers return, they will pay you for anything I can't cover."

The old man opened the envelope and counted the contents. "I will find a safe place for this. You're such a little thing, I doubt you eat enough to make a difference. When the time is right, we will put this money to good use for you."

Little. Maybe. But I could eat as much as any boy. Two boys. And smart as three. Poppa always said so.

The old man took my bundle and placed it near the stove. I thought he meant that I should sleep there, then he opened a door onto a narrow staircase tucked on the other side of the wall behind it. "This leads to an attic. It has no heat register, but there's a bed, and privacy."

The kettle whistled. The old man beckoned me to a central table surrounded by benches and covered in tools. The headline of an Italian-language newspaper lying against a shoe form assured, L'INFLUENZA DI PHILADELPHIA È CONTROLLATO. The influenza outbreak was under control.

At that time, the building was new, one of many constructed to house a population exploding with workers who flocked to high-paying factories because of the war in Europe. Despite the beveled trim crowning the room, the intricate birds carved on a wooden chest beside a cot on the far wall, and the trim on the window curtains, the space felt run-down. Lifeless. A place to eat and sleep and work. Nothing more.

The old man picked up a porcelain teapot, perched on the table's corner. Painted with yellow flowers, the teapot was a delicate incongruity amid the awls and leather punches. He indicated the bench, palm up, fourth finger and pinky crooking like the priest's when he raised his hand to give a benediction. "Sit, Fiora Vicente. You must be hungry. Tonight you are my guest."

The last of my bravado collapsed. I had a place to sleep. Food to eat. My knees went shaky with relief. I dropped onto the bench, ducked below the level of the table and made a show of checking the alignment of my stockings, hoping I didn't faint and tumble headlong under it.

I wouldn't have fit. The space was scattered with baskets and leather scraps, a box of iron rings and a cylindrical clay pot, brown and plain as dirt, filled with twine-wrapped bunches of dried verbena.

I plucked one from the container, breathed a nose full of lemon and nostalgia, then popped my head up, and waved the verbena at the old man. "My mother used to hang this at our windows and doors. Why do you have so much?"

He took the verbena from me and placed it in the exact center of the table. "You never know when it might be needed."

He fed me toast and apple slices layered with cheese and put plenty of sugar in my tea. He didn't talk beyond the necessities of eating, but he smelled of the same shaving soap as my poppa and didn't reach for his food until I'd reached for mine. When we finished, he took a pipe and tin from a shelf, filled the bowl with tobacco, tamped it with a thumb, struck a match from the box behind the stove, and drew deep, the glow casting shadows under the hollows in his cheeks.

He lifted the lid on the carved chest, pulled a sheet and blanket from it, along with a towel, and handed them to me. "We share a bathroom and toilet with the lady on the second floor. Her husband is away at the war, so it is not busy."

I took the linens from the old man, and he added, "She's a little older than you."

A friend. Maybe. Hope ignited.

The old man doused it. "But she's expecting. So . . ."

I would need to be careful. I hefted my bundle up the stairs, braid swinging across my shoulder and disappointment close on my heels.

The attic was a narrow space suffused in moonlight. The bed, plenty big for two, was pushed up against the short wall, its mattress sausage-rolled at the end of its metal springs. Boxes and baskets crammed into the corners. Fabric piled along shelves. The room's single chair, draped in dustcovers, cozied up to a dressmaker's form. The form wore a hat, feathered and flowered and old-fashioned as petticoats, its brim large enough to take on passengers.

Discouragement faded. I balanced the hat atop my head and peered into the wavy glass of the room's single window. My reflection, pointy and pensive, peered back. I pinched my cheeks to bring up the color, then remembered Mamma wasn't there to dose me with cod liver oil to cure the paleness. I pulled the hat from my head, flung it onto the bedpost, threw open the sash, and shooed the memory into the damp September chill.

A panorama of the curb market on Ninth Street spread out four floors below, one storefront after the other, marching parallel to trolley tracks embedded in the drizzle-covered cobbles.

PRODUCE. FLOWERS. MAGAZINES. BREAD.
GROCERY. SEAMSTRESS. CHEESE. PIES. PANINI.

I measured the window with my arms, pleased it faced east and, therefore, the rising sun, then turned around, looped thumb and forefinger before my eyes and squinted at the ceiling slope shortening the attic's opposite wall and imagined the effect in daylight. I pulled Mamma's Big Ben alarm clock, always my constant in a crisis, from the blanket-wrapped bundle, wound it, set it on the night table, and stood very still, as Mamma had taught me, while its *tick-tick-tick* settled into the room's unique rhythm.

The church tolled the midnight hour.

I shivered.

The tailor's wife didn't think the old man's death mattered. Because he had no purpose. She was a silly, shortsighted woman who didn't understand the importance of what she had done.

Until she dumped me at the old man's door, he had no reason to live.

TWO

The kettle whistled again at dawn, followed by the aroma of espresso wafting up the stairs. I opened an eye, waiting for Mamma's call. "Fiora. Come down. Help me set the table."

The call didn't come. Mamma was gone, lying with Poppa under the dirt at Potter's Field, or so the men who came to collect them claimed. I shook off the sadness along with the covers, quick to get into my clothes: cotton stockings, ankle-length skirt, and a plain long-sleeved blouse with a square collar—what we used to call a waist, for shirtwaist. I rolled my sleeves up over my elbows. In those days, I had a bad habit of dragging my cuffs through my food.

The room looked smaller in daylight. Not so long, nor so wide, the ceiling lower, its slope steeper than I remembered from the night before.

Not the window. It loomed three times larger than recollection. I thought of the black velvet drape still hanging in my parents' bedroom, flopped onto the bed, and bounced a frustrated fist to the bedcover, the landlord's parting words ringing unfair and final. "Curtains and cutlery stay with the apartment."

A sharp knock *rat-tat-tatted* on the old man's door. I hurried down the attic stairwell, paused at the bottom step, and peeked around the jamb to see who was there.

The tailor's wife. I drew back.

"How are you getting on, Fiora?"

I kept my eyes on my feet, pegging them into place, but all the good manners Mamma had foisted on me carried me into the room. "Fine," I mumbled.

She jangled her key ring. Like a jailer. "Good. Keep yourself busy. Make yourself useful. In time, everything will work out."

Useful.

The tailor's wife was a robust woman, with cheeks chunkier than a chipmunk's. Her skirt was dark enough for a funeral, twice the necessary width, and so out-of-style my fingers ached to transform it into the modern slim-fitted fashion. I told her so, adding, "I'll sew the extra material into a very useful sack. Suitable to stuff things, starting with your bluster."

The tailor's wife took on the look of somebody who needed to eat more roughage. She stepped toward me, and I thought I might get to make good on my offer, but the old man stepped between us. He led the signora onto the landing, his voice conspiratorial and constricted.

I tried, I really did, even stooping to put my ear to the keyhole, but I couldn't hear a thing.

The church tolled the seventh hour. I reached for the old man's Big Ben, the move reflexive, and wound it.

The old man stepped back inside, cloth piled under his arm. The left side of his mouth took a downturn. He took the clock from me and set it on the table. "What were you doing?"

Every answer seemed obvious, so I kept them to myself.

He handed me the pile of cloth. "Mending. With the parade only two days away, the Lattanzis cannot keep up. The signora will pay you what her customers pay her if you will help them keep their good reputation."

I flashed on Poppa's upholstery scissors, as long as my forearm and worth the earth, lying on Mamma's kitchen table beside his box of threads and cording, forfeited in the landlord's haste to evict me. A flash of the dress form in the old man's attic, the piles of fabric, followed. The old man seemed to apprehend my train of thought because he pointed to a basket on the bench. "You can't do proper work without proper tools. My wife was a seamstress. You may use hers until we get back your own."

"But . . ."

"What the landlord did was illegal. What's yours is yours. Maybe this afternoon, we will take a walk and speak with him."

"He said it was to pay for the extra days."

"Why didn't you pay him from the money you had?"

"Poppa told me rents are climbing everywhere. If the landlord had known about the money, he'd have charged me for every little thing until it was gone and put me out anyway."

That made the old man smile. It crinkled across his face like crepe fabric across a doorway, the corners stretching all the way to his eyes. He set a bottle of milk on the table, the cream layered at the top. "It's chilly today. I'll warm this for you."

I now know he meant to be kind, but at the time he made me feel like a baby needing a bottle. I half-expected him to hand me a bib.

We ate sliced bread and espresso, mine swimming in the warmed milk. Then we worked.

Hem. Button. Button. Button. Another hem. Patch. Torn pocket. Pulled lining. Frayed collar. Cuff. Every stitch even, as regular as the old man's Big Ben. Every stitch money in the pocket, a pebble on the path toward freedom. I tied off a knot.

The tailor's wife had found me on the street corner, teeth chattering, my coat soaked through. She was the only one of the dozens who passed me who stopped to ask if I were okay. Because none of them saw a girl in need, all they saw was somebody who could be a threat to their family.

Not Signora Lattanzi. She saw me as somebody who could be a threat if she *didn't* help me. Maybe her thinking went against her. I was doing her work, earning her money, because the old man told her. Because she didn't dare refuse. Because she called him *don*. I tied off another knot.

I bet she was sorry she didn't take a different route home that night.

The Big Ben's seconds ticked into minutes, the minutes into hours. The sun climbed. I envisioned it streaming into my attic as the moon had on the previous night, unfettered, without direction, the light splashing across the slope on the opposite wall.

Button. Button. I bet the signora would collect an extra nickel on each repair. An extra nickel wasn't much. The old man would never know.

Seam. Hem. Button.

I stood. "If we do go back, I need my mother's curtain."

I put down my needle and went downstairs to use the toilet.

The landlord proved reluctant, rubbing at a poorly washed ear. "She took what she could carry. I am not a warehouse. It seemed fair. Her parents should have been in the hospital. It cost me plenty to disinfect the place after she left." His gaze slid over the top of my head, then down my side to my shoes. He put out his hands. "Had I known she'd go to you, Don Sebastiano . . ."

"You could have taken her to the Holy Sisters, or spoken to the priest."

"I am a busy man. She's old enough to take herself and I told her so. But she insisted her brothers were coming."

Exasperation opened my mouth. "My brothers *are* coming. The moment the war is over they will return."

"Return? How? They are fighting with the Italians."

"What do you mean how? On a ship, same as everybody." The sound of squabbling, high-pitched and tinny, wafted from his open door. I tilted my head, eyes narrowed, shoulders tensed. "You have children?"

Silly question, my family had lived there since before my brothers went to fight in the war. Of course I knew he had children. And of course he knew I knew.

He jerked back, like I was delivering bad news. He partway closed the door until only his bulbous nose and beady eyes, perched atop the middle rectangle of his body, were visible. "I only meant . . . your brothers are in the Isonzo, no?"

The old man laid a hand on my hair. "Fiora, wait outside. I will settle things here."

"But my mother's curtain."

The landlord sucked in a breath, his neck going bulgy around the top button of his collar. "Impossible. The apartment is already rented."

"Fiora." The old man's voice grew stern. "Please."

He disappeared into the landlord's apartment. I climbed the stairs, as I used to, two at a time with a little kick-step on the third bounce.

Go to the Holy Sisters. I can imagine the reception I'd have receive there. They'd have gone through my things, Mamma's things, with much muttering of prayers and pleas to the Virgin. The items they didn't understand they'd have tossed on the fire.

The moment the war was over, my brothers would return. They'd march up the steps to the old man's attic, medals bright across their chests, and want to see our mother's curtain.

I stood outside the door, the door that led to my home until the landlord closed it on me and shoved me down the stairs.

My brothers were brave. So brave. Something quavered above my breastbone.

I wanted to be brave, too. I knocked on the door.

A signora answered in a haze of tomato gravy. She was young and tired-looking with a baby on one arm, a wooden spoon in the opposite hand, and two little ones clutching at her skirt. She looked past me when she answered. Up the stairs, and down. Like maybe she'd expected somebody else.

No. Not expected. Worried. "Can I help you?"

"I used to live here," I told her. "I left a curtain in the bedroom."

"The beautiful velvet one? With the embroidery?" Dismay filled her voice, whiny and weak. A flush crept past her collar. "But the landlord told me . . ."

"It doesn't matter what the landlord told you."

"Of course it matters. That curtain goes with the lease. It will cost a week's rent to replace it. Food from my children's mouths."

A week's rent. A month's rent. A year would not replace what that curtain meant to me. I peeked past her to a kitchen in the midst of meal preparations, then grabbed hold of her arm. "It will cost you a lot more to keep it. Your husband is fighting in the war, correct?"

The signora stepped back, like the landlord, her expression shifty and suspicious. "How could you know that?"

Because dinner was on the table and there was no plate at the table's head. "Because the signora who lived here before you was Rosina Vicente."

The signora's hand flew to her mouth.

I didn't care. That signora slept in Mamma's room, cooked on Mamma's stove, ate at Mamma's table. Mamma's curtain hung surrounded by objects it did not recognize, handled by people it did not know. Dormant. And dangerous.

Besides, Mamma always said I liked to be dramatic.

"Nobody is blaming you," I lied, letting my voice get resonant and round, "but I must have that curtain. My name is Fiora. Rosina Vicente was my mother. The curtain was her burden, now it is mine. Because I'm the fortune-teller's daughter."

Almost as ancient as the land that birthed it, Mamma's curtain was black, of the heaviest velvet, and embroidered over in signs and symbols that shifted with the circumstances. Mystical shapes, mysterious markings. Restitched and patched the moment a thread frayed, or color faded.

The curtain told stories, of yesterday and today, tomorrow and beyond. Stories not of when, but if, not why, but how. Stories of the heart, the soul, that moved to a unique rhythm, sang a unique song, and swelled into an imagining reserved for the angels.

Or so Mamma always said.

The old man and I left the landlord with the curtain folded under my arm and the landlord's promise he'd send the rest of my belongings. I walked beside the old man, my manner solemn, bearer of the burden, all but bursting to be back in the attic, get the curtain hung, and see if I could make it work.

I couldn't.

The curtain refused to cooperate, making the rod droop under its weight.

So I nailed it to the window frame, first to one side, then the other. The first nail fell. So did the second. I tried again, using two nails to a side. And again, using three.

The old man took back the shoemaker's hammer. "Next time, ask permission before you use my tools." He studied the setup. "This rod is iron, plenty strong to hold the material. The supports need reinforcement."

He went to work, turning screws deep into the studs. I fumed, nostrils flared, embarrassed I hadn't thought of the simple solution myself.

Ten minutes later, the old man stepped back to admire his handiwork. The knotty place inside my stomach unwound, giving my relief somewhere to settle. "The curtain fits."

It didn't always.

Iron grommets spiraled at set intervals from the curtain's center, each fitted with a flap, which, when buttoned, prevented even the tiniest bit of light from exiting its aperture.

The old man traced one of the grommets.

I reached past him and undid most of the flaps, repeating the explanation I'd heard Mamma give the few times a visitor strayed into her bedroom and caught a glimpse. "To let in the light, but maintain privacy." I raised the window sash an inch. The breeze set the curtain fluttering. Sun-filled pinpoints danced across the room. "See? Like fairy lights."

The old man didn't find what I said adorable, didn't say, "How charming," the way the biddies who came to Mamma for advice always did. Instead, he closed the flaps, spiraling down, outer to inner, heading toward the centermost grommet.

The fairy lights dimmed, one by one.

I fixated on his fingers in the artificial dusk, how his pinky and ring finger crabbed, and waited on the coming night, but the old man did not close off the centermost grommet. He stepped away.

The room stopped its descent into twilight. The light entering the final grommet strengthened, concentrated by the single aperture.

My heart did a thumpety-thump louder than any Big Ben. I'd had no idea, would never have thought it possible. How could more come from less? Light from darkness? I swiped by my ear, confused by a low-pitched buzzing sound. We were almost to October. It was too late for mosquitoes. Drawn by an incomprehensible pull, I turned away from the curtain. And caught my breath.

A projection of the Ninth Street Market splashed across the opposite wall. Every cobble exact, every roofline distinct, every red-and-orange-turning treetop bright in autumn sunshine.

Except upside-down and reversed, the signs all backward, like the old man and I stood on our heads, scarves dragging across the trolley tracks and feet in the clouds.

I traced the outline of the grocer's awning, sweeping upward like a giant coal bin beneath piles of tomato and *zuchetta* squash fixed to crates suspended from tables which appeared tacked to the ceiling. I placed my palm over the single grommet; the scene disappeared into the dark. I opened a second grommet; the scene bleached to nothingness. I returned to the single aperture, watched the scene again develop, and remembered something. "This isn't magic. It's science. I learned about it at school. That single grommet is like the lens on a camera." I patted the ceiling slope. "And this wall is like the film."

"I know the principles." The old man crossed to the curtain's far end and peered into the topmost corner. An upside-down cat curled beside an upside-down barrel. He traced along the cat's back. The cat arched, like it could feel the old man's touch.

I went to stand behind the old man. The mosquito buzzing swelled to a swarm. I traced along the cat's back, too. Nothing happened. "How did you do that?"

The old man studied me for what felt like a forever minute. "You have no idea how to use this, do you?"

The buzzing stopped, along with my wonderment. Thorny prickles of indignation clawed their way up my throat. "Do you?"

Three

The next morning I spent ten lazy minutes watching the upside-down market wake with me—vendors setting out stalls, carts making deliveries, street cleaners and cops making their rounds. Ten minutes stretched into twenty, and would have stretched into thirty, except my stomach grumbled. Loud.

I hopped out of bed and got in close to the projection. The cat from yesterday had returned, sleeping beside a barrel. I ran a finger along its projected back, as the old man had done, but the cat didn't react. I tapped the wall beside its projected paw. The cat didn't stir. I poked my nose right next to its projected whiskers. "Boo."

The cat slumbered on.

I opened the curtain and let sunshine displace my discontent.

What the old man knew about the curtain, he'd kept to himself. I dressed and headed downstairs, determined to wheedle the information out of him.

He sat at his workbench, face drawn, shoulders drooping, like he'd lined his sleeves with iron. He shook a pill from a paper packet and slid it under his tongue.

Something cold and crampy clamped my midsection. "Are you sick?"

He swept his opened palm over his forehead, down his cheek, and across his mouth, an actor donning his mask for the performance. He slipped the packet into his shirt pocket. "Sometimes, I get a little tired."

He turned over the newspaper at his elbow, hiding a headline which started with the word DISASTRO, then slid a plate of polenta—left over from the previous night's dinner and provided by the tailor's wife—across the table. I shoveled piece after piece into my mouth, my mood again set to a rolling and optimistic boil.

The old man watched me, fork suspended over his plate. I looked to my blouse, ran a hand down my braid, searching an undone button, a ribbon trailing in the cream, some reason for his scrutiny. "What is it?"

"I went through your father's papers last night. I cannot find his Petition of Intent. That's the document he would file to say he intended to become a citizen."

It felt odd to hear the old man speak English. "How do you say it?"

"Pe-ti-shun a In-ten." He found a pencil among the flotsam on the table and wrote the words on the top of a box of tacks. He showed them to me. "I can write the immigration and ask if your father ever filed one, but if I do, they will know about you."

I stopped dribbling honey into my bowl. "Know what?"

"That you are orphaned. With the Petition of Intent, that is not a problem. You could take the test for yourself and make your own oath of citizenship. Without it, you cannot make a claim until you are twenty-one. But I do not know what would happen in the meantime, and I do not want to ask anybody. You have no guardian, and they may move you."

He meant to an orphanage. I'd read about them in stories. There'd be many girls, our hair tied with bows starched stiffer than our pinafores. We'd sleep, one cot after the other, like a tray of *canneloni*. Eat at tables arranged in rows. Stand in orderly files, littlest to biggest, when prospective parents came to look us over.

The prospective parents decided me. "You could be my guardian."

"I am an old man and I am not a relative."

"Then my brothers. Everybody says the war will be over soon. If we write to them, they can say you can take care of me until then."

"I already wrote to them. Yesterday, before you were up. Young Carlo took the letter to the war office for me."

Young Carlo. Probably a neighbor kid. "I won't be a bother. You'll see. I'll cook and clean."

"You can cook?"

"Not a lot." Not at all. What for? Mamma had done all the cooking. "But I could learn. All kinds of things. I could even iron your clothes."

The old man shoved aside dishes still sitting on the table from the night before. I snatched them, circumscribed a wide arc around the signora's pile of mending, and set the dishes in a sink already piled to overflowing. I turned on the tap.

He arranged a set of spats, their buttonholes stretched and useless. He placed them inside out, lay snippets of leather over the holes, I presumed for reinforcement, then threaded a needle, one that curved more than his pinky. "Signor Lattanzi irons my clothes. He has a press downstairs in his shop."

The heat crept up my neck, reminding me of what I might do with an old scarf. I looked to the door, picturing the tailor's wife on the other side, listening, as I had.

Pompous old pincushion. Let her iron clothes. I was meant for bigger things. "Poppa wanted me to take a secretarial course. So many girls are learning the typewriter now. They dress up every day and go to offices. I see them sometimes. They take the trolley."

The old man scratched under his right cheek, at a mole near lost amid the fine-grained cracks of his skin. "Very modern. But those girls don't get married."

"Who says I have to get married?"

"Don't you want children?"

What did he care if I wanted children? What did anybody? The world had plenty of children. It'd do fine without mine. "You sound like Mamma."

"But not like your poppa." He tied off a length of thread. "Do you speak English?"

In those days, not everybody did. "Oh yes. I went to school. Poppa placed great importance on education." I placed my hand over my heart, as the nuns had taught us, and swallowed to get my mouth ready to form all of English's harsh angles. "I pledge allegiance to my flag . . ."

I had been born in Italy, but I pledged to America, because to me, the *bel paese,* the beautiful country, was a distant tangle of torturous closed-in streets filled with dogs and donkeys and people. So many people. Living wall to wall, exploding out of every corner, filling every chair, crowding every fire, and scraping every last bean from the pot.

I pledged to America, with an accent that still had plenty of trailing "uhs" and "ohs," because my parents had scrimped and saved to make the long voyage. I pledged to America, because America was where my loyalties lay, where my hopes were forged, and where my dreams would realize. I pledged to America, because America was my future, and that pledge made me American, no matter what the immigration said.

The old man listened to my recitation with a grave respect. "You may need to know that for the examination. For citizenship."

He glanced at the clock, then at the signora's pile of mending. "So, Fiora Vicente, will you go to school today?"

I headed out and into a hustle and bustle bountiful with possibility. School? Ha. I was a woman on my own, free of encumbrances, and I had ambitions.

The trolley approached, trundling past storefronts and stalls. Each bore a poster reminding of the next day's parade, the parade for which the tailor and his wife so busily prepared. I stepped aboard, handed my fare to the conductor, and found a place among the tight pack of people, my plan to head to parts of the city I'd never been. I'd stayed up late to peruse the classifieds in the old man's newspaper and found a school that would teach me skills. Skills that would let me travel that trolley into the future, my braid looped into a twist at the back of my head, like the other typewriter girls.

It was a beautiful day. Sunswept. Overflowing with life.

And while I didn't know it then, soon—swift, swift, swift—it would all steamroll to a stop.

Four

Saturday, September 28, Parade Day, dawned clear and cool. Planned for weeks, the parade was to launch the fourth issue of Liberty Loans. Without the money those loans generated, we were told, we couldn't finance the war against the Kaiser. So everybody bought a subscription—Poppa had one, tucked somewhere in those papers the old man had checked—and everybody was going to the parade.

Except, it seemed, the old man.

I pointed to a lineup of shoes, half-disassembled. "Aren't you going?"

"No."

"But . . ." There would be bands and Boy Scouts and even a sham airplane battle fighting in the skies above Mifflin Street. Veterans and war workers marching shoulder to shoulder. Four Minute Men making short and stirring patriotic appeals to the spectators. To support our doughboys, beat back the Hun, and buy those Liberty Loans. A closed-in crowd, lining the banks of Broad Street. Singing the same songs. Shouting the same slogans.

Breathing the same air.

The old man removed a stitch. "The DiGirolamos ordered a new pair of shoes for their oldest and would like the rest resoled before Monday. They are bringing the children by so I can measure them before the parade begins." He gave me an address. "Do you know where that is?"

"Of course." Mamma had been there a few days before she got sick. "Give the druggist my name. He will know what is needed. It's already paid for. I meant to send Young Carlo, but perhaps Parade Day has him busy. Maybe you could go for me now."

The DiGirolamos were shuffling the shoes, passing them down, and putting away the smallest pair for the next baby. And the old man did not want me, Rosina Vicente's daughter, making them nervous. I clutched at a brochure stuffed deep in my pocket and squeezed until my knuckles hurt. A brochure picked up during my disappointing journey downtown, a brochure detailing the high cost of typewriter school and how little time I had to earn enough money before the next session began.

The old man handed me a few coins. "In case you get hungry."

I put the coins in my pocketbook, then shrugged into my coat and wrapped my scarf under my chin. "Be sure to deduct this money from what I gave you when I arrived."

He rapped the table, the angles along his cheekbones going sharp. "When I need your money, I'll ask for it."

Somebody knocked at the door. The old man handed me another coin. "Pick out a couple of peppermints. If you like them."

I headed out, sparing the briefest of nods to the crowd that waited for entrance: a mamma, a poppa, and five children, two girls and three boys, the littlest no more than three.

The parents shielded their children's eyes from me.

I caught the signora's and signore's gazes and held them.

The old man had handed me money. For candy. So I could be gotten out of the way. And then I went and did the thing he most wanted me not to do.

I raced down the stairs, chagrin charging after. And ran headlong into the pregnant girl. She stepped aside, hand held protectively over a bulge rising beneath her apron like dough on a summer day. She smelled of fresh bread and roses, and I wondered when the baby was due. Soon, I supposed.

I couldn't ask. She'd think I was putting a curse on her.

I dropped my gaze, ashamed to have given her a fright, ashamed of my behavior with the DiGirolamos, like maybe she'd seen and worried I'd hurt her.

She retreated to her apartment, rapping on the jamb to get my attention. She gave me a shy smile, then closed the door with a solid click. I continued down, my pace more sedate. Something whizzed past my nose and crashed into the wall beside me.

A wooden biplane, the kind powered by a rubber band.

I picked it up. "You can come out now," I said good and loud—much like the tone Mamma would use—to let the little troublemakers know I had no intention of moving until they did.

Something rustled in the open space beneath the stairs, a place I'd noticed the tailor's family had commandeered for storage. I peeked around the railing.

Two well-dressed urchins plastered themselves against the wall beside a collection of galoshes. The tailor's children, I presumed. I held up the airplane. "Is this yours?"

The younger one pointed to his brother, coal-colored gaze directed into mine. "He did it."

"It was an accident." The older grabbed a hunk of his brother's dark-brown mop and tilted his head down. "Don't. Mamma said."

Don't look the girl on the third floor in the eyes. Don't let her look into yours. If you do she will steal your soul.

The little one swept his brother's hand off his hair. "Stop. Maybe she's the good witch."

I didn't know much about children. Few people let the fortune-teller or her daughter near theirs. We're fine for telling them if they would find a husband, or if their future would be bright, but there was the uncooked side of the *crespelle*, the assumption anybody who can see so clearly may see more than they should, and may use that knowledge against them. The part of me I kept tight-wound and secret, the part too wrapped up in myself to understand the boys were parroting the behavior they'd been taught, wanted to grab both by the chins, force them to look me in the eye. "Good witch?"

"Like in the book." The bigger one brought it from behind his back.

I knew that book, knew the green cover. We'd read it in school. *The Wonderful Wizard of Oz*.

The smaller boy took the book and paged through. He pointed to an illustration of the Emerald City, rising beyond a field of scarlet poppies. "Someday, we will fly an airplane there."

The older one put a hand over the illustration. "Don't be ridiculous. We can't fly there. Poppa says this kind of book isn't real."

Poppa sounded very practical. "You read English?"

The older boy shook his head. "The lady on the second floor does. She gave us that book."

I handed him the airplane. "Next time, watch where you launch this. Somebody might get hurt." I slipped out the side exit. I wasn't the good witch. I was Dorothy, tossed out of my familiar surrounds by an act of nature. Still, the little one's generous estimation had me turning right at our stoop, to avoid upsetting Signora Lattanzi by casting my shadow on the window of the tailor's shop. I headed to the heart of the market, careful not to catch my heel on the trolley tracks.

The market seemed twice as busy as it had the day before, bustling by at double speed: a hailing whistle, answering shout, the *rappa-tat-tat* as one merchant after another dragged out metal poles to raise their awnings.

Banners draped across storefronts, celebrating the parade, celebrating the Sons of Italy, celebrating our part in this great American achievement. Naval workers, shipbuilders, welders, riveters, craftsmen, laborers from every corner of my homeland, the end of the war in their sights, and working day and night to bring that day forward, finish our tasks so our boys could finish theirs. And come home.

Already, trash blew down the alleys. Pyramids of honey jars and canned tomatoes, peach preserves and sweet potatoes beckoned, the air redolent with spicy sausage and Parmesan. Merchants in billed caps and ladies in aprons, skirts swishing, were eager to conclude their business before the procession started on Broad Street. They leaned over their boxes and crates, calling to passersby dressed in Sunday clothes, starched and ironed to hold their shape, how their quality was high, their prices the best.

This was a simpler time, when even the window stiles were made one by one in a factory peopled with men, not machines. The parade was a major event. Anticipation swelled like overcooked lentils, squeezing me past barbers. Lacemakers. Confectioners. Flower sellers.

I applied at them all, or so it seemed, moving from shop to stall to stand. At each, the excuse was the same: Business is slow. Maybe next week. Talk to me in a month.

"But you have a sign saying you're looking for help." I pointed, again and again, to where the sign was posted: in a window, tacked to a table, by the register.

Smack of palm to head. "How silly of me to leave it there. I filled that position last week, last night, this morning."

And always the averted eyes, the whispers behind hands, the veiled politeness, despite the need for help because of the worker shortage caused by the war and the influenza.

Finally, finally, the fishmonger seemed tempted. "Don Sebastiano is a friend, but . . ." He rubbed at his neck, "I need somebody more permanent."

"I will be here a long time. Even if the war ends tomorrow, it will be months before my brothers return."

"Women always say that, but look at my daughter. I thought she'd stay close, be here to help in the shop, then she married and she and her husband moved to Camden."

He went back to his work.

I pushed on, but the spring went out of my step, the stuffing out of my spunk. Shoppers swept past me, an outgoing tide heading for Broad Street. Band music wafted down the cross streets.

A group of boys wrestled a cart along the road, the wheels picking up speed as momentum bumped them over the cobbles. A little girl separated from the crowd and darted past me. I didn't think, not like in a real thought, "Oh, I'll go do that now," after I weighed all the options, pro and con. A deeper part of my brain determined my next action, a part which calculated the little girl would enter the street exactly when the cart moved past. A calculation which responded with reflex. A reflex that grabbed the girl by the skirt, and dragged her back from the curb. A reflex that would have left her on the curb while I moved on except the girl looked up at me with big dark eyes very much like the tailor's sons, and I thought as I had with them, *Kids don't think much past their noses.* "Careful," I told her. "You'll get run over."

A woman pulled the girl from my hands so hard, the little girl's doll dropped to the sidewalk. The woman buried the girl's face in her skirts. "Did you say she'd get run over?"

I had, so I saw no reason for agreeing. The woman crossed herself. She spit over her left shoulder, then addressed a clot of people standing around a nearby stall. "Rosina Vicente's daughter said *my* daughter would get run over. My little Grazia. Run over. God forbid. And after what happened to Rosina Vicente."

People turned, stared, muttered to one another, stared some more. Grazia's mother extended her pinky and forefinger to make the sign of the horn. Protection from the evil eye. From me.

My mother's reputation descended. My spirit shrouded, my appetite to join the festivities quashed. What did the everyday people have to do with me? I was like the curtain, separated from them by superstition and fear.

My gaze swept the receding throng, seeking something to distract me from my awful solitude, and picked out a display of apples piled prettily in wooden boxes under a green-striped awning. Last of the local harvest, in a week, maybe two, they'd be coming in from places with names like Georgia, and Carolina, and prices would double. I thought of the cinnamon sticks in a tin on the metal shelf behind the old man's stove, the jar of cloves beside, and picked out six large fruits of variegated red and yellow. I could cook them down like Mamma used to, serve them on a cold autumn evening, maybe not feel so alone.

The signore held up seven fingers. I shook my head and held up two. The signore dropped the hand holding two. A second later, he folded the thumb on the other hand, then added two more apples to the purchase.

Perhaps he felt bad for not hiring me. Or thought I deserved some recognition for saving the girl from the cart. He dropped the apples into a paper bag, and I counted out the coins, leaving them by the cashbox, lest my fingers touch his palm.

Hooves clip-clopped over the cobbles. The signore slid his cap off his head. The din of pushcarts and peddlers, deal making and dickering quieted. Even the breeze dropped off. A wagon trundled past, three boxes, one atop the other two stacked in its back, their shapes unmistakable—coffins.

The murmuring picked up. A lady examining a display of handkerchiefs crossed herself. "And on Parade Day. How could they?"

The grocer's wife drew her children close. A man at the stall beside muttered something to his friend. He nodded in my direction.

One by one the bystanders fixed on me. Nervous. Wary. Their silent accusation pressing in. My heart went heavy and my feet sore, but I couldn't return to the old man yet. I still had his errand to complete. I moved on toward the pharmacy, one block, then two, wishing I were back in my attic, back with Mamma's curtain, wanting to lay my forehead on its smooth black velvet. And cry.

A snatch of song pulled my self-pity up short. A bit of opera beloved by my poppa. I turned and found myself staring into eyes of the lightest blue, an unusual color, even in our village, which had many blue-eyed men. These shone like sunlight on the Adriatic, or how I imagined the Adriatic to be from Poppa's stories, with green and yellow flecks near the pupil and irises rimmed in indigo. The eyes were large and honest and perfectly distributed on either side of a strong nose above lips, full and smooth, set into a face the color of cappuccino.

Beautiful eyes, housing a beautiful soul, a soul filled with music, and truth, and the conviction life is best when lived.

An eternity passed. Then another. I tore my gaze from his, turned to continue on my way. And tripped on a cobblestone.

The grocer's bag flew from my hand. The apples scattered. I dove after them.

The young man dropped his satchel and dove after them, too, corralling one after the other. He returned the fruit to their bag, helped me up from the sidewalk, his fingers strong and sure around mine. He gathered them close.

"What cold little hands," he said, echoing the Puccini he'd been singing, then released me and gave the apple bag back. He slid his cap off a shock of soft curls, brown as dried fava beans, and bowed, foot extended, an exaggerated arm across his midsection. "I am at your service, Fiora Vicente."

He straightened, hoisted the satchel back onto his shoulder, and went about his business, whistling a happy tune. I watched his progress through the crowd streaming its way toward the parade, my jaw agape, so dumbfounded he'd spoken to me when no other would, I never wondered how he knew my name.

The bell over the pharmacy entrance jingled. The sign tacked to the door clattered:

HALT THE HUN.
OUR BOYS DEPEND ON YOU.
YOUR LIBERTY BOND SUBSCRIPTION PAYMENTS
CAN BE RECEIVED HERE.

The druggist, mouth and nose white-masked against the influenza, looked up. "Yes?"

"Don Sebastiano sent me. I am here to pick up his order." I peeked around a display for cough drops and cold elixirs. "I am also looking for work. I'll stock shelves. Mop. Do windows. Anything."

A white-masked lady swept over before the druggist answered. "But you are so much more talented than that, aren't you, little one?"

Behind the woman's eyes, dark and doe-shaped and twinkly as stars at midnight, lay a bed of moss, soft and spongy, begging me to come forth, find a comfortable spot within, and yield all my secrets. I shook myself. "Who are you?"

She tapped a finger to my brow, soft and smooth and smelling of cinnamon. "Silly, you already know."

Suddenly, I did. "You're the *guaritrice*."

The village healer.

The apples of her cheeks lifted, and even though she wore the mask, I knew the lady smiled. I also knew her teeth were white and even and her cheeks dimpled. She put a finger to where her lips would be. "We don't talk about such traditional things here. This is America." She tapped a finger to her temple. "Only modern thinking."

We'd found common ground, she and I. Fellow travelers, meeting by chance on the same trolley, each knew the other knew something and each knew nobody else understood how.

She looked past me, her gaze sweeping corner to corner. "Young Carlo normally collects the don's prescription. He's not ill, I trust."

She spoke in that cautiously inquisitive way people do when they want to know one thing but ask about something else. I looked behind me, too, thinking maybe she was looking for this Young Carlo and I'd see what he looked like.

All I saw was the expanse of the pharmacy's display window, and the street beyond. I turned back, but the guaritrice had been replaced by a shadow—spindly, and spiky, and far too small. I blinked, presuming the brightness from the window had blinded me. "The don expected him, but I think he forgot."

"The young are always forgetful, are they not? Still, he should be more reliable. He's the don's heir." Her voice came out of the shadow, distant and doubtful.

"Don Sebastiano has a son?" My construction of a neighbor kid collapsed, replaced by a young man with better things to do, one who no doubt slept under the table the few times he managed to drag himself home. No wonder the old man had balked at the idea of being my guardian.

"He doesn't have a son. The don and his wife lost their children. However, Young Carlo serves a purpose."

My new manufacture of a carefree young man fizzled. "My mother always told me things have purpose. Not people."

"Your mother was very wise. Yet, you may refer to Young Carlo the same, once you meet him. Maybe at the parade. Everybody is there. All the young people, our best and brightest."

My eyes finally caught up with the light level, and the shadow resolved. The guaritrice waved her arm, like the best and brightest were standing in the room with us and she meant to show me. "Why are you not with them?"

"I meant to go to the parade."

"But you got lonely. Poor little soul." She patted my cheek, then drew me close, like Mamma used to, smelling of lavender, as Mamma had. Then talked, as Mamma once did. "Life is filled with so many maybes. So many wants and wishes. Your mother used to tell me all we imagine, we can make true. Whatever we like. Such a good soul, your mother. She cared so much for you. Wanted to see you happy. Settled. And now she's gone and left you."

Her words rolled over the heavy places in my heart, molding my memory of Mamma into what the guaritrice spoke—a good soul, dedicated to my well-being, able to imagine all I wanted might someday be true. "You knew her?"

"Like a sister." She heaved the most melodic of sighs, one that started high and in the back of her throat and ended in a breathy mush. "But change comes to all, little one. We must be strong. Must be practical. I hear you're going to typewriting school."

Every fuzzy curve in the guaritrice's voice went sharp. Mamma's memory deflated, melting into a pile of ill-formed sentiments. Something pricked at my thumbs. "How do you know about typewriting school?"

"People talk, little one. Oh, how they talk. And so shall we, but come." She wrapped her arm around my shoulder. "I'd like to introduce you to my Tizi."

She moved me toward the back of the store, an alcove which felt disconnected from the rest of the pharmacy. There was a counter there, with a strongbox centered on its top, and a map of the city tacked to the wall behind. Red dots speckled the map, a scattered bloom that coalesced around the market. Beside the map was a doorway, curtained in beaded strings of many colors.

I tilted my chin at the map. "What's that?"

"We must keep track of our deliveries." The guaritrice gave me a squeeze, then released my shoulder and clapped her hands. "Tizi."

A light went on behind the beads. One side drew back, and a girl stepped into the room, bearing two steaming cups. "I was making tea."

Masked like the guaritrice, with hair three shades lighter, Tizi was half a head shorter than me, and at least two years my junior. Her brows sloped down toward the sides of her eyes in a way that made her look sad. She fixed me with a blue-gray stare. Frank. And familiar.

The guaritrice lay a palm on the girl's head. "Your mother visited the other day, and I'd hoped you and Tizi could play together, but your mother did not bring you with her. So protective, your mother. She did all she could for you. A mother must. Sometimes life is not easy. And now look at you, all grown up and able to think for yourself." She put her hand on the small of Tizi's back and pushed her forward. "But listen to me going on while Don Sebastiano's order needs to be filled. Tizi, why don't you give our new friend my tea. I'll have a cup later."

I plucked at the guaritrice's sleeve. "But, I—"

She turned to me. "No, I insist. It is an honor to serve Rosina Vicente's daughter." She worked her index finger around a tendril of Tizi's hair. "Isn't that right, Tizi?"

"Yes, Mamma."

"Good. Keep our guest company until I return."

The guaritrice ducked behind the curtain.

Tizi handed me one of the cups. I took a sip, lavender and . . . something I couldn't quite place. Cloves, maybe?

Tizi watched me. "Mamma says people don't treat you nice because of what happened to your mother."

I spat my mouthful back into my cup, set the cup back on its saucer and the saucer onto the counter. I fixed Tizi with one of my stares, but she laughed it off. "Don't try that with me *Rosina Vicente's* daughter."

Fine. I picked up my cup. "How can our mothers be such good friends? I've never seen either of you before."

"People like our mothers don't have to see each other to know everything they need to know. Besides, we just arrived."

"From where?"

"Here and there." Tizi flopped her palm left, then right, then left again. "We started in Kansas. On a hog farm. It stank. But Mamma says if we want to make an elephant, sometimes we need to start with a flea. We hitched a ride out of there with a soldier home on leave. Mamma was so grateful. She gave him a bright red scarf as a thank-you."

Kansas. I'd heard of it, of course. Like in the tailor's boy's book. Dorothy. Oz. A cyclone-tossed house that crushed a witch. "Mamma says that, Mamma says this. Someday your mamma will leave you. Then you'll have to speak for yourself."

The curtain flew back. The guaritrice swooped in. "We must watch our words, little one. We never know who might be listening."

Tizi's eyes went wide and beneath her mask, her complexion paled. The guaritrice scooted her into the background. She pressed an envelope into my hand. "Don Sebastiano's medicine. The instructions are on the label." She pressed a paper bag into my other hand. "Tea. My own mix. Brew this for him. And a little for yourself, if you like it. Twice a day. It will make you feel better."

I opened the bag and sniffed. The mixture smelled of cinnamon and cloves. It would be perfect with the apples. "You know Don Sebastiano."

"Everybody knows Don Sebastiano. And he knows everybody. How fortunate Signora Lattanzi brought you to him. It's what your mother would have wanted. Such a good woman, the signora, to do what your mother would have wanted. We all must try to help you in that way." She leaned toward me, her expression soft and sad. "Your mother left you her things, yes?"

Beautiful things. Useful things. I thought of Mamma's curtain dancing light across the roof slope in my attic.

Powerful things.

The guaritrice tapped my elbow. "How tragic you almost didn't get them back."

"You heard?"

"How could I not?" She let go of me and walked back and forth before the counter, wringing her hands. "That horrid landlord. I went to see him, brought him a little tea as a peace offering, but I found you'd already collected the curtain. How very smart of you. How very wise of Don Sebastiano to make sure it was returned. Who knows what mischief it might have gotten up to if it'd been left on its own."

"Mischief?"

"The most chaotic of mischief. Have you any idea the power the curtain commands?"

"Of course I do. Kind of." I glanced at Tizi, standing smug and certain beside her mother, secure in a relationship I'd never had, wearing an expression that said she knew I was lying. "What I mean is, Mamma never actually explained how any of it worked."

The guaritrice stopped pacing. "We should talk. About your mother. About her things. The things that matter. The things to which we return. It is foolish to not make the most of our burdens. Especially when a burden can help you enter a world you never imagined. A world where you earn money, money to pay for your typewriting school, money the people in the market are too silly to let you earn in other ways. There is nothing to it once you know. Swish of a finger, twitch of a wrist, and you are there. But you must learn the proper way. Bring your burden to me and let me teach you." She took hold of my chin. "Because there's a price to pay if you do not use things properly."

Her tone was ominous, the low rumbling that followed, real.

"And you must get to know my Tizi." She again put out her hand and Tizi again stepped under it. "How nice if you became friends."

Time to leave.

I tucked the medicine into my pocketbook, my feet already

heading for the door. She walked with me and tapped the tea. "Keep this between us. Don Sebastiano is a proud man. A stubborn man. How awful if anything happened to him. How very sad for you. Just a little, twice a day and you will be free to do as you please."

She opened the door to the pharmacy, and before the jingle faded, I found myself outside on the sidewalk, my temple throbbing and a sensation, like butterflies, fluttering against my ears.

Five

The day after the parade, I pushed out of bed, eyes grainy. The projection of the upside-down market flickered across the ceiling slope like a movie in the cinema. A great wheel turned over the cobbles, the people who'd attended the parade fled before it. The young man from the market whistled from the sidewalk, his tune no longer happy.

I blinked and woke up for real, the projection showing a market moving in its familiar and upside-down everyday routine.

I dressed quickly and raced downstairs.

Change was coming. Perhaps I hoped to escape the wheel, too.

The old man was not at his workbench, the cloth not laid, the stove cold. I put on my scarf, thinking . . . I'm not sure what I thought, maybe that I had to find him.

The pregnant girl stopped me on the second-floor landing. "I wondered," she said, eyes downcast. "Would you like a coffee?"

Coffee. And . . . conversation?

Sunshine broke through my clouds.

The old man was probably running an errand. Or taking a walk. Wherever he was, the old man wasn't home. So he didn't have to know. About coffee. Or conversation. Or anything I didn't want him to know about. I looked down the stairs, like he'd heard my thoughts and would come charging up to stop me.

All that came charging up those stairs was a hacking cough. "Is that coming from the Lattanzis?"

The pregnant girl leaned over the banister. "The signora says it's a cold. She didn't look bad. The newspaper says every sniffle is not the influenza."

She clasped her palms before her chest. "Forgive me. Your parents. I did not think."

"No. It is fine. We all say things we wish we hadn't." I looked at my feet, all the things I wish I'd never said bubbling like dirty water from a bad drain. "My parents were good souls."

And they'd gone and left me.

"Of course they were good. They were very good." The girl stepped away from her door. "Please. Come in."

She led me into a room even smaller than the old man's. A curtain hid a corner where, I presumed, she slept. A bassinet dominated another corner, all lace and pleats and pretty little bows. A bookshelf stood beside it, piled in titles. "You like to read?"

She nodded. "It helps my English. And to enter another world." She curled her fingertips together, then exploded them outward and swept her arms to either side. "Like magic." She leaned toward me. "Signora Lattanzi says it is a waste of my time. How about you?"

"I love it, too. I read all the time. Every chance I get." When I couldn't get out of it. Stories were fine for babies. I wanted to see the *real* world.

The girl crossed to the window. She pressed two fingers to her lips, then to verbena twined into a ring hanging from the casement. She faced me, fist over her heart, expression sheepish. "For protection. Don Sebastiano says windows and doors let things in. They also keep things out."

I went to examine the ring. Iron. Like the door knockers. "What is he trying to keep out?"

She held out her hands, palms up, her expression shifting to amused. "I don't know. He didn't tell me." She motioned to the table. "Come. Sit here."

A ball of dough rested on a marble slab beside a collection of little rectangles, pinched in the middle to make a butterfly shape, what we call *farfalle*.

She laid a small cloth before me, set out a cup and saucer, placed a sugar bowl and creamer beside. I ran a finger along the cloth's edging. "Did you crochet this? The stitches are so tiny."

She dipped her head, looking pleased at the acknowledgement. "I did everything. The napkins and the curtains. Even the sheets and pillowcases." She reddened at the mention of sheets, color washing across cheeks plump as pomegranates. She poured the coffee. "So silly of me. Of course there are sheets and pillowcases." She laid a hand on her belly. "And obviously a bed."

All I knew of that aspect of marriage I'd learned from watching dogs. It didn't look comfortable.

The aroma rose from my cup. "Your coffee is lovely. Do you brew it with cloves?"

"I don't know what's in it. Signora Lattanzi gave me the mix. Says it will help the baby grow." She wafted the scent under her nose. "Smells like strawberries to me. My favorite. But summer is over and I can't get them anymore." She tapped her chin, then yanked her hand away. "Oh dear. I'm not supposed to touch my face when I crave something. The baby will have a mark. But I do love strawberries." She smacked herself on the rear. "That should fix it. At least the mark won't be visible."

She giggled, the sound fluffy as whipped cream, then waved at the dough. "I hope you don't mind. If I don't roll it now, it will dry out."

She set to, laying her full weight against the wooden pin. Tendrils escaped her rich brown coif to feather about her forehead. She pushed at a wisp with her forearm. "I wish I had a separate counter for this. Every job is easier when you have the proper tools, don't you think?" She tossed a little more flour onto the marble. "It's only me, so it doesn't much matter, but Nicco says when he returns we will buy a house, big enough for a dozen children, and marble slabs in every corner."

"Only rich people own houses."

"The Lattanzis own this house, and they're not rich."

The revelation struck me like a match. One thing for the tailor's wife to bring a stray into a place to which she had no attachment, but to bring a stray into the heart of all she had, all she was, took courage.

"I thought Don Sebastiano owned this house." I looked to the iron rings, to the verbena, thought of how the signora and the pregnant girl deferred to him. "I mean, he sure acts like he owns it."

The pregnant girl sliced the flattened dough into thin strips, then rolled a crimper across their breadth to make the rectangles. "What Don Sebastiano owns is not easily seen. How fortunate he took an interest in you. When you get married, you will understand better."

And there it was, the slight denigration, the smallest jab that maybe I shouldn't consider myself like other people. Or maybe I should consider myself *exactly* like other people. Maybe I should be quiet and nice and do exactly what was expected of me.

The pregnant girl's coffee went cold in my stomach. "I'm not getting married. I'm going to typewriting school."

She looked up from her crimping, her face bright and interested. "Typewriting school. There's a girl over on Twelfth Street who went. Now her clothes are always stylish."

I nodded. "Those jobs pay plenty. Enough to go to Atlantic City. You know, take the train and spend the whole day. Maybe even overnight."

"So much ambition." She opened closed fingers between us, casting her disbelief to the heavens.

"Why shouldn't I have ambition?" I tapped my forehead. "This is America. Only modern thinking."

"Yes, but you'll still need somebody to take care of you."

Take care of him more likely. Cleaning, cooking, keeping the buttons on his shirt. I pushed the coffee away, and made a show of looking from one corner to the next. "What do I need? Look at you. Making your own pasta. All alone and taking care of yourself just fine."

"I'm not alone. There's the Lattanzis. And Don Sebastiano, of course."

"You knew him before you came to live here?"

"Everybody knew him. He is from our village. Like your parents."

This was why Signora Lattanzi brought me here, why she thought she owed my parents, my mother, some responsibility. "We all come from the same village."

The pregnant girl drew her head back. "You didn't know? You must have been very young when you came over. Signor Lattanzi's family used to make everybody's christening clothes. And Nicco's grandmother, the don's wife. Like this." She interlocked her index fingers. "So when Nicco went to enlist, Don Sebastiano told him it would be best if I came here."

The pregnant girl's explanations ushered me into a new world, like the pregnant girl claimed happened with her books, a world in which I was no longer a stranger, no longer an interloper, a world in which I was more like a . . . cousin. How come Mamma hadn't told me? "Why did the don think you should come here?"

"Because I was planning to go with my aunt. She lives in Coatesville. Her husband worked in the mine, but there was an accident and he died, so now it is only her and my little cousin. She owns her house, and we always got on well, but . . ."

"But what?"

"But . . ." She picked up another ball of dough and slapped it to the marble. "Don Sebastiano says I shouldn't bring life into a house so soon after someone has passed. He says time needs to find a new path after a great upheaval."

Nonsense. "He was being philosophical." The nuns at my school had loved philosophical.

"Maybe so, but when Don Sebastiano makes a suggestion, it is a good idea to take it."

"Everybody seems to think that."

The pregnant girl moved her hands toward her, fingers splayed, like she was gathering in the pieces. "Including Nicco."

Men. Even when they think they know something, they don't know anything. I cast about the room, looking for something, anything to distract the conversation, and latched onto a camera, what we called a Brownie, sitting on a shelf hanging on the wall behind a doily-covered parlor chair.

The Brownie was supposed to be affordable, a camera for everybody, but up until then I'd only seen one in magazines. I snatched it up, ran a finger along its stitched leather casing, along the slider the ads claimed I only needed to push to expose a frame. The lens, so like the grommets on Mamma's curtain, the light flowing through the aperture. The image of the pregnant girl, her floured palm prints on her apron, captured on the film. A moment in time. Enshrined forever.

I held the camera and turned toward her.

She put her hands out, palms forward. "No. Don't take a photo. It might be bad luck. Nicco says that camera is for taking photographs of the baby."

Nicco sure had plenty to say for a guy who wasn't even there. "Fine. We'll take photographs after the baby is born, then. We'll go to Atlantic City. Take a dozen photos for Nicco. The ocean is good for babies. The air is healthy."

Her fingers moved over the rectangles, giving each a pinch to make the butterfly. They reminded me of little birds, pecking in the ground for seeds. "I can't think about that right now. Maybe after the baby is born. Maybe when the war is over. Maybe when Nicco comes home. Maybe maybe maybe. Life is filled with so many maybes. So many wants and wishes."

Her sentiment reached me from a far-off place, carried on a voice cloying and convincing and nothing like hers. I flicked at my ear. "What you can wish for, you can make true. Whatever you like."

She tossed a handful of the strange wheat and rice mixture we had to use for baking in those days onto the marble. Dust rose in a happy puff. "Right now, I'd settle for some decent flour. I'll swear the grocer's substituting his wheat ration with talc. I don't know if I should cook with it, or sprinkle it over my skin after a bath."

I sneezed, then sneezed again, trying to keep both to the right, so the luck I was expelling would remain good.

She buried her face in a towel and sneezed with me. "My parents are still in Italy. I wish they could be here. I imagine what that would be like, all of us gathered around the table, talking about the future. Nicco says he will help them come over, but they don't want to leave. My cousin told us he would care for them, but he is in the army, with the Italians, like your brothers, and with all the rumors . . ." Her hand flew to her mouth.

My heart hitched. "What rumors?"

"Oh. Nothing. With all the fighting, people go on about every little thing and I go on more than any of them. My grandmother used to tell me my tongue is like an unbridled horse." She sat beside me, leaned toward me in a conspiratorial way. "I am a silly, fearful girl. My mother would be so ashamed. I bring you here, offer you coffee, hoping to attach a string. But I have no right."

"Right to what?"

"Every little thing worries me these days." She patted her stomach. "This little one more than anything. Will he be healthy? Will he be strong? Will I be a good mother? Will he even be a boy? The doctor can't tell me. Nobody can. Except maybe you?" She said the last in a rush. "I . . . I can't pay you. Except, possibly, in pasta."

She was so earnest, so innocent, her offer of friendship so sincere. Never had I shared a confidence with another as I had with her. Mamma had warned against it. *"You never know who might be listening."*

The girl put her palms on her cheeks. "Take the pasta, anyway. I make so much because I'm not supposed to eat it. I'm getting fat." She threw her hands in the air. "My mother told me the only time a woman can eat all she wants is when she is having a baby, and the doctor tells me I shouldn't." She tapped her head, the movement exaggerated so I would know she was imitating me, and she was only doing it in fun. "Modern thinking."

I put my hand over hers in the companionable way I'd seen Mamma do so many times. The girl's hand was soft, but strong, and I wished I could gather it close as the young man in the market had mine. I concentrated, but all I got was a glimmer around her edges, peaceful, and . . . powerful.

I released her.

She clenched at the collar of her shirtwaist, her eyes taking on the alarm of a trapped rabbit. "What is it?"

"Nothing. I got a cramp." I flexed and unflexed my fingers, uncertain what to make of the jolt that had coursed through them, then stood and gathered my scarf. "Do not worry. About anything. I am not my mother, but sometimes I get an idea. If I do, I will let you know."

She let go of her collar. "Then I will wait, Fiora Vicente. And be patient."

I was back upstairs and in my attic before I realized. She knew my name, but never offered hers.

Mamma said the power in her curtain rose with the sun. "For the light exposes everything." I put a finger on the thick velvet and traced a pattern of leafless branches in the lower left corner that sometimes reminded me of summer, sometimes of autumn, then closed the flaps as had the old man, spiraling through, outer to inner, as he had done, the room darkening with each closure, until the last final miracle when sunlight expanded through the final aperture to splash the upside-down market at midday across the opposite wall.

Now what?

Swish of the finger, twist of the wrist . . . who had said that? I searched my memory, found nothing. No matter. I tried.

Swish. Twist. Swish. Twist.

Swish and . . .

TWIST.

Nothing.

Mamma used to tell me, "Approach the simplest of acts with great purpose, imbued with your deepest emotions, and you will have success. All else can wait. Except burning food and crying babies."

Beautiful words. Useless words. *How does one see the future when the present feels so hopeless?*

I crossed to the wall, my shadow looming in the light entering from the grommet, noting, without noticing, how the upside-down clock in the fishmonger's upside-down window and Mamma's Big Ben here in the attic showed the same time. I pressed myself to the plaster, the attic's behatted and fabric-covered dress form to my right and a projection of the grocer and his stand to my left, and imagined myself part of the scene. Imagined myself seeing as Mamma had, concentrating on the pregnant girl, on her baby, on what might happen next.

Big Ben ticked off a minute. Then another. Five minutes that felt like ten.

I grew twitchy. No great purpose propelled me, no deep emotion drove my act. Just a desire to please my new friend, and a vague notion somehow, someway, Mamma's curtain would help me where Mamma hadn't.

The wall remained hard, the plaster cold. I rubbed at my temples, head achy, cheeks hot, wishing I'd told the pregnant girl *no*.

No. I cannot tell when you will deliver, have no idea if the baby will be healthy, haven't a clue whether it's a boy or a girl. And as to your mothering abilities, the only thing certain is you would be better than me. A turnip would be better than me.

Me. Rosina Vicente's daughter.

Unremarkable. Ungifted. Unable to look at a sky filling with clouds and predict so much as a rainy day.

All my talk of typewriting school and train trips to the seashore.

I couldn't even get a job sweeping floors.

I smacked at the projection, aiming my frustration at a collection of crates stacked alongside the grocer's upside-down stand. I hit the wall hard, my fist seeming to sink into the plaster. A shiver, like electricity, hopscotched up my arm.

A clatter, a crash, another clatter like a giant game of dominoes, *clackety-clackety-clacked* beside me. I whirled, my hand coming away from the plaster with a sucking sound. The dress form was fine, standing prim and proper, but in the projection, something had changed. The collection of crates, stacked so neatly, had toppled, scattered in a confusion beside the grocer's stall.

Coincidence. Somebody must have happened by while I wasn't looking. Except I noticed something strange. The fishmonger's clock, the one in his window, showed a time five minutes further along than

Mamma's, like it had moved two minutes for my every one. Pushed by my impatience.

I shook out my shoulder, snatched up the Big Ben. And checked again.

Impossible.

"Everything is possible, Fiora. Except for all that is not."

"Mamma?" I swung around, expecting to see her, hands on hips, dark waves coiled atop her head, their red highlights glinting in sunlight the same way she always said mine did. I looked up, presuming Mamma would tower, though, in life, she stood an inch shorter than me, even in shoes.

The attic was empty.

But I was not alone.

Something laughed at my elbow. Strident. And shrill. And not at all friendly.

I bolted for the stairs, Mamma's Big Ben in hand, and out the old man's door, leaving my coat, my hat, and the last of my composure. I hurled myself down the steps and onto the street, into the scene that danced across the walls of my attic, except three-dimensional and right-side-up and stinking of horseshit and straw.

The grocer's stand looked as it had, a collection of crates stacked to its side.

I headed over, meaning to examine the stack. See if it matched the specifications I'd noted when I first saw it in the projection, for height and twist and order of the crates, six in all, with the topmost upended sideways into the fifth.

A crack, and a thud, like the sound of a fist smacking plaster, stopped me shy of the trolley tracks. The grocer whipped around. He threw up his hands. I followed his gaze.

The collection of crates had toppled, just as they had in the attic. Mamma's Big Ben pinged.

I held the clock to my chest and did a few calculations. How many readings? How much should they pay? How fast could I get the curtain working the way I wanted?

I was going to make a fortune.

The old man ate early that evening, scooping beans into his mouth with the same precise movements he used to cut shoe leather. I watched, looking for the least indication anything other than a collection of crates had toppled, worried because I did not use things properly.

I cleared the dishes, accidentally knocking over the first in a file of shoes, each beside its shoe form, lined up at the table's end. I set the footwear back into place. Red descended in a choking cloud. The cloud spread out until it filled all my vision and made obvious the sound of sobbing, deep, heaving gasps. I snatched my hand back.

The old man looked up. "What did you see?"

"See? Nothing. I . . . I thought the DiGirolamos wanted these today."

He picked up the shoe, ran a finger along the buttons, his face pensive. "They did, but Carlo forgot. He'll deliver them tomorrow. Then he can check the fit."

And make sure the DiGirolamos don't risk another eye-to-eye encounter with Rosina Vicente's daughter. So, Forgetful Young Carlo had shoemaking skills. I guessed that was why he was the old man's heir. "Why does everybody do what you want?"

"Almost nobody does what I want." The old man put the shoe back with its form. "Some do what I say. Most don't listen to me at all." He removed his napkin from his collar, and pushed his plate aside. He put on his sweater. "Come. Let me show you something."

He led me to a door I'd presumed led to a fire escape, but opened onto a flat rooftop. I took the time to figure out the geometry. "We are over the second-floor bathroom."

Boards crisscrossed the space to provide walkways. Quilts, ragged and weather-beaten, draped beneath the edges of a lineup of old sashes, panes intact. The panes topped a wall of wooden crates. Inside the crates were a collection of clay pots, planted with tomato and zucchini, basil and oregano, summer sage and rosemary, and, of all things . . . strawberries.

I'd seen this in a schoolbook. "A greenhouse. These windowpanes, the quilts, make a special world. Protect the plants from the outside."

The old man seemed pleased I understood. He removed a sash. A row of candles squatted in the dirt, one to a pot. He pulled a box of matches from his pocket, struck one against the bottom of his shoe, cupped his hand around the flame, and lit the candles, one after the other. "The warmth keeps the plants from freezing. Soon it will be too cold, no matter what I do. For now, they thrive. Long after summer has withered."

I put my fingers under a strawberry, large and red and ripe enough to pick, closing my fingers around its comforting weight. The old man turned to me, his gaze meeting mine, and I saw another hand making the same movement in his mind's eye—a woman's, gentle, but worn with work and years, the veins on its backside prominent.

The old man hadn't made the garden.

She had.

The fine grain of the old man's skin smoothed. "My wife wanted strawberries when she was expecting our last. Ate so many, she started to itch. The midwife said she'd developed an aversion. There's only a few plants here, not enough to harm the pregnant lady. In two days, maybe three, they will be ready. Perhaps, you could bring them to her. With my compliments."

So, he knew I'd met the pregnant girl. The tailor's wife must have told him. The only material she stitched was black. "I thought Signora Lattanzi was sick."

"Her hearing is fine. And so is her tongue."

"Tell the signora I left my broomstick on the pregnant lady's landing. All we did was drink coffee."

"How much did you charge her for making predictions about her baby?"

And he knew about that, too. Maybe from picking up the shoe after me. Maybe I'd left that knowledge with my touch. But who cared? And how dare he anyway? I was a modern woman, able to think for myself. Who was this . . . this old man to tell me what to do?

I lurched. The strawberry fell away from the vine.

The old man retrieved it. "Fiora."

"Nothing. All right? Not a penny. I didn't charge her anything. Because I can't tell her much of anything. Except she's not delivering in the next five minutes."

The old man tilted his head, expression quizzical.

"The curtain's . . . stuck. On the market. Five minutes into the future." No matter what I did, no matter what I tried. No matter how many times I reset Mamma's Big Ben, or punched the projection, or imagined myself there, or here, or later, or earlier. Mamma's Big Ben always reset to five minutes more than every other clock I checked, and the market was always five minutes ahead.

The old man went to work replacing sashes, and draping quilts, shutting the plants away for the night. "The curtain's not stuck. You're stuck. Because you think you need the curtain to follow your plan."

"I need to make some money to follow my plan. I have to be able to take care of myself. My mother collected money for her readings. Did that make her bad?"

"Your mother was good. She collected only what the client needed to pay her. Not a penny more."

"So she was powerful."

"She was good. Good is better than powerful. Good is the most powerful power there is."

"Ha. A lot of good her goodness did her." I headed back to the kitchen.

The old man followed. He put the strawberry by the sink. "I had a visit this afternoon from the Children's Bureau. Somebody must have informed them."

Everything warm inside me went cold. "The landlord?"

"Perhaps the undertaker who collected your parents. It is no secret you are here."

"What did you tell them?"

"That your brothers have given permission for me to be your guardian." He handed me a letter. "I picked this up from the war office this morning. The notice arrived via the Italian army."

"This isn't either of my brothers' handwriting."

"It's transcribed from a wireless transmission." He flicked his fingers toward me. "Read."

I did so. Out loud. "'. . . and handle any other circumstances as you deem fit, acting in every way as if you were our sister's grandfather.'" I looked up. "What do my brothers mean? What circumstances?"

The old man took the letter back. "Whatever should arise. It may be months before your brothers return home. Unfortunately their permission may not be enough for the Children's Bureau."

The old man's tone pulled my spine taut. "How can my brothers' permission not be enough?"

"Your brothers are not yet of age themselves, neither are they citizens. The people from the Children's Bureau accepted the letter. For now. But with so many sick, the orphanages are understaffed. A strong girl, an older girl, like yourself, to help with the younger children . . ." He drew himself up. "In difficult times adults don't always make the best of decisions. So we must be ready, in case the Bureau comes back."

"Be ready. How?"

He pulled a wooden box from under his cot. He set it on the table and opened it. About the size of the Oxford dictionary the Reverend Mother kept in her office, the box had a carved lid like the blanket chest. It was stuffed with papers. He took back my brothers' letter and placed it among them. "Until your brothers' return, this is your home. That makes us family. And as family, we must accept. I am old. Sometimes I do not feel so well. That means we must prepare. I have your approval to act as your guardian. Tell me, Fiora Vicente, do I also have your trust?"

Six

The next morning, I woke to sun rising over the upside-down roof-tops of the market five minutes into the future. I drew the curtain aside, fixing it behind a nail I'd hammered into the jamb for that purpose. The curtain fell free, casting the room into darkness which lightened by moments until the market again projected across the ceiling slope.

I hooked the curtain behind the nail a second time. A second time the curtain fell free.

I hooked it again, looping a length of ribbon around the velvet to tie the curtain into place. The curtain kicked back.

Deliberately. Defensively. And with determination.

I left all the flaps undone; the curtain rebuttoned them down to the centermost grommet. I closed that grommet off; the curtain reopened it.

The air grew tingly, my scalp hairs tense. I got dressed, yanking the waistband of my skirt up over my hips, my shirtwaist over my head, grabbed my stockings, grabbed my shoes, thinking I should get out of there. Now.

I stumbled down the stairs. The door at the bottom of my attic wouldn't open. I pounded on it, straining for the *tap-tap-tap* of the old man's hammer, but all that returned was an overwhelming silence. Up the stairs, in my attic, came the sound of struggle. Knocking. And scratching, and the oddest slithery sound. The stairwell fell into darkness. The curtain must have fallen free. I gave the doorknob another try. "Mamma. Please."

The door flew open. I flew through it, my feet barely touching the floor, grabbed my coat and scarf, and flung myself onto the landing.

The tailor's sons were there, peering soulfully up at me. "We're hungry."

"Hungry? What? Ask your mother."

The older one answered. "She's sleeping. So is Poppa."

A fit of sneezing exploded from downstairs. "Well . . . sounds like they're up."

The older one took the younger's hand. "C'mon, let's ask Signora Bruni."

The pregnant girl had a name. I wondered what her Christian one was. "Keep your distance. You don't want to get Signora Bruni sick."

The bigger boy didn't seem to like me telling him what to do. "How can she get sick if we aren't?"

I wasn't sure she could. But at school we'd learned germs traveled on a sneeze. And if they traveled on the sneeze, maybe some of their parents' sneezes had landed on them. If they went to sit in the pregnant girl's apartment . . .

I saw the influenza in my mind's eye, falling from the boys' clothes as a dust, red as a . . . kerchief, the kind of kerchief a young soldier from Kansas might wear.

The girl would take the boys' coats, maybe put an arm around them, and the dust would cling to her hands. Her hands would carry the dust into the streets, perhaps touch a peach or an apple in the market. She'd tap a finger to her mouth while she made the decision, then bite her lip. The dust would find a way into her lungs.

She'd feel tired. The headache would start. The fever would come and she'd sneeze, then cough, bringing up blood in bursts to splash another red across the sheets and maybe even the wall.

Then she would die. Meanwhile, another customer would pick the apple the pregnant girl hadn't chosen. And take it home to her family.

I turned the boys around and shuttled them down the stairs, the vision so clear, my head throbbed with the impression: a city covered in red dust, traveling with the people.

The younger boy tugged at my skirt. "Are you all right?"

The vision fled. The throbbing in my head ceased. "Let's go. There must be something in your icebox. And be quiet. If Signora Bruni sees you, she'll want you to eat with her."

"How do you know that?"

I'd long ago stopped answering those kinds of questions. "Move. I haven't got all day."

They hurried, pushing open the door to their apartment.

Dishes piled in the sink, laundry in a tub beside it. The tailor's wife sat by the stove, face drawn, skin cracked, a cup of tea in hand. Its steam, cinnamon-laced and friendly, smelled familiar. "What are you doing here?"

"The boys are hungry."

"Then I will feed them." Her tone was sharp enough to slice tomatoes. "Etti, Fipo. What did I tell you about bothering the don?"

Ah. The boys had names, also. "They didn't bother the don. The don isn't home." I thought of what waited in the attic, the incident already taking on the unreality of a dream. Still, I wasn't eager to go back up there alone. "I thought I'd make some oatmeal."

"Do you know how?"

I didn't, but how hard could it be?

The signora pointed to a shelf behind the stove. "The canister is there. If you'll bring it down and leave it here, I'll make it myself. We're fine."

"All due respect, Signora Lattanzi, you don't look fine."

"You're wrong. Fipo fill that pot with water. The small one."

The older one climbed onto a stool and turned on the tap. "How much?"

I took the pot from him. It was crusted with what looked like dried tomato gravy. "At least let me clean this first."

The signora grabbed my fingers and turned my palm up. "With these hands? Signora DiGirolamo told me the dishes are piled to the ceiling in the don's apartment. Have you ever washed a dish in your life? Your mother, always so soft on you. And now look at what's happened."

I yanked my hand from hers. "Don't you talk about my mother." I remembered words, the right words, the ones that would sound appropriate. "She was a good soul."

"Yes, a very good soul. I've prayed for her. Prayed for your poppa. Lit a candle. Gave you my mending. You've no reason to fault me for this. No reason to bring foul fortune on my family. The young man is lucky. Lucky, I tell you. God bless you. God bless him. You'll see. He's a good match. Almost a citizen. Now leave the pot and leave my house. I will see to the oatmeal."

Outside the Lattanzis' apartment, I leaned against their door, my rage enough to push any worry over freethinking curtains out of my head. Match. Lucky. The signora's fever must be raging. Did she think she was sick because of me? I sat on the bottom tread and pulled on my stockings, then my shoes, dropped there on the way in.

Well, fine. Her decision. Although oatmeal was sounding pretty good to me, even cooked in a dirty pot. I hadn't eaten breakfast.

But, no. Signora Lattanzi didn't want my help. She didn't need it. She'd looked pretty good. Nothing like my parents. Maybe the pregnant girl was right, maybe all the signora and the signore had was a cold.

Another fit of coughing burst from the Lattanzis'. I picked up my coat and scarf, also lying on the floor.

Maybe not.

The doctor's office was shuttered. A sign instructed: LEAVE NOTICE OF PATIENTS NEEDING ATTENTION.

Sheets of paper were tacked to the jamb, a pencil hung from a string beside. I wrote the Lattanzis' name and our address, tore off the page, and slid it beneath the doctor's door. Then I turned. And halted.

The young man from Parade Day, his shock of soft, brown curls falling over his forehead, stood on the other side of a store window, talking to a man at the counter.

I hurried past, stopping on the far side, then reversed direction and strolled by the window again, staying close to the curb so I could read

the awning stretched across the facade: LEATHER GOODS: BOUGHT
AND SOLD.

Poppa always told me to cultivate my curiosity. Mamma told me to
be careful it didn't kill me. I couldn't cross the window again. What if
the young man looked up and saw?

I compromised, crossing the street to pass the shop, wondering
whether the young man was purchasing or selling. When I looked
again, the other gentleman was gone, and the young man had moved
to the other side of the counter, bent over a pile of items I couldn't
identify. Perhaps he wasn't buying or selling. Perhaps he worked there.

I crossed back. A trolley trundled past, then a cart. I ducked around
the first, dodged the next, eager to get back to the curb.

The young man stood on the sidewalk, carrying the same leather
satchel he'd carried on Parade Day. "May I help you, signorina?"

I straightened my coat and rearranged my scarf, aware I hadn't
thought to grab a comb in my escape from the attic. "Why should I
want your help?"

"This is the third time you've passed the shop. And yes, the shop is
most impressive, still I cannot remember I've ever seen anybody give
it such careful and constant attention."

"Don't be absurd." I stepped close to the lamppost, tried to pretend
I'd only meant to read the notices tacked there. The first week of the
fourth Liberty Loan subscriptions were due. And, apparently, accord-
ing to the flyer, keeping a happy spirit would ward off the influenza. "I
must be on my way."

"Excuse me, signorina, but which way? You appear to be undecided."

His smile, warm enough to melt ice cream in a blizzard, displaced
the last of my dignity. I pointed to the banner overhanging the shop.
"I am looking for work. You're not the owner, are you?"

"Today I am the delivery boy." He hefted the satchel to his shoulder.
"Signor Minora is the owner. He just left. If you will come back tomorrow, I will introduce you."

"How can you? You haven't introduced yourself." I didn't need
this young man's introductions. Didn't need his presumptions, or his

insinuations, or his service. I was a woman who could go out and make my wishes, a woman who'd never let her pile of mending climb higher than her aspirations. This was America.

I turned, chin high, and started up the street.

My wrist refused to follow.

I twisted it, this way, then that, doing my best to look like I wasn't doing so.

The young man watched me. "The button on your cuff is caught on a bit of metal."

Attached to the lamppost. A nail. Or a screw. A piece of wire.

Because I hadn't taken the time to fasten it.

Embarrassment flooded places I didn't know I had.

"Do not fret, signorina. All we need is the proper tool. As Fortune would have it, in this one thing, I *can* be of service." He put down his satchel, pulled a buttonhook from his coat pocket, took hold of my elbow, ran his hand down to mine, and expertly extricated my cuff from the fray.

Excitement firecrackered up my arm, an unexpected rush that barreled past my shoulder and lodged in my throat, like I'd jammed my finger into a live socket.

Well. My goodness.

Had the same thing happened to him?

If it did, the young man didn't let on. He pocketed the buttonhook, retrieved his satchel, tipped his cap to me, and headed down the street.

I stood there a while, trying to look like I meant to be standing there, to prove to those rushing past I had some purpose, some promise, some part in life's grand performance.

Only modern thinking.

I washed the dishes that evening. I dried them and I put them away. One. By. One.

The old man watched me. "Something wrong?"

I explained to him about the Lattanzis, about how sick they were. I poured his tea and slid the cup before him. "Their lips were blue."

"Carlo meant to find the signora's sister today."

"But he forgot?"

"He has other things on his mind. I'll send him tomorrow." The old man picked up his cup, and sniffed at it, his face going strange. "Where did you get this?"

"From the . . ." From the what? An image surfaced of somebody closing my fingers around the bag of tea, but I didn't remember who. "From the market," I decided. Where else could I have gotten it? I went to take a sip.

The old man knocked the cup from my hand. Hot liquid, tinged in red, splashed across the table, and soaked the contents of the sugar bowl. "No market sold you this. Have you had some already?"

"Yes. Of course. I've been drinking it since . . . since . . ."

"Since you got back from the pharmacy?"

His question came at me like a cannonball. "I didn't go to the pharmacy."

He held up his box of pills. "Of course you went. Was she there?"

I had no memory of the pharmacy, yet there was the box of pills.

He gripped the handle of the teapot. "You didn't give any to the pregnant lady, did you?"

"No. We drank coffee." I remembered the aroma, so rich and inviting, smelling of cinnamon and cloves. "Her coffee. And we rolled pasta."

The old man eyed me. He emptied his tea into the sink, emptied the pot after, and dumped the sugar down the drain. He rummaged through the baskets and tins on the shelf until he found the bag, then opened a window and scattered the contents. "I was stupid to let you go. I wasn't thinking. I haven't seen her in such a long time. But of course she would be there, now, with so many sick, so much need."

Doubt pulled at my insides, like knotted thread. "Who are you talking about?"

"The guaritrice."

It came rushing back, somehow overshadowed by everything else that had happened since. The woman. The girl. The masks. The strange little alcove at the back of the pharmacy. I followed after the old man and examined the bag the tea had come in. "She told me to give you a cup. Told me it would make you feel better."

"If she meant it for me, why did you drink it?"

"Because she told me to make a cup for myself, too. And why shouldn't I? It smells good. Fragrant. Lavender." Like my mamma used to wear.

He smacked the sash shut, drew the curtains, and snatched the bag from my hand, stormed out to the rooftop garden, struck a match, lit the bag, and cast it over the side. It streaked to the cobbles, and, I'd swear, landed with a tiny scream.

He looked over the edge. "The tea smells like whatever will bring you the most comfort at that moment. For me, it is almond and fig. You couldn't have known. And the tea made you forget. She gave you the suggestion and you did as she suggested."

His reaction seemed ridiculous. The guaritrice was a good soul. She worked so hard. A mother must. And she'd offered me help where the old man had none. "It's only tea mixed with herbs. But for the leaves, I could bake with it."

"It's more than tea. It makes you go to sleep. Not for real. In here." He tapped at his temple. "You do things you otherwise wouldn't dare, imagine things you otherwise wouldn't dream. Wish for things that will come to no good. Tell me everything she said to you. Every little thing."

My attitude, rarely more accommodating than a mule's, retreated into a shell plastered over in stubbornness. The old man and I were temporary, cobbled together by tragedy, and, despite his assertions we were family, little more than strangers. He had no false comforts to offer, nor confidences to share. Five days after my arrival, the space between us remained veiled, mist hovering over water before the sun rises. "There's nothing to tell. I was only there long enough to pick up your order."

He marched back into the apartment, his face all angles and annoyance. "I don't expect you to understand me, but I do expect you to obey me. Never accept anything from the guaritrice again."

"But—"

"Nothing. Not even a greeting. You can sell your soul without even knowing and never collect a penny on the contract."

Seven

The old man was gone again in the morning. He left the icy remnants of the previous evening beside a roll and a plate of sliced apples—a note propped against a medicine bottle: "To whom much is entrusted, much is required."

Followed by an explanation how he was delivering the DiGirolamos' shoes, and I should give the medicine to the Lattanzis, one spoonful, three times a day.

I pried the cork off the bottle and sniffed. It smelled like the anisette Poppa took to help with the cough. I took a sip. The liquid burned all the way down, then fought to come back up. The urge subsided and a subtle heat spread through my insides. How come how often the Lattanzis took their medicine was *my* problem? Let the increasingly forgetful and no-doubt-useless Young Carlo worry about it. He was the old man's heir.

Awls. Shoe forms. Leather cutters. Punches. And the carved wooden chest.

I again raised the bottle to my lips.

I bet Young Carlo had a harelip and a squint.

Would he want the flowered teapot? I ran a finger along the handle and traced one of the painted daisies, thinking how accustomed I'd become to seeing it on the table.

Maybe Young Carlo had a wife, a wife who wouldn't want the teapot. The old man and I were supposed to be family. That would make this wife my . . . what? Sister-in-law? Aunt? Maybe she would give the teapot to me.

I took another sip and let the warmth wash all the worry away, replace it with imaginings of myself in this unknown woman's place, owner of the teapot and my hare-lipped, squint-eyed husband off running errands. The pregnant girl, pregnant no longer, would visit. We'd eat cookies made with proper flour that maybe she'd taught me to bake as good as hers, while the baby did . . . whatever it was babies did. I skipped that part of the imagining, because, truly, at the time, I hadn't a clue, and moved right to where she taught me how to roll my own pasta so I could make dinner for my brothers who would finally be returned from the war.

There. I liked that imagining. I bent to adjust my stockings, get a deep breath of the verbena, then maybe go downstairs and see if the Lattanzis were dead.

The bundles under the table were gone. All of them. So was the box of iron rings.

I looked to the old man's windows. Verbena twined into rings hung from each of the iron rods. I dashed to the rooftop door. Another bundle, twined in another iron ring, clattered against the wood. And yet another at the old man's entrance.

So many bundles. So many rings. These few were only a fraction. Old World superstition, meant for protection.

From somebody the old man didn't like. Somebody the old man didn't trust. Somebody who had offered me kindness, and caring, and the one thing the old man wouldn't—answers to my questions.

Because the old man didn't like her tea. And maybe the old man likewise didn't care if I ever made enough money to get to typewriting school.

Well. I'd see about that.

I ran upstairs, scribing as wide a circle around the curtain as I could manage. There'd been nothing scary about it in the night, just a piece of velvet that stayed hooked on the nail like any bit of fabric should. But it had been hanging down, projecting my five-minute-forward upside-down market when I woke.

I arced around it, then arced around it again. "Don't hurt me, all right?"

The curtain didn't answer. How could it? It was only fabric, and a little embroidery. But it seemed the branches I'd traced along its corner had changed, branches that reminded me sometimes of spring, sometimes of autumn. The branches had filled out and flowered, looking like summer. I took that as friendly, came in close, and gave the curtain a tug.

It released from the rod. A shower of verbena rained down with it. I folded the material, wrapped it in canvas pulled from the fabric piles on the shelf, then hefted it onto my shoulder as the young man had his leather satchel. I went downstairs, grabbed my coat, and headed out the door.

I had to know.

I stood across from the pharmacy, the bell over its door jinga-jangling every time a customer exited or entered.

Tizi spotted me through the window, face lighting around her mask. She pointed to a sign tucked in the display between a collection of cough drops:

HELP WANTED

APPLY WITHIN

Hope rose like cream on a cold day. I near skipped across, then stopped in the middle of the cobbles, the old man's admonishment constructing a brick wall fifteen steps short of the curb.

Tizi disappeared from the window, and reappeared at the entrance, her stance bouncy and boisterous and brimming with joy, a sharp contrast to the cautiously caustic attitude of our first meeting. She beckoned, pinky and ring finger crooking with the downward motion "Fiora. Come on. Mamma says you would be perfect."

I shifted forward an inch, maybe two, the welcome I'd received warm in my memory. The guaritrice's hand on my shoulder, how kindly she'd spoken of the mother everybody else feared to reference. Then the harsh memory of the old man throwing the tea down the drain. Setting fire to the package. How the empty bag shrieked as it fell.

Tizi put hands on hips as round as her cheeks and suited to somebody older than the adolescent I met on the day I picked up the old man's prescription. She tilted her head, her expression confused. "Fiora?"

I glanced to my feet, to the trolley tracks forming the iron line I dared not cross. "You come here."

Tizi took a step. Rather, she tried. Lifted her foot, moved it forward, brought it down. To land right where it had been. She lifted the other foot, moved it forward, brought it down.

Nothing.

Confusion choked the cheerful from her face. She looked up.

I looked with her. Attached to the doorway's bell. An iron ring. The same as hung at the doorway of the old man's apartment. Twined with verbena.

Tizi's hand flew to her breast, and she sucked in a breath, a breath that made her breast appear far more developed than what I'd expect from the young girl I'd met on Parade Day. Then Tizi sighed. The last of her girlish good spirits slid from her shoulders. She took on a sadness of a full-grown woman, exaggerated by her eyebrows' gentle downward slope. She shook her head. "I can't."

She stepped back into the pharmacy. The door's spring mechanism pulled it shut behind her. The verbena jangled with it.

Keeping things out.

Or keeping them in.

I thought of the bits and pieces that had showered down with the curtain.

Or keeping them from crossing the trolley tracks.

Preposterous. Superstitious nonsense. I stepped again, one, then two. Me, Fiora Vicente, bearing Rosina Vicente's burden, the burden that belonged to me and me alone. To seek guidance. "Nothing more."

The weight on my hands dissolved. I looked down.

The canvas remained, limp and empty and quivering in the breeze.

The curtain was gone.

The doctor was in the old man's apartment, a hand on the old man's shoulder, a stethoscope to the old man's chest. He listened, then pulled out the earpieces and packed the stethoscope into his bag. "The DiGirolamos are very sick, my friend. You shouldn't have gone." He nodded to me—"Keep him home. Do his errands for him."—then handed me some small white pills. "For the tailor and his wife. They need one every few hours."

"But, I—"

"You haven't caught it yet. You're probably resistant. Boil everything you can. Keep the boys away from the pregnant girl. And for god's sake, get them something to eat."

The doctor might have said something else. I didn't know. I grabbed the old man's Big Ben and dashed up the stairs, heart pounding an uncomfortable rhythm.

The curtain was there, hanging unsettled and skimpy on the rod. I pulled it to the left; it gapped on the right. I pulled it right; it gapped on the left. I stretched it from the bottom; it wouldn't reach the sill. I felt silly talking to it. But I did. "What's wrong?"

"The curtain chooses the window," the old man spoke, husky and matter-of-fact, from the top of my attic stairs. "The curtain can unchoose it, also. Have you made it angry?"

I whipped around. "Angry? It's a piece of cloth."

"It is powerful and profound and not to be trifled with to earn a few dollars at carnival games."

I thought of typewriting school. Of all the money I didn't have to pay for it. Whatever the curtain wanted from me, it hadn't liked going to see the guaritrice. "What do I do?"

"Don't use it. Put it away. The curtain provides a path, but if you do not respect the road, you may not like where it leads. For now, the Lattanzis need you."

"The doctor cannot order me to care for his patients. The Lattanzis are his responsibility, not mine."

"How fortunate for you Signora Lattanzi did not take the same attitude when she found you in the alley."

I lay a hand on the curtain's edge. "Is that what you want?"

The curtain relaxed, settling past the window's edges. Darkness fell. I undid the centermost flap. Light arrowed into the room, splashing the Ninth Street Market across the far wall, in all its glorious upside-downness.

Fine. I stomped past the old man, opened the door, and descended the stairs, my attitude firmly in tow. The curtain and the upside-down, five-minute-forward market would be there when I got back. So would the old man.

The Lattanzis? I sat on the bottom tread, listening to them cough for a full one hundred and twenty-three seconds.

Maybe not.

I might have sat there for a hundred and twenty-three more except the tailor opened the door.

Shivering, skeletal, whiskers sprouting in all directions.

I'd never met him, only seen him in the neighborhood, an earnest, carefully dressed man, walking with his sons.

He shuffled past me, heading to the street door. "I thought you were Fipo. I sent him to the market."

"I'll go look for him." I took the tailor by the arm, turned him around, pushed him back toward the apartment, and into a scene of devastation.

Dirty dishes piled in the sink, dirty towels across the floor. The younger boy stood in the corner, thumb in mouth, diaper sagging to his knees. He clutched a blanket and stared wide-eyed at his father. I crouched in front of him. "Aren't you too old for diapers?"

"He doesn't talk anymore, either." The voice came from the still-open door to the hall. Small. And defiant.

Fipo, the older boy, clutching a paper-wrapped bundle. He crossed the room and placed it on the table. "I got oatmeal and carrots." He tapped the side of his palm to his stomach. "I'm hungry."

The tailor pulled a box of matches off the shelf. His hands shook. "I have to light the furnace. There's no heat."

"I'll do that. You start the oatmeal." I took the matches off of him, ran down to the basement, shoveled coal into the furnace, and did my best not to blow anything up. I'd never lit a furnace. Never made oatmeal. Never worried about feeding anybody else. Not even when Mamma and Poppa were sick. They died so fast, I was still eating leftovers from our last dinner together on the morning the men came to collect their bodies.

I returned to the kitchen. Fipo was stirring the oatmeal. It bubbled over. I grabbed a swatch of my skirt and pulled it from the heat. A generous arc splashed across my shirtwaist, and into my hair. I set the pot on the floor. "Fipo, don't use the stove."

"Poppa had to sleep. If you ask Mamma for help, she could tell you how to make us hotcakes, instead."

"Maybe later." I took the spoon from him. "Go find your brother a clean diaper."

"We call him Etti. And if he had a clean diaper, I'd have already found it."

"Why didn't you get me sooner?"

"Because you made Mamma sick."

I cooked and cleaned. Scrubbed and washed. Every plate, every towel, every gummy corner. Etti tugged at my elbow. He pointed. A smell more aromatic than beans rose from behind the stove.

I put a hand over my nose. "Did you try to change your own diaper?"

I threw open the windows, scooped the diaper into a bucket, marched to the bathroom, and emptied the contents in the toilet, flushing again and again. Fipo found me. "Poppa threw up."

I stopped flushing.

I'd already done this for my parents. Cleaned puke and piss and poop, washed snot from towels, and mopped blood off floors. Hour after hour, morning to evening. For one day, then two days, then three. Inexpertly, inadequately, because Mamma had always done the cleaning, and when none of what I did helped, when none of it made Mamma or Poppa better, I escaped to the roof, lost myself under the stars, imagined they were windows on the infinite, and wished—oh how I wished—I could find a way to push through to the other side.

But there was no other side. There was only more cleaning, more scrubbing, this time caring for people I barely knew. Because one had plucked me out of the rain rather than risk running afoul of an irrational fear.

The contents of the medicine bottle bubbled up onto my tongue, bringing with it a vision of the flower-painted teapot that would someday go to Young Carlo. Young Carlo who got to run errands and didn't have to clean up poop. Young Carlo, whom, I'd decided, also had a hunchback.

I slammed the bucket to the floor and flung myself at the entrance to the Lattanzis' apartment, near twisting the knob off its screws. I yanked the door open, pulled it shut behind, then leaned against it, chest heaving, heart pounding sternum to backbone.

The pregnant girl stood on the bottom tread of the stairs. "I came to help."

"The doctor wants you to stay away."

"Then I'll take the children with me."

"The doctor wouldn't like that, either."

"If the children were going to get it, they'd have it by now. If they don't have it, I won't get it. So get them. And we'll get you cleaned up." She looked me up and down. "Because you don't want to go upstairs like that."

My gaze followed hers to take in my vomit-stained skirt, the poop-streaked stockings. "Don Sebastiano won't care."

"Not Don Sebastiano, silly. Carlo. The young shoemaker. He's upstairs."

Oh. Curiosity, even reluctant curiosity, was a welcome distraction. "What's he look like?"

"You've been living there this whole time and you've never seen him? My goodness, Fiora, how can a fortune-teller be so blind?"

"What are you talking about?"

"He comes every day since Don Sebastiano told him about you."

"Me?"

"Of course. Carlo's working harder than ever. Saving his money. There won't be a shoe needs repair for ten blocks by the time you get married."

"Married? Why would I get married? My brothers are coming back. I'm going to school. I—"

The girl put her hand to her mouth again, like when she talked about how her tongue was an unbridled horse. "Oh dear. You really didn't know. I thought you were teasing me the other day. Thought you thought I was being nosy. From the way Signora Lattanzi spoke, I thought it was all arranged."

Like a flower in a vase.

I thought of the fishmonger rubbing at his neck—*"Don Sebastiano is a friend, but I need somebody more permanent."*

"This is the reason nobody will hire me." Not because of my mother. "Because they presume I'll quit."

Because I'd. Be. Married.

To a man I didn't know. Cooking. Cleaning.

Keeping the buttons on his shirt.

I pulled the medicine bottle from my pocket, pulled the stopper, and took a generous swig.

So this was the old man's definition of trust. *Hand me a husband; his responsibility is satisfied; my problems are solved.*

I took another swig, imagining this young shoemaker, his hunch grown to mountainous proportions and his squint so pronounced he was all but blind in that eye. He'd probably expect me to thread his needles.

I took a third swig, and thought of my brothers, their letter to the old man—"*. . . and handle any other circumstances as you deem fit.*"

Fit. To wrap me up and hand me over.

Like a bowl of fruit.

I turned and turned again. The landing was full of doors. To the street, to the shop, to the basement, to the Lattanzis' apartment. Not one led to freedom, not one to my heart's desire.

I headed for the stairs, ire clearing a path. The pregnant girl stopped me. She put a hand on my arm. "Fiora. Please. Let's go to my apartment. Wash your face. Brush your hair."

The jolt that accompanied her touch made the one I'd experienced with the young man when he extricated my cuff from the lamppost seem like a pinprick. Had I been carrying a bag full of apples, I'd have dropped them. The heat crept up my neck and I knew I was blushing.

I let her take the bottle from me. Let her ascend the stairs with me. Let her lead me to the entrance of her apartment. "I have a fresh waist you can borrow, and a clean collar. So pretty. I know you're angry, but don't rush off. He's a good match. Soon he'll be a citizen."

Signora Lattanzi had said the same.

The pregnant girl's touch turned to ice. I dropped her hand, took hold of my skirt, vomit stains and all, dashed up the steps, barreled through the door to the old man's apartment. My tongue reared on its hind legs, and charged the old man at a gallop. "You can tell my brothers I wouldn't marry your short, crooked-backed, half-blind Carlo if he were a citizen of ten countries. I'm going to typewriting school. I'm getting a job in an office. And then I'm going to Atlantic City."

The old man looked up from his work. He flicked his head in the direction of the rooftop garden, where a broad set of shoulders obscured the open doorway. "May I present my assistant, Carlo Lelii. Carlo, this is Fiora Vicente, a young woman of strong ambition."

I turned to this . . . this Carlo, swath of oatmeal-laden hair hanging over my eye, smoke all but billowing from my nostrils. He stepped into the room, and I stared into eyes I already knew, large and honest and of the lightest blue, shining as sunlight on the Adriatic, like the stars overhead, windows onto an infinite filled with music, with truth, with the conviction life is best when lived.

The young man slid his cap off his head, threw an arm across his midsection, and bowed.

As he had on Parade Day.

I lunged for the attic stairs, scooping up the old man's Big Ben on the way. I burst into the attic, slammed the door behind, and lobbed myself across the light arrowing through the curtain's single open aperture with one well-formed, whole, solid desire: to escape the path everybody expected, and find the one meant for me.

The light flung me forward, propelling me like gunpowder onto the projection opposite, where trolley tracks rode street cobbles crossing the ceiling and chimneys stacked along the baseboard. Where the grocer, the fishmonger, and the lady with the freshly made tomato pies worked above awnings which yawed toward my floorboards, presided below stands which should have fallen at my feet. Where the world was as upside-down as my real life had become and always five minutes ahead of where I'd ever be.

A pop, a fizz, and the scariest of sucking sounds barrel-rolled me through the plaster. My stomach did a topsy-turvy, blood rushed to my head, the world went pale, my feet slid like ice covered the cobbles, cobbles I couldn't believe were somehow supposed to suspend me. I clutched the old man's Big Ben to my chest, an anchor in the tide. Then took a breath. On a world foreign, and familiar, and moving too fast.

The old man's Big Ben *tick-tick-ticked*, its pace moving ahead of Mamma's clock still in the attic room and still five minutes ahead of the rest of the world. The old man pounded on the attic door, but the rate did not sound urgent. "Fiora," he called, his voice elongated and low, "Thiiiis . . . iiiis ri . . . di . . . cu . . . lous. Coooome ooout. We wiiillll talk."

I wanted to answer, but couldn't keep the air in my lungs. Wanted to tell the old man to go away, not open the door, to leave, and take his Carlo with him. I was trapped in the image the curtain projected, a Ninth Street market in which I hung upside-down and uncomfortable. A world that would overexpose in too much light, and disappear in the dark. I had no idea what would happen if the curtain were thrown back, or another grommet opened, or if I lingered here past sunset. I was castaway on a magnifying shore, ticking to the increasing pace of the old man's clock. And the curtain was my only road back.

The knocking stopped, my sigh of relief whisked into the curtain world's advancing minutes, then an hour, another hour, half a day, into what had not yet happened. My every inhalation expanded beyond the previous; the subsequent exhale ended before it emptied. The future branched and branched again, an unfathomable complexity, in which one thing happened, and the other thing did, and still a different thing happened. The grocer passed me, time and again. I watched each of his eventualities unfold. Sometimes he turned to the right, sometimes to the left. Sometimes he raised his awning, and then laid out his produce. Other times he laid out his produce first. Each subsequent movement changed the movement that followed.

For the merchants, the people in the market, the schoolboys playing in the streets.

My ribcage blossomed with the incomprehensible enormity. My eyes bulged. My sinuses ballooned. My heart swelled with compulsion.

Examine each path. Explore every possibility. Extrapolate every consequence. Then move to the next.

The old man's Big Ben ticked its way to infinity. It dragged me along, prisoner to this new perspective. Until the future expanded past my ability to draw another breath.

Time snapped, like a cable released from its pulley, screeching me back through the days and hours and minutes, a deep tug that tossed me back into the attic and dragged me to my knees.

Dizzy. Disoriented. Fixed to the floor. Forearms crossed over my face.

My chest collapsed. My eyes sank back into my sockets. I had no idea. Never imagined. The future was big. It was so, so big. And not meant for mortals to travel.

Mamma's clock had advanced a full half hour, the amount of normal, everyday time I'd passed in the market projection's strange tangle of possibility. The clock *tick-tocked* at what sounded like its typical pace. The old man's Big Ben still slowed, its hands moving in reverse. I grabbed hold of the chair and pulled myself up, my excitement effervescing like seltzer. And gazed on a scene of confusion moving upside-down and cockeyed across the opposite wall.

People of the market gathered on the sidewalk. Most leaned over, and one pointed, his gesture so strong, I almost heard his silent shout: "Hurry. Hurry."

The old man's clock continued its backward tick. The crowd followed, sliding back to wherever they'd started. The object of their concern, a man motionless on the sidewalk, rose from fingertips to feet in a way that told me when he'd fallen, it had been all at once. He clamped a hand to the lamppost, the other to his chest, features contorted.

The old man.

Terror shot down my spine. Panic took the upward path, exploding down my arms, and past my fingertips, outstretched to the projection.

I checked the time. Five minutes from then. That was how long the old man had.

Five minutes.

No. Fiora, no. Reimagine the scene, splice a better ending, overtake the unthinkable outcome. Gather your strength. Don't let what will happen, happen. Do it now and do it with every part of every piece that is you, Fiora Vicente, Rosina Vicente's daughter.

I froze.

So did the image.

The old man's Big Ben stuttered, like it'd been tossed off a track, ticking toward Mamma's in seconds slower than it ever had in the mending pile. Slower than the moments between when I'd watched Mamma take her last breath and when she let it out. Slower still than Poppa's final coughing fit.

Giving me plenty of time to think.

Should I do this? Could I stop?

The old man was there, suspended between now and never. This world and the next. And there I teetered, a girl on the edge. Alone. Afraid. Blindsided by my past, blind to my future.

And as I tilted, so would the world.

Tick. Tock. Tick. Tock.

Tick.

The seconds accumulated, stalled by my indecision. They pooled at my feet, stumbled down the steps to my attic, shimmied under the old man's door, tumbled off his landing. They suffused the second floor, and the first, oozed over the stoop, cartwheeled off the curb, extending outward from the curtain, the circle perfect, until their edge arrived at the lamppost. At the exact moment as did the old man.

The world took a breath.

A breeze blew past the scene in the projection. Awnings rattled. Men grabbed at their hats, women at their skirts, vendors at their tables.

Then the breeze stopped.

Dead.

The people in the scene waited, looking one to the other. I waited with them, expecting a great gust to come from the opposite direction and scatter all those accumulated seconds.

None came. The old man's Big Ben slowed. Mamma's gathered speed. Until the two *tick-tick-ticked* in tandem.

A door closed. The path the world was supposed to take, in which the old man fell to the sidewalk and left his orphaned, immigrant ward to fend for herself, disappeared. Another path opened. Where it would lead, I had no idea.

The market resumed its activity. The old man swayed, then stopped, hand clamped to the lamppost. He looked about him, as if taking stock, then put a palm to his chest and rubbed at it in a circular motion. He looked up, and I could tell he focused on my window, dark and covered from the street. But from his upside-down perspective along my attic room roof slope, it seemed he saw me, inspected me from a great chasm, eyes squinting, expression damning.

The wheel had turned.

Change had come.

Development

Eight

My sleep the night after the old man didn't die was deep and complete under air which felt bulkier than my blanket. I woke an hour past my usual to the upside-down market flickering across the attic's ceiling slope, its projection slowed, like movies of the time, each frame exposed in increments longer than they had been the day before. I checked Mamma's Big Ben, compared it to the old man's. Five minutes still separated them. Five elongating and interminable minutes.

I slid out of bed, dressed carelessly, then made my way down the narrow staircase, shirtwaist half-untucked, stockings puddled at my ankles. I shuffled past the table, rubbing at sleep-sand crusted in my eyes. "Don Sebastiano?"

A half-eaten apple lay beside the newspaper. The stove was warm, the milk cold, the door to the old man's landing open. I pulled back the curtain's heavy crochet, but the beam entering from the street side yielded no more than a dull illumination, burdened by cloud cover.

I took the apple with me and descended the two flights to ground level, my every step landing like two. The street door seemed too heavy, its hinges too slow. I pulled pulled pulled for what felt like minutes, then hours, then stumbled down the stoop, looked this way, then that, half-expecting to see the old man's disappearing form turn the corner.

All I saw was a dog worrying at a pile of refuse.

The market still slumbered. I fought the urge to slumber with it.

I took a bite of the apple, then spit it out. It tasted mealy, and flat, nothing like the other apple from the batch I'd eaten the day before. I tossed the rest into the gutter and trudged back inside. Etti and Fipo waited outside their door. Fipo piped up. "Did you bring breakfast?"

"There was plenty of oatmeal in the pot when I left yesterday."

"We ate it."

Etti showed me his shirt, opened and flapping against his belly. "I lost my buttons."

Fipo shook his head. "He didn't lose them. They ripped off. He was climbing to get to the flour and caught them on the stove. We wanted to make hotcakes."

I grabbed Etti, checking him for burns. His shirt was a mess, streaked with grease. "I told you to stay away from the stove. Why can't you obey?"

Fipo took my hand off his brother. "You're not our mother."

Mamma used to tell me to count to ten when I thought my temper might get away from me. *"Twenty if you're really upset, Fiora."*

That morning, I counted to thirty, ticking each down like the seconds on Mamma's Big Ben, slower than seemed normal. Etti stood on tiptoes and reached his mouth to Fipo's ear. "What's she doing?"

"She's thinking up an excuse to ignore us."

In a crowd of a hundred, even with their faces hidden, Fipo's criticisms would have marked him as the signora's son. "Inside."

The boys didn't move.

"You heard me." I waved my arms. "Inside. Inside. Now."

Etti's eyes went wide. "Are you making a spell?"

"You got it, you little smart mouth. Inside, quick, before I cast it."

Etti took hold of the door's knob, turning it this way and that.

Fipo stood his ground. "There's no such thing as magic."

Hmmm . . . maybe he was his father's son also. I turned and continued my way up the stairs. Fipo's voice followed. "You're taking terrible care of us."

Inside the old man's apartment, I noticed what I hadn't before. The old man's coat hanging on its iron hook by the door.

Oops.

I found him on the rooftop, examining his plants. He lifted leaves, bent stems, poked a finger into the soil. He looked over the alley and beyond, slid off his cap, and scratched his head.

I went to stand beside him. "What are you looking at?"

"The trees." He pointed to several blowing in the next block, their tops visible from our vantage. "Now look at the market."

All was peaceful.

"Don't you see? Look at the papers by the wall. The awnings. Nothing is moving."

I pointed down the street. "Those awnings are moving."

He licked his finger and held it in the air. "I don't feel it. How can the wind be down the street, but not here? And this haze." He peered at the sky. "It should have burned off by now. Look." He pointed to a shaft of sunlight reflecting off a window several doors down. "Since when does sun shine on one house, and not the next?"

A nervous feeling tugged at my insides.

He again looked across the alley. "Those roofs are frosted. The cold came in overnight." He returned his attention to the plants. "Even with the candles, some of these should be suffering. They look exactly as they did. And here I stand without my sweater. How can it be cold there and warm here?"

His question hung heavy as the air, growing weightier with my silence. I backed to the door through space so thick I thought it should push my skirt forward.

The old man halted my retreat. "Fiora, what have you done?"

My explanations fell, one over the other, my fingers fluttering in an expanding arc to demonstrate how the seconds accumulated, how they rippled outward. "Like I threw a rock into a pond. I had no time. I couldn't think. I . . ."

The old man rubbed a palm to his forehead. "I saw you. Yesterday on the street. Like a dream without sleeping, a path I never lived. I was on the ground, my chest tight, but also standing by the lamppost.

In both places. And neither. Like I had a choice, but no options. For a long, long moment." The old man turned his remarkable blue-gray gaze on me. "You have to make it go back."

My stomach dropped to my ankles. No. No. I couldn't. "If I do, you'll die."

"I won't die. I will only pass to someplace different."

"I would be alone."

"You are not the center of all concern. And you don't understand. You can't chain time. All that should be happening will fill the spaces. Here." He touched his head. "And here." He touched his chest. "Until it chokes us and everybody caught within." He ran his thumb along the base of his throat. "Take a breath. Tell me that's not true."

I did as directed, dragging at air that felt thickened with flour. I thought how the pregnant girl must be feeling, the Lattanzis. Thought of entering the curtain world, the enormity, the expansion, the way my chest near exploded. "You fix it," I said.

He shook his head. "The curtain is your burden, your action. What results belongs to you. Don't use the curtain. Put it away. Perhaps your . . ." he waved his hand to indicate everything around us. "Perhaps whatever this is will fade."

I thought of how I tried to take the curtain to the guaritrice. "I don't think I can. The curtain wants to be at that window."

"Then you must destroy it."

Dismay took hold of my heart and twisted. "No. I can't. I won't. That curtain is all I have of my mother."

I grabbed my scarf and coat, ducked out the door, down the stairs, and into the street. Afraid. Of the old man. Of myself. Of what I'd set in motion.

The area directly outside our stoop felt stagnant. Like somebody had trapped it into a big glass bottle. Shoppers wandered past, pace listless, words muffled, their clothing drab. I took one step, then another, my gait leaden.

Gravity pulled at my shoes. My footfalls plodded. Sweat trickled under my collar. I removed my scarf, unbuttoned my coat. One step.

Two. Persevering to the place I'd seen the old man fall. I clutched at the lamppost, as the old man had.

Objects hold memories. Even now, if I concentrate hard enough, I remember them, too. The only memories that lamppost held were of people rushing past and the occasional dog, lifting its leg to relieve itself.

A newspaper, already discarded, crinkled against the post's base. Photos of the day's parade of dead, local soldiers all, headlined the page, along with news of battle victory somewhere, as well as details where to bring peach pits being collected for use in the manufacture of gas masks. The sidebar admonished all to buy their subscriptions to the Liberty Loan, to keep payments up to date, and informed that the incidence of influenza was decreasing, the crisis well in hand. "Stay warm, get plenty of rest, and salt water gargle."

I pushed myself south, past one shop, and another. A half block past the lamppost, I stopped.

Then started.

Then stopped, my impression that I'd entered a wall of gelatin.

A woman lumbered by, shoulders stooped. She hesitated at the gelatin, the way one does when faced with a crack in the sidewalk, then moved on, shoulders straightened, step lively, the green trim of her brocade scarf suddenly bright against her coat. A gust ruffled the edge of her hat.

I shored up my courage, and followed.

The veil lifted. The day grew sunny, the air fresh. My coat flapped in the breeze. I exhaled all the way, threw out my arms, and scooped in another lungful.

The temperature also dropped. I tightened my scarf and continued my way, progressing to a different pulse, the everyday rhythm which had already begun to feel foreign.

On that second day of October, contrary to the newspaper's assurances, a menace bloomed. A menace which transcended all borders, of race, of gender, of social means. A menace more destructive than any war, more fearsome than any nightmare. A menace which killed with perfect democracy.

I looked behind me and squinted to where I had been, not yet cognizant of the coming catastrophe.

The subtlest of shimmers marked a perimeter, a rainbow of iridescent swirls curved along its surface, like a soap bubble. The change I'd conjured in the old man's attic had a boundary. The events that would happen because of that boundary did not.

Nine

It seemed the crepe fabric appeared overnight, announcements of mourning which vied for space amid parade announcements which had not yet been removed. Black for the elderly. White for babies. Mamma used to tell me birth is sometimes too much for a tiny soul and it gives out, overwhelmed by life's enormity.

Nobody expected how much appeared for those caught in between. The young and vibrant. Mothers and fathers. Students and laborers. Carpet layers, wallpaper hangers, seamstresses, and shop clerks. Like dried lamb's blood, deep purple draping those doorways declared, "Stay away. Do not visit. Death lives in this house. Its name is Influenza."

Beneath that cloying cloud of despair, my fingers looked as they always had, nimble and able to handle a needle. My arms strong, able to scrub for hours. My legs steady, able to walk miles. Beneath my cotton nightgown, my breasts were high and round, the skin smooth, ready, when *I* decided the time was right, for a lover's caress. Yet my heart felt shrouded, tender. And bearing a banner: Do not talk to this girl. Do not notice. Turn away, for misfortune follows her kind.

Three days after Carlo broke on my horizon, I woke spitting a sprig of verbena from my mouth. I pushed out of bed, brushing bigger clumps off the blanket, my pace slower than the ever more sluggish sun. Bunches were tied to my bedposts. Leaves crumbled across the sheets. I pulled a bundle from Mamma's curtain, twined within an iron grommet, and shuffled downstairs, an afghan draped across my shoulders. I found the old man reading his newspaper.

I dropped the verbena on the table. "I'll be picking this out of the grooves in the floorboards for weeks."

The old man turned a page. "I mean it as a protection."

"From what? She's a widow woman, a peddler of remedies. Hang all the verbena you want, twist it into every keyhole within a block of the pharmacy." I thought of the guaritrice's tea, so fragrant and friendly. "The only thing you're protecting me from is herbs."

The old man looked up. "You returned to her. After I told you not to."

"I returned to the *pharmacy*. They have a job." The lie slid off my tongue with ease, like I'd been licking grease.

The old man's face went serene and studied, and I had the impression he was more powerful than he appeared, more observant than he let on. Able to see my thoughts, sense my movements, anticipate my mistakes. I needed to watch myself, take him seriously. "Is there espresso?"

The old man nodded toward the press, still steaming on the counter. I lifted the lid and sniffed. "What's wrong with it? I don't smell anything."

"The oatmeal is tasteless, too. I think it's your . . . what should we call it? Your bubble?"

"Don't be ridiculous." I emptied the coffee into the sink. "You probably didn't use enough beans. I'll brew more." I shoved the verbena into my skirt pocket and set the kettle to boil, using both hands to lift it to the stove—it felt laden with stones—then took a glass off the shelf and turned on the faucet.

The old man rattled the newspaper. "Wait for the kettle. We're supposed to boil the water." He showed me the headline, in a sidebar on page one: WATER PLANT WORKERS OUT SICK. PRECAUTIONS NEEDED.

Below an attention box reminded us to BEAT THE HUN. KEEP YOUR LIBERTY LOAN SUBSCRIPTION CURRENT.

Papa's subscriptions, tucked in with the money I'd given the old man for safekeeping, were already behind. If I kept them up, maybe—*maybe*—I could borrow against them for typewriting school.

I leaned over the old man's shoulder and pointed to the headline about the plant workers. "With so many sick, somebody must need help. Somebody who isn't convinced I'm getting married. Unless you've already taken out an advertisement setting the date."

"The Lattanzis will need you."

Yes, the Lattanzis were still alive. Sneezing. Hacking. Rasping so much I could use them as sandpaper. But alive. "I will check on them before I leave."

Every wrinkle on the old man's face tightened. He shoved his newspaper aside. "The children need more than a minute of your time. Children must always be watched, with careful and constant attention. What will you do when you have your own?"

"You can't order me around. You are not my father. They are not my children. I cannot spend hours every day cleaning their messes. They are not my responsibility."

"No. They are your moral imperative."

I wasn't sure what a moral imperative was. Something the nuns would make us do whether we wanted to or not was my guess. "I have to find work."

"There is plenty of work at the Lattanzis."

I showed him my apron, stained, my fingertips, raw, my palms, cracked and coarse and smelling of carbolic. "I *have* been working. I will not be trapped by ancient superstitions, boxed in by old-fashioned customs. This is America." I tapped my temple. "Only modern thinking."

He rose, put on his coat, and slapped his hat on his head. "Fine, then I will leave you to your modern thoughts." He nudged a leather satchel by the door. "Young Carlo forgot this the other day. He is coming to pick it up and deliver another. Perhaps you could find it in your modern heart to speak to him with at least the respect you would reserve for a dog."

"I won't be here when he arrives. I have things to do."

"What could you possibly have to do? You, a modern woman with no responsibility to your neighbors, to your benefactor, to your culture."

Did I answer? No. But only because the old man slammed the door after him.

I switched off the gas, threw on some clothes, and headed out. I was in no mood for tea.

The pregnant girl stood on the second-floor landing, clutching the rail, her face pinched. Sweat beaded over her upper lip.

"Are you all right?"

"I'm melting. The paper claims today's weather is cool and breezy." She swiped at her forehead. "The person who writes the report never gets it right. He should just look out the window."

I poked in my coat pocket for a handkerchief to give her. It exited with a cloud of verbena.

She pulled a twig out of my hair. "I see the don is making sure to protect you, too."

"He stuffed all my pockets."

"Leave it. If you clean them out, he'll only put in more." The pregnant girl was still in a bathrobe, belted carelessly over the bulge under her nightgown. She pulled it more modestly around her and peered up the stairs.

"He's not home. He had a load of moral imperatives he needed to deliver."

"Oh dear. Sounds like you and the don had a fight." She tapped a finger to her lips. "Not about Carlo, I hope."

"Why do men think a woman alone is a problem that needs to be solved?"

"Because a man alone is helpless." She rubbed at her neck, then shook the hem of her nightgown. "I can't sit in there any longer. Every window is open, but it still feels like I'm standing in a vat of tomato gravy. I'm desperate for a breeze. I was going to open the door to the street."

I imitated the tailor's wife's key ring jangling. "The signora wouldn't like that."

"The signora won't care. She keeps a key in the flowerpot beside the stoop and another wedged between the casement and the brick. You never noticed? Never mind. We'll have tea. So long as you're not in a hurry. The water's taking forever to boil."

She patted her hair and cocked her head in an appraising way, then reached for my braid and twisted it in her fist. She leaned forward, awkward around the baby's bulk, and looped the twist behind my head. She pulled a couple of pins from her chignon. "Take off your hat and turn around."

I did so, her attention sweeping my grumpiness to the side.

She fixed the braided loop into a loose bun and secured it with the pins. Her touch tingled against my scalp. She took me by the shoulders, turning them until I faced her, then set my hat back into place. "There. Now you look like one of those typewriter ladies."

I touched the braided bundle, feeling the need to stand taller, put my shoulders back, to counterbalance the new weight.

The pregnant girl shrugged out of her robe. "Tell you what. Forget the tea. Forget everything. Give me a minute to get dressed. We'll show off your new style to the world." She took my arm. "Walk with me."

Oh how I wanted exactly that, to wander the market, arm in arm, friends forever. With her by my side, the shopkeepers might not be so quick to refuse me, ashamed to appear petty in front of such a gentle soul, but . . .

"The doctor said you should stay inside." Something about pregnant women being more susceptible to the sickness.

She laid a hand over the bulge. "He also said exercise might help this little guy along. Honestly, if he gets any bigger, I'll pop."

Did babies grow in the bubble world? Did anything? I didn't know. I glanced to my fingernails—they seemed the same length as the day before, and the day before that. "Why do you think you're having a boy?"

Her mouth compressed and her eyebrows lifted, like my question surprised her, like nobody had ever asked her that. "I'm not sure. Nicco always talks about the baby like it's a boy. 'Sloppy and sticky and full of mozzarella,' he says. I guess he worries about a girl. Worries she'll break. Men always think boys are tough."

Tough. I thought of my brothers, fighting with the Italians. Maybe that's why men liked to send other men to war. Because then the war won't worry them. I glanced to the bottom of the stairs, to the Lattanzis' door. "The boys will be hungry."

"I left bread for them this morning."

Alarm zigzagged between my shoulder blades. "You talked to the children?"

"The older one. He's a scamp. He opened the door a crack, told me you said he couldn't talk to me, but that didn't mean I couldn't leave butter or jam if I had any. They'll be fine for a quarter hour."

Two Fioras debated her invitation, the Fiora who wanted to be like everyone else and walk with her friend in the open and the other Fiora who worried doing so might bring danger upon that friend.

But . . . fingernails didn't grow. Germs probably didn't either. "Don't forget your coat."

"In this heat?"

The front door opened. In stepped the young shoemaker. My good mood went glum. The pregnant girl pushed me forward. She retreated to her apartment. "Don't wait for me," she said, loud enough for him to hear. "I forgot something." Her latch clicked. Firm. Final.

Carlo gazed at me for at least a dozen of those lengthy intervals which now passed for seconds in our cramped and stagnant little world. He slid his cap off his head and fell to one knee. "Excuse my bad manners, signorina, but, to see you, standing at the railing like Giulietta . . . I am overcome."

I glanced at the pregnant girl's door, aware no power on heaven or earth would open it while Young Carlo, once so blessedly absent and errand-running, waited below. I descended the rest of the stairs through space thick as honey and tried not to pull where it stuck my clothes to my skin. I swept past him. "Wait there, Romeo. I'll get you some smelling salts."

He scrambled to his feet, beating me to the street door. "I know you're not happy with me. Never did I intend to deceive you when first we met on Parade Day. Certainly not when you passed by Signor

Minora's shop. I didn't want any gossip. You had no parents, and we had not yet been properly introduced. You know how people talk."

Yes. I knew exactly how people talked. "Don't you have something to pick up from the don?"

He smacked his forehead. "I forgot. A half hour won't matter. The don thought it might be a good idea for you and I to get acquainted."

"The don thinks a lot of things. Excuse me, please."

He stepped aside and let me pass, but chased after. "But when the don thinks, things happen." He slid his cap back on his head. "Where are you going?"

"South."

"Excellent. Exactly where I was going, too." He got two paces ahead, turned around, and walked backward, his step too lively for the new sedateness the bubble required. "Any place south in particular? Or are you going there in general?"

I switched directions.

So did he. "And now you go north. Why, signorina? To the north there are only monsters."

That stopped me. "The pharmacy is north."

"But you're not sick."

"I'm going to the pharmacy to inquire about a job they posted."

"So you can earn enough money so you can go to typewriting school so you can take the trolley to your job every day and maybe take the train to Atlantic City."

My jaw dropped.

Carlo scratched at the back of his neck, mouth and forehead scrunched to one side, like somebody drew them together with a stitch. "My apologies, signorina. You did mention a lot of that the other day." He looked at his feet. "And, as I said, you know how people talk."

About everything, and everybody, and every chance they got.

"I'm not trying to distract you from your ambitions. I'm asking for a few minutes of your time." He put out an arm. "Walk with me."

On the heels of the pregnant girl's invitation, his felt prescient, the feelings elicited with both, similar, the contrast, disconcerting. Memory of the day I'd watched the old man falter on the sidewalk took center stage, and I again saw myself as I had then, blinded before a sea of possibilities, crossed swords balanced against my chest, the growing pressure intolerable.

Oh bother. A little time now, maybe after he'd leave me alone.

I took his arm, hooking my hand in his elbow. It felt nice, secure, the muscles taut and strong. Nothing like the pregnant girl's. I sometimes wonder how differently those same five minutes might have gone had Carlo waited an equal number to cross our threshold.

He turned us and headed west, slogging me across a street that felt packed with snowdrifts. At a half block and another half block past the lamppost, I paused and put out my arm, anticipating the wall of gelatin.

Carlo waved his arm in the space before him also. "What is it, signorina?"

Nothing. It was nothing. Or rather, more of the same. No gelatin, no border. Just more sameness. I pulled my arm from the crook of his elbow. "I don't have to explain myself to you."

The bubble had expanded again in the night, as it had the night before, and the night before that. As it had every night since the old man did not have his heart attack.

Tomorrow, the bubble would expand again, and again, the day after, and again, the day after that. For how long, I didn't know. To what result, I couldn't imagine. The weight of my responsibility piled before me, insurmountable.

I turned around, ditched Carlo. And went home.

Ten

That night, I dreamed of colors. Tomatoes red and tossed with basil. Skies blue as turquoise. Yellow hair ribbons. Roses so pink they looked like a kiss.

The tomatoes got me out of bed. I was hungry.

I headed to the old man's garden and peeked under the quilts. But the fruit hanging from the vines was hard and green and far too pale, bleaching, like everything else in this bubble world. Hopelessness settled around my shoulders.

Somebody knocked on the old man's door.

Fipo. He held Etti's hand. "We're hungry."

"Signora Bruni didn't leave you bread?"

"Signora Bruni's sleeping. The don said to ask you."

How come nobody worried if I was sleeping? I followed the boys downstairs. "Where are the cannelini?"

"We ate it. I gave some to Mamma. She threw it up."

I tried not to think about the puke likely still lying on the bedroom floor. "Fipo, ask your mamma if there is money someplace so I can go shopping."

He darted into the bedroom and returned with a box, slim and silver and etched with flowers. He handed it over. "It's Mamma's. Poppa decorated it for her."

I lifted the lid. "I don't see any money."

"Are you sure? Mamma says everything important is there."

The box contained a photograph of the boys. Fipo, seated and serious, Etti in his lap.

Well and fine, but I couldn't trade sentiment for oatmeal. The signora must keep a little money somewhere. I rummaged in bowls, behind picture frames, upended vases, and shoved aside furniture, finally plowing my way to the bedroom across a floor that gelled like pudding and dreading what I'd have to do next—speak to the tailor's wife directly. "Signora Lattanzi?"

Her response came with a cough, hard, and hacking, and tinged with blood. "How long will this last? How long will this punishment last?"

I opened a window, but the warm, moist, bubble-compressed air that sloshed over the sill, only accentuated the stench. "Nobody's punishing anybody, Signora. You're out of food. I need to buy more."

"You've done enough of my mending to eat for a month."

The signore turned over. He put a hand on his wife's shoulder. "Shhhh." Then he pointed to the dresser. "There's an envelope stuck under the bottom drawer." He fell back to his pillow. "Thank you."

I checked and found plenty of money. Indignation turned my burners to high. Like with her keys, the signora probably had stashes all over the house. And here she wanted me to hand over the money from all the mending the old man forced me to do. Money I had yet to see because nobody had paid me.

The signora raised herself on one elbow. "The gas bill is due."

Yes, and the coal was getting low. The handkerchief with its tight-twisted coins I kept secure between my breasts suddenly felt petty. What would the tailor and his wife do when the money in their envelopes ran out? I returned to the kitchen. "Boys. Get dressed. Let's go shopping."

They clung to my skirts the entire time, Etti's hand wound tight in mine. We stopped at the grocer's. The apples looked pale, the sweet potatoes washed out, the prices higher than the newspaper said they should be. "Don't you have something nicer?"

The grocer kept his gaze firmly on the boys. "My deliveries are not so regular these days. Too many are sick."

I could try another stall. Maybe a block and a half or so, but the thought of braving the boundary, especially with the boys . . .

The grocer slid a squash across the table, a pumpkin with warts, what we call a *zucca barucca*, big and bright colored, the stem cut from where it had been harvested still raw. I rapped on its shell. The sound resonated deep and rich. The squash must have been newly arrived from beyond the bubble's border, and, given the shortages, better than I'd have expected the grocer to sell to me.

He dipped his head toward the boys, "For soup," then turned away, his part of the negotiation done.

Fine. I'd pay his ridiculous prices. People were watchful, casting me sideways glances. I made a big show of placing the money beside the cashbox.

Etti tugged on my wrist. He tapped under his eye. "Nobody's looking at us."

"Because they are all jealous of Signorina Vicente's luck to be accompanied by two such handsome young men." The voice came over my shoulder, light, familiar, and friendly. The pregnant girl. Welcome as water ice in August. She bent to the boys as best she could, given her condition, and held out her hand. "For you."

"Peppermint!"

They sucked happily while I stood in front of them, a human shield against their germs. I opened my mouth, but she placed her fingers over my lips. "They're fine. I'm fine. Let me help you. You look ready to drop."

Her hat rode so regally on her head. Her hair coiled so cooperatively at the back of her neck. I imagined the beautiful crochet collar of her shirtwaist covered in snot, the perfect pleats in puke, imagined her scrubbing and mopping, soaking and washing, ladling up bowlful after bowlful to feed two stomachs that seemed bottomless, and two that couldn't hold anything down. Then I imagined her sitting outside all the mess, keeping me company while I did the nasty work. I imagined her making tea and whispering encouragement, making funny comments, keeping the boys occupied. I imagined how beautiful she would look putting them to bed, telling them a story, running a hand over their foreheads and telling them not to worry, how everything would be all right. I imagined a world in which we could be friends, and people did not look on me with suspicion. "What is your name?"

Sellers and customers at the nearby stalls grew quiet. No good could come of asking for what had obviously never been offered.

The pregnant girl looked from one stall to the next, delicate and defiant. She lay her palms on either cheek, then released them to the heavens. "All the talks we've had. Living in the same building all this time. How silly I haven't told you already." She took my hand and squeezed. The pall lifted. The day brightened. Had a bird found a way to squeeze past the bubble's barrier, I believed it would have begun chirping. "I am pleased to meet you, Fiora Vicente. My name is Benedetta."

Benedetta.

Next morning, I woke with her name on my lips. Lips that let each and every one of the name's four syllables roll off my tongue with a click on the *t*. "Ben-a-det-ta."

Benedetta.

Somebody who brings blessings. Of course that was her name. It couldn't be anything else. I hopped out of bed, tossed on my clothes, and skipped downstairs, moving faster than I had in days.

The old man wasn't around.

Good. Better a morning without Don Dismally Disapproving. I was tired of feeling depressed. I wound the old man's Big Ben, eager for its chipper *tick-tick-tick,* but its hands pushed forward with the same reluctance of a visit to the dentist.

Tick.

Tock.

Tick.

Tock.

Plenty of time to notice the previous night's stew took forever to warm, the espresso to brew, the milk to steam. My shirtwaist suddenly felt cumbersome, my skin tacky, and my braid dragged on my neck like I'd tied it with a ribbon of iron.

The old man's curtains drooped to the sill; the windows refused to open. I flung the door to the garden wide, not to let the air in, but to let some of its awful denseness out.

Towels hanging on the line strung between the vegetable pots were still soggy in the bubble's damp warmth. I retreated inside, swept the old man's shoe forms off the carved wooden chest, and lifted the lid, intent on finding something fresh to dry the dishes.

A doily embroidered in pink roses greeted me. Roses like the ones in my dream, their color deep as the day they were embroidered. I traced along the design's edge, so like the blush along Benedetta's cheek. An afghan followed, appliquéd in red apples. Next came a shawl, *trapunto* speckled across its frothy white like fresh-fallen snow.

I climbed atop the table and wrapped the shawl around the hanging fixture's plain metal frame, then pulled the chain. Soft glowy patterns cut through the bubble's growing gloom and dismissed the doldrums.

I pushed the old man's tools to the benches, scrubbed the table, and laid a cloth, bright with embroidered strawberries. Benedetta would love this. Maybe I could invite her up. Tea and a little conversation. Like other people.

I dug deep into the wooden chest, seeking napkins. I found a photograph instead, framed in filigree and colored in the sepia of the time.

Three crosses, draped in white crepe, rose from a freshly turned plot in a walled garden. One cross was so small, it all but disappeared in the bulk of the other two. An ancient fig tree protected the crosses, and hand-tinted *poleggio* and *pervinca*, flowers meant to comfort the spirits of dead children, sprouted from the surrounding stones.

A couple knelt beside the grave. About the Lattanzis' ages, they dressed in traditional clothes found in old family trunks. The woman's sleeves were long and wide, gathered at the wrists, her skirt voluminous with vertical creases, and her headdress tied under her chin in the typical sign of mourning. The man's jacket was short, close to his body and buttoned to his neck. He held the lady's shoulder. His posture spoke of sadness, deep and profound and too heavy to bear.

The old man. I'd know the hollow of that cheek anywhere.

It felt strange to see him strong, younger than my poppa. His hair had once been so dark and full, his face unwrinkled. I presumed the woman to be his wife, the lady responsible for the contents of the chest, for the old man's garden.

Her face was turned away from the camera, revealing only the downward slope of an eyebrow and the curve of her cheek. I put a hand to mine, smooth as hers in the photograph, and imagined a time, in the far, far future, when my skin would crinkle as hers did in my vision by the strawberries.

Without the sickness, I'd never have known of her, nor the old man. Would never have met Benedetta. Good things sometimes came from bad. Mamma used to say so. Did good things ever come on their own?

"What is going on?" The old man stood in the doorway, a familiar leather satchel under an arm, his expression steel, his tone granite. He looked to the tablecloth, the afghan, the doily, the shawl shading the ceiling fixture.

I slid the photograph behind the stove. "I wanted to surprise you."

He laid the satchel on his bench. "You were successful."

"You don't like it."

"I don't understand it."

"You told me this is my home. That we are family. I wanted to make it pretty."

"Ah. And as a modern woman you don't need permission before pawing through my things."

"If I marry Carlo, these would be my things, too. That's part of the agreement. Take Rosina Vicente's daughter off everybody's hands and he doesn't have to wait for his inheritance."

The old man tilted his head. "Is that what he told you?"

"Well, no. Not exactly." Not at all.

"Exactly what did he tell you?"

"Nothing. We went for a walk. Look, that's not important. What's important is that everything in the chest is so beautiful. Somebody loved these items. Somebody wanted them to be used." I retrieved the linens, hands shaking, folding and refolding, but they refused to reassume the compact and precise arrangement in which they'd been laid. I gave up and slammed the lid. "I don't like the world I created. It is heavy, and harsh, and slow as sludge. But the one you've created is worse. Work and sleep, work and sleep, work and sleep. Life is so big. It's so very, very big."

The old man took his place at his table. He unrolled a length of leather. "And yet you placed yourself into a bubble."

Fine.

I went to replace the shoe forms, smallest to largest, huffing. A red cloud descended. My throat tightened, my stomach cramped, my palms went moist. Every part of me filled with the awareness, the awful finality. "The DiGirolamos are dead. That's why you didn't send Carlo to deliver their shoes. You knew they were sick, and you didn't want him to catch it. You're like me. You're exactly like me. You see things, know things."

The old man took his time about answering, like my words were a package in need of careful handling. "I know everybody knows the DiGirolamos were here on Parade Day, that you saw them, saw their children." He pointed to the satchel. "Mending. Perhaps it would be better if you stayed home today."

I took a step back, gaze darting corner to corner, though where I thought I would go I still don't know.

People die. They die all the time. And at that place, in that time, they were dying from a sickness, a sickness carried on a sneeze and spread by a war we hadn't caused, we couldn't cure, and we were helpless to control.

Yet people still blamed me. I was trapped, caught in a bubble far more compact than any the curtain had manufactured, populated by every superstition our backward world could produce.

I shuffled through the shoe forms and saw the feet those forms had measured, the shoes made with them permanently emptied. Boys and girls, mothers and fathers, teachers and seamstresses, cooks and cabinetmakers, a congregation sucked into an ever-widening sea of red. A sea filled with the lost dreams, the unfulfilled talent, and the unrealized promise of their unlived years.

Eleven

In the normal world, a week measures no more than seven days, each of those days lasts a mere twenty-four hours, and each of those hours slips past minute by relentless minute. In the bubble world, time ceased to have meaning. Every stuporous second extended into an infinity in which all things happened, but nothing progressed. What did hours and days matter when each resembled the last? I slept. I woke. Prepared food and took baths. The sun rose. It set. So did the moon. The world turned on its axis, yet in the bubble, all we perceived was an increasingly unwieldy, unrelenting, and inexorable Now.

And despite the lengthiness of every moment, the typewriting school's deadline for making an application loomed. I needed a job.

Etti pulled on my skirt. "What if Mamma and Poppa die?"

I wrung out the mop and set the bucket into the corner. "They won't die."

"What if they do? Mamma says we cannot stay with you."

I combed that question out of my hair, tucked my clothes in properly, straightened my skirt, and checked the set of my collar. "You boys be good. I'll check on you later."

"There's no more bread."

"There's soup on the stove. Don't touch the burner. Eat it cold if you have to. There's tea already brewed if your parents want it."

"You make a lot of tea."

"It makes your parents feel better."

"Can you make them hotcakes? Hotcakes would make them feel better, too."

Not my hotcakes. "Maybe I'll do that when I get back."

Fipo called me into his parents' room. "Poppa threw up again."

I sent Fipo for the mop, wrung out a cool cloth from the basin on the dresser, and placed it over the tailor's fever. His breathing was labored, his face hollowed and haggard.

Germs didn't grow in the bubble world, so the Lattanzis did not get worse. Germs also didn't die, so the Lattanzis did not get better. They still needed to breathe, still needed to sleep, still needed to use the toilet, so I held to the hope that given the time, the Lattanzis would build resistance. Meanwhile, they needed to eat, but if they could not keep their food down, the Lattanzis would starve.

I headed out the door. I had to do something. Find something to take away the *agita*. The old man wouldn't like it if I went to the pharmacy, but the reasons for his disapproval grew fuzzy. Something about not liking the pharmacy lady's tea.

Benedetta called to me from her landing. "Are you going out?"

"Yes. Is there something you need?"

Her hair was tousled, her face wan. She lay a hand over her bulge. "Find me a box of sleep. What I wouldn't give to be able to lie on my stomach again." She moved toward the bathroom. "So sorry. Can't wait. I'm bursting."

Now I had a double reason for going to the pharmacy. Maybe the druggist had something to make Benedetta more comfortable. I could bring it up to her. I warmed to the idea. An excuse to see her that didn't involve the boys or my fortune-telling.

The old man's warnings suddenly seemed laughable. He got his pills from the pharmacy. No logic I shouldn't go there to get something to help Benedetta, to help the Lattanzis.

Unless Carlo's warning about the monsters were true.

"Signorina?"

Like my thought had poofed him into existence, Carlo stood between me and the street door. "I didn't mean to startle you. You were lost in thought, gazing to the ceiling like you saw stars. Are you going out?"

I had on my coat and hat. Of course I was going out. "How do you keep getting in here? How come you never knock?"

"I have a key, signorina."

A key. Like he was one of the family. "Excuse me, please. I don't have time to chat."

"The don had mentioned it might be better for you to stay close for a few days."

I clenched my fist, letting every nail slice a groove into my palm. "And because you have a key you think it is your job to keep a list of everything I should and should not do? Maybe you should see the don now. See if he has any further restrictions."

"Please, signorina." His tone went from conversational to contrite. "At least let me accompany you." He indicated the satchel under his arm. "I'll bring these to the don and come right back. He doesn't have to know."

I stood to the side so he could pass.

"Five minutes. No more." He darted up the steps, his pace demonstrating none of the damp despair which pulled at all else in the vicinity.

Of course I didn't wait. Carlo belonged to Don Sebastiano. He wouldn't like me going to see the guaritrice, either.

There were one hundred and seven steps from our stoop to the grocer. Before the bubble those steps were without effort, accomplished without notice. In the unrelenting Now, the steps felt twice as many and mired in mud, weighted by the gravity of a hundred disapproving stares.

The grocer's offerings were slim, the activity in the market subdued. Shoppers passed, aromatic with the scent of camphor and onion necklaces, worn to ward off the sickness. I looked over the stalls, feeling hopeless. This is what we had come to, camphor and onion, probably sold by the guaritrice, a woman only trying to feed her daughter, a woman whose tea upset the old man.

The clip-clop of horses cut through my sloth. A wagon approached, much like the one on Parade Day, filled with what I first took to be rolls of blankets. As they had on Parade Day, men slid caps off their heads. Ladies crossed themselves. Children were admonished to "hush."

Down the block, a jumping rope rhyme rose in the sudden stillness. The rhythm of a little girl's shoes slapped the cobbles in complement to the rhythm of the hooves:

"I knew a little bird,

Her name was Enza.

I opened up the door,

and IN-FLU-ENZA."

The wagon driver stood, his voice rising over the child's. "Bring out your dead."

The blankets in the back of the wagon weren't rolled. They were wrapping bodies.

We all looked, one building to the next, waiting for a window to open, a door to unlock, some notice of who had died in the night.

All remained silent. There were no takers. There couldn't be. Not that day. Nor the next. Nor the next day after. Inside the bubble, nobody could die.

But that didn't mean we lived.

The market activity resumed, solemn, and cautious, the shoppers wary, the merchants suspicious. A man pointed to the wagon receding down the cobbles, then pointed to me.

One woman whispered, "*Strega.*" Witch.

Another, "Remember her mother."

A different man, two stalls down, muttered, "She needs to be controlled."

"The don isn't thinking straight."

"That Carlo should be careful."

"Shhhh . . ."

"Not now."

"She'll hear."

And other voices, springing to protect:

"Stop it. A sickness is carried by germs. She's only a girl."

"She has her mother's curtain. That's how."

"*Pfft.* It's a piece of fabric. Leave the girl be, she's not bothering you."

I went on my way. The kind speakers faded, their attention returned to everyday tasks. The fearful followed, their menace coagulating in my wake.

"Her parents died, but she did not even get sick."

"The DiGirolamos saw her. They said she looked them in the eye."

"She has her mother's curtain. What other mischief might she cause?"

Return to the old man's apartment seemed impossible, the path behind crowded with enmity.

A tub of water overturned on my shoes. An odor, fetid and sharp, rose before me.

"I was washing the trays." The fishmonger's wife retrieved the bucket. She spit over her left shoulder. "You should watch where you step."

Somebody jostled me and something damp and pasty soaked into the front of my coat. A rotten squash. I scraped at the clod, the seeds embedding under my fingernails.

A handkerchief appeared. I took it and scrubbed it across the stain. A gelatinous swath smeared into the mess. Snot. I dropped the hankie and looked to see who had handed it to me, but the once familiar countenances of the people in the market contorted. They melted into a featureless mass of gray. My face went hot and the inside of my nose stung.

I shed the coat, threw it over my arm, and pushed on, plodding to a new rhythm marked by anxiety and fear. Ten steps, then five, repeated once, then twice. And still, the people followed me, the pharmacy in sight.

"Get out."

"We don't want you."

"Cover your eyes. Don't let her look in them."

I pushed into the pharmacy, the crowd pushing in behind. The druggist, eyes shadowed above his mask, *rappa-tap-tapped* on his counter, pointed to a notice tacked to the wall behind him—BE POLITE. GET IN LINE. WAIT YOUR TURN.

I wasn't going to be polite, wasn't going to get in line. I was tired and tattered and smelling of fish. A finger tapped my shoulder. A voice whispered in my ear. "Take their rage, swallow it whole, turn their emotion against them."

I obeyed, consuming their hatred, their fear, in chunks and shards. I let it pound in my temple, beat against my chest. I imagined my tormenters sick, lying in putrid piles around me, the red dust coating the insides of their lungs and their bodies stacked like cord wood.

Power gathered behind me, like sunlight behind the curtain, except this power was dismal and desperate and determined to find a way out.

Another hand came out of the chaos, pulling me back from the entrance.

Carlo. All he got was my coat. "Don't go with her, signorina. All you will find is monsters."

The guaritrice emerged from the mess. She pointed to the crowd. "I think she's already found them."

The pharmacy filled. Carlo got in close, got hold of my hand. He stepped this way, then that, trying to keep himself between me and the people. So many people. I circled with him, but the crowd seemed to multiply. They pressed in. From every angle.

The guaritrice's voice rose above the hubbub. "Let us through."

She might have been Moses, or rather, Moses's wife, for the way the crowd parted, falling away to either side.

Tizi rushed forward. "Are you here about the job? I knew you'd come. I keep telling Mamma, 'Don't worry, Fiora will return.' We've been so busy. So many orders to fill. You have no idea. There are so many more here than in the last place, and—"

A hand fell on Tizi's shoulder. "Enough, my love. We are not so busy we forget our manners. Have you even said 'Good afternoon' to Fiora's young man?"

I let go of Carlo. "He's not my young man."

Tizi played with the end of her braid, twirling it and untwirling it as I used to when I wore my hair that way. Why had I thought she was older when I saw her from the trolley tracks? She appeared even younger than the day we first met. She looked Carlo up, then down. "If he's not your young man, what is he?"

The guaritrice lowered her mask. She looked over Tizi's head at Carlo. "Don't be rude, Tizi. Signor Lelii is our Fiora's friend of course. And how nice. We can all use a friend."

Our Fiora. The designation puffed me up. Lightened the effect of the bubble. Nobody had referred to me as *our Fiora* since that last time my parents introduced me to somebody. *"And this is our Fiora."*

Tizi turned her back on Carlo. "Well, I can be Fiora's friend, too."

Carlo touched my elbow. "Come on. Let's go. The don will be expecting us."

The guaritrice stepped between us. She wisped a hand by my hair, at the chignon helping my hat to sit at a jaunty angle. "And look at you, little one, all grown up, and so fast, doing a woman's work before you've even had time to be a girl."

She wrinkled her nose and slid her mask back into place. She eyed my coat, still slung over Carlo's arm, eyed the snot on its collar, then side-eyed Carlo. "But friends should protect each other, don't you agree?" She put an arm around my shoulder, turned me so she and I faced Carlo, where a moment before, Carlo and I were facing her. "Perhaps I can help."

Carlo reached across the chasm. "Thank you signora, but we only need to see the druggist and we will be on our way."

"I insist. Look at that line. Where men founder, women can often move events forward. Tizi, why don't you get Fiora's . . . *friend* some tea." The guaritrice stepped away, drawing me with her, like I was pulled with a thread, sucking me into a sphere which did not include Carlo.

"You don't have to go with her." Carlo's fingers grazed the back of my blouse. "You can think for yourself."

Of course I could think for myself. I looked over my shoulder. "You don't need to stay."

The guaritrice snapped her fingers and a wall of people filled the space behind us. I lost sight of Carlo. "Don't worry about him, little one. Tizi will get him settled. Men. They think they know what's best. Too often, they don't know anything. Tell me, why are you here? Nobody braves the streets these days without a mission."

I explained about the Lattanzis. About Benedetta. She took my arm and led me toward her little alcove. The wall of people followed, like iron shavings chasing a magnet.

"Please, signora, I've been waiting hours." A man, frantic and familiar, broke from the pack, beady eyes flitting back and forth above a bulbous nose.

The landlord.

The guaritrice went to stand behind the counter. "We expected you yesterday, signore. Tizi was up before the sun preparing your order, but you went to the druggist first."

The landlord took on the air of a hunting dog. Eyes forward, ear cocked. "How could you have expected me? They got sick only yesterday morning."

"Word travels, signore. How sad you did not come right away. I'm told your children are much worse, especially your oldest."

"So many of my tenants are sick. Collecting rents is difficult. I thought possibly the druggist might have something . . . less expensive."

"Ah, yes. We all have to make hard decisions. Each mixture is unique, compounded for the individual. Yours is spoiled. Tizi can make you another batch, at least enough for your oldest, but we will have to charge you extra to cover our costs."

The landlord clutched at his cap. "I hoped—"

"We would be able to provide enough for your whole family." The guaritrice finished for him, her voice smooth as polished metal. "We should be able to get you the rest tomorrow, maybe the day after." She glanced pointedly at me. The landlord followed her gaze. "It is proper to do right by our neighbors."

The landlord seemed petty and small, nothing like the imposing figure who'd put me out in the rain. My heart soared to see his heart brought low. My spirit lightened to see his spirit in the dirt. I bet his house was filled with snot. I bet there was coughing and hacking and nights without sleep. I bet he scrubbed and mopped and washed blood from the sheets without end. I stared at him the way I'd stared at him the day the old man brought me to get my things. Open and angry and full in the eyes.

He looked away.

And I bet he was sorry he'd tried to keep my mother's curtain.

The guaritrice put a hand on the strongbox. "We will take your payment now. Come back in two hours. Do not be late. Or we will need to do this negotiation again."

The landlord lowered his head. He dug into his pocket, and counted out the cost. He laid it on the counter. "Thank you, signora. Two hours."

The guaritrice turned and marked another red X on the map tacked to the wall behind her. The pattern had changed from the bloom rising along Broad Street on Parade Day. Now the Xs made a spiral four blocks to the east, a spiral circling the market. The landlord's X was on an outer ring, right at the spot where Mamma and Poppa and my brothers and I had lived. The crowd pushed forward, swarming to fill the landlord's place. The guaritrice sniffed at the air. "Tizi. We have customers."

Tizi popped out from behind the curtain, two steaming cups of tea in hand. She placed one before her mother and slid the other before me, then took her mother's place by the strongbox, handing out bags that looked much like the one the guaritrice had handed me on the day we met. She named prices, collected the money, and marked the map. One signora's face squinched. "But that is twice as much as yesterday."

Tizi looked to her mother.

"Because demand is so high." The guaritrice pointed to the map, to the multiplying red Xs. "We would never think to put a price on your family's survival, but our suppliers' prices are rising by the hour, so we must pass the cost on to you."

The signora did not appear to believe her. Nobody in the crowd did. Still, they continued buying, their pleas growing more desperate as the minutes passed. I drank my tea and watched, letting the lavender remind me of all I had lost, how very fortunate these people were to even have the guaritrice's tea. She came and settled beside me.

I wasn't feeling very friendly. "How come you did not make a mix for my parents?"

Her face went sad. So very, very sad. Like the responsibility of every bad thing in the world suddenly took up residence in her forehead. "Your mother did not come to me soon enough. When tragedy strikes, we must not be overly cautious in our decisions. We must move quickly, do what is recommended, or miss our opportunity." She put her hand over mine and gave it a squeeze. It felt squishy and cold. I pulled away, lay my palms in my lap.

The guaritrice's face went hard. "Ah, I see you don't agree. But, look at you, little one. So busy. So very, very busy. But have you money to show for all that busyness? Has it brought you one step closer to your ambitions? No. It's produced tomatoes that won't ripen, babies that won't be born, and sick people who refuse to get well. I told you there is a price to pay when we do not use things properly."

Her recitation washed over me like acid. "How did you know?"

"How could I not? People may not have a name for their prison, but all feel the effects."

"I call it a bubble. And I don't know how to make it burst."

"Burst?" Her eyes went wide and alarmed. "Oh no. You cannot allow that to happen." She cupped her hands before her face to demonstrate a bubble, then splayed her fingers, and threw her arms wide. She waved them, moving them chaotically in all directions. "You cannot control the result."

Fine. I guess there wasn't any reason for me to be there. I stood and straightened my hat. The guaritrice reached a finger and lifted my chin, as the old man had when the tailor's wife first brought me to him. "You are a smart girl. A wise girl. You went down a road you did not intend. And now you return to the place where you might find counsel. Yet you arrive empty-handed, looking for remedies, not for a cure. I owe your mother a debt. A great debt. But without the proper tools, I am helpless."

I thought of the verbena, my attempts to bring the curtain to her before. "It would be better if you came to my house."

"Don Sebastiano would not like that."

Her words were pointy little pinpricks of annoyance. "I don't have to listen to Don Sebastiano."

"But Don Sebastiano thinks you do. Men. So helpless on their own. So certain they know what is best for us." The guaritrice handed me two bags, bags very like the ones Tizi dispensed. "The large for the Lattanzis. A little before every meal and all will be well. The second for you, my own blend. Take them and take yourself. Return with your mother's curtain. Don Sebastiano is a good man, a wise man, but men do not always know the best way to proceed and not all are wise enough to let a greater wisdom prevail."

She put a hand to her nose, and I again became aware of the fishmonger's stink, the stain on my collar, the embarrassment, the fear of being left on my own.

"It is late little one. Don Sebastiano will wonder where you've gotten to." She looked to the front of the pharmacy. "And your young man will be waiting."

I followed her gaze. Thought of Carlo waiting, when I'd told him to leave. How he'd followed when I didn't wait. The pinpricks became spikes, driving a wedge of resentment between who I was, and who everybody wanted me to be. "I told you. He's not my young man."

She dug into her bodice and pulled out a key. She went to the door behind the counter and drew back the hanging strings of beads. "Ah, then I will let you out a side exit."

"But, but . . ." I picked up the bags. These weren't enough, only a fraction of the help I needed. How could I bring a curtain that refused to be brought? How could I control a bubble that was bound to burst?

And there was Benedetta. "Her time is now past. Is there nothing you can do for her?"

All the guaritrice's edges went soft. She pulled me close, her scent mixing with that of the tea's lavender, again the comforting presence I craved. "It has been many years, and now there are so many modern methods."

She was talking about the knife, about cutting out the baby. My stomach cramped with the thought. "You know about these things."

"I used to attend many births." Her voice grew vague. "It is easier if the help is sought willingly. You will know what to do when the time is right. If it seems necessary, bring the girl to me. Such a privilege to help Rosina Vicente's daughter. Such a privilege to help her friend. But don't tell Don Sebastiano. He's such an old-fashioned man. Set in his ways."

"How could Don Sebastiano not know? Carlo came in with me. He will tell the don I was here."

The guaritrice led me down a dark passage, more crooked and looped than would seem possible, one we navigated mostly by touch. She turned the key in the lock and twisted the handle. "Do not worry about Young Carlo. He won't be telling Don Sebastiano anything. He has been drinking my tea."

Twelve

Outside, in the alley behind the pharmacy, my pricklies sputtered in the humid and far-too-warm-for-October afternoon. I looked to the sky, squinting to see past the dullness. I wanted to rejoin the world of light and time, feel my heart beat to a pulse growing faint. Yet my every effort fell short of my expectation. My every idea withered without exception. My every hope doused in an ever-expanding deluge of responsibility. I had to find a way to resurrect my dreams, or they would bury me in disappointment.

A newspaper page flapped against the pharmacy's back stoop, dog-eared and damp. Beneath a listing of dead heroes was a boxed admonishment:

DON'T BE LATE.
THE HUN WON'T WAIT.
KEEP YOUR FOURTH LIBERTY BOND SUBSCRIPTION
UP TO DATE.

News of the influenza again occupied a sidebar, advising the populace its spread had been "considerably checked." In war news, American and British troops were smashing through German lines, and Italians in the Isonzo were preparing for a final push.

The Isonzo.

I knew nothing about war. My brothers' letters always spoke of life in tents, sometimes bad weather, complaints the food was not as good as Mamma's. I imagined them standing in files like little lead soldiers, their rifles shouldered. Somebody would give the order to charge. They would. The pieces would scatter, then everybody would pick themselves up, scrape off the mud, and head back to camp for dinner.

The paper's dead heroes were young, often smiling, proud in their uniforms, a reason to pause for pity, to say a prayer, to bring pasta and pastry to their grieving relatives. They were dead in theory, not for real, not like my parents, cold and irrefutable and hardening under their bedcovers. And until somebody showed me otherwise, none of those dead heroes would ever belong to me.

I kicked the paper to the side and adjusted my scarf to cover my mouth and nose. Carlo still had my coat, but the stench of the fishmonger's wash water remained, rising from my shoes, soaked into my stockings. I picked my way south through the trash heaped along the alleyway and onto a street quieter than a Sunday morning in a January snowstorm.

A confectioner across the street was closed, a notice tacked to the doorway: OPENING TOMORROW. FUNERAL. A milliner's, a stationer's, a tinker's stand, all silent.

The trolley rumbled to a stop.

I shook my head, fuzzier than the air, to let the white-masked conductor know I wasn't riding. The trolley rumbled on, the people aboard packed close as matches in a two-penny box.

Catacorner from where I stood, a bakery was closing up shop. I plodded across the cobbles, and bought two rolls.

The baker bagged them. "I'll give you a good price on the rest."

I thought of Etti and Fipo, and plunked down another coin. I slipped one roll into my pocket, twisted the bag containing the others into my scarf.

Down the street, the girls still jumped rope, their pace sedate, their rhythm sapped of rhyme. A few doors down, a group of boys crouched, playing marbles, coats unbuttoned and shirttails dragging on the sidewalk. Farther on, a little girl sat on a stoop and cuddled a doll.

I knew her. Grazia. The little girl who darted past me on Parade Day. I looked at her tangled hair, remembered the neat braids. Her mother must be ill. A little boy, looking enough like her I guessed he was Grazia's brother, sat on the stoop beside her, face dirty, head resting on her shoulder. I moved toward them. I'm not sure why. Maybe I thought I would give them a roll. The little girl saw me coming. She took her brother's hand, and disappeared inside the house.

Grazia's mother had been so angry, though I'd saved her daughter. She likely told the girl to beware, likely told her I'd brought her a curse. The pricklies returned, poking from under my collar. I continued down the street.

A half a block on, a dog barked, then growled. Children's voices, which I at first assumed were rising in play, turned frightened. I gathered my skirt and ran.

"Hold him. Hold."

"Watch your hands."

"Get it. Quick."

Then a scream.

I rounded the corner into an alley and onto a group of boys, piled into a trash heap. A dog bounded away, something tight in its jaws. The boys picked themselves up. I grabbed the biggest by his collar. "What happened? Who screamed? Are you hurt?"

"It was in the trash."

"What was in the trash?"

"Cappacoli. C'mon signorina, the dog had it, we tried to get it. We didn't do anything wrong." He thrashed under my grasp, grabbed my scarf.

I held tight to the guaritrice's teas. The rolls went tumbling. The children fell on them. And scattered.

The boy stopped struggling. He looked after his departing friends and let out a wail, then raised a dirt-streaked face to mine. "Do you have more?"

The boys had been rummaging in the trash for food. They were hungry. Their parents were sick, and there was nobody to care for them. I imagined their apartments, piled in dishes and dirty clothes, overflowing basins and snot-filled hankies. Imagined the children pawing through empty iceboxes, empty canisters.

It'd been more than a week, days and days. Pay packets would be spent, rent due. Appeals to relatives would go unanswered because they would also be sick. Within my bubble nobody died, yet children cowered in corners while their parents vomited all they tried to eat, coughed to exhaustion, and burned under the fever.

My feet got numb, like they weren't connected to my body. My head grew heavy. I twined my fingers in the boy's collar, needing something steady and sure, something familiar with which to connect. "Take me to your house."

Worse than the worst the Lattanzis' had ever been. Every dish crusted, every cloth soiled. The boy's parents coughed in their room, his brother curled into a corner, thumb in mouth. Like Etti.

I picked up a bowl, and put it into the sink. Picked up another and did the same. I ran the water. Cold. I thought of the Lattanzis' furnace, wondered who was responsible for making sure the one in this house stayed lit. Did they even have coal?

Outside the bubble, time had become precious, each second lasting no longer than it should, the moments which happened between them impossible to retrieve. Inside, the suffering never ended. I was one girl. One confused, dejected, and exhausted girl.

Stinking of fish.

I reached into my pocket for a handkerchief. The last of the baker's rolls tumbled out and fell to the floor. The boy turned around when it hit. His brother pulled his thumb from his mouth. They fell on the roll.

Like dogs.

I walked out of the kitchen, out of the house. I closed the door behind me.

A long, long quarter hour later, I turned the corner onto Ninth Street. "Fiora."

The doctor. White-masked. Wan. Heading my way. He had the old man on his elbow.

My pace picked up, along with my heartbeat. "What happened? Is he all right?"

The old man didn't look happy to see me. "Where have you been? Where's Carlo?"

All the umbrage of the past few hours flew forward and knocked my conscience into the gutter. I lied. "He had work to do. I went looking for Signora Lattanzi's sister."

The doctor shook his head. "I saw the signora's sister this morning. She will not survive the day." He nudged the old man. "Get him upstairs. Find his pills. His heart can't take this."

The old man shrugged him off. "I have my pills. They're on the shelf."

"They should be in your pocket." The doctor handed me a booklet. "For you. For the pregnant girl. In case her time comes and you can't find me. I have to go. And for God's sake, that scarf won't work. Get a mask."

He was off.

The old man held on to my shoulder and let me walk him a painful step, then another. People gathered, sideways glances cast my way.

The old man told them not to worry, told them he was fine. "Fiora will see me home."

But the men insisted. Two formed a chair with their arms. Two others lifted the old man and sat him between them. They trudged together through the thickness which now defined our world, trading stories and jokes.

I trudged behind. This is how regular people talked. People whose mothers were not the neighborhood fortune-teller. Easy and friendly with one another, containing a lightness which defied the bubble's growing density, their words allowed to exit unmeasured, unexamined. Unnoticed.

They knew the old man, knew he knew things. Yet they treated the old man with respect and remembered my mother with fear.

It wasn't fair.

The old man made the men leave him at the stoop. "Go," he told them. "Fiora can help me from here."

They slid caps from their heads, each backing up a step with a deferential nod. Then they turned, replaced their caps, and were gone.

The old man took his time taking the stairs. In the apartment, he took his place at the table.

I rummaged among the canisters on the shelves. "Where are your pills?"

"The doctor gave me one."

"Then where are they in case you need another?"

"By my cot." He reached for a leather punch. "What did the doctor give you?"

The booklet. I pulled it from my pocket. It was in English and titled *Childbirth in the Home*. I paged through, blushing at the illustrations, at anatomy the nuns told us we should keep to ourselves, appalled at the apparent physical impossibility. "I can't do this."

The old man stopped working. He gathered a hammer and a few tacks. "Come with me, Fiora Vicente."

He opened the door to my attic and mounted the stairs. He took it slow, his feet landing with a soft thud on each tread. I followed, shutting the door behind us. His hand grazed the bedpost, then the back of the padded rocker. He ran a finger along the brim of the gigantic flowered hat, then took a seat. It seemed the chair enveloped him, as Mamma's curtain did me. He sighed and his shoulders slumped, and it became clear why these items were up there and not downstairs where they should be. "You miss her."

"To have someone to miss is a blessing to be embraced." He gazed at the projection of an upside-down market moving five minutes ahead of us across the far wall, at shuttered stalls and streets emptier than I'd ever seen. "But I do not think it is bad to sometimes wish to not be so blessed."

He pulled the curtain aside. The market bleached out. He reached into his shirt pocket and withdrew a pamphlet, not so thick as the doctor's booklet, but larger in dimension. He handed it to me. "Unfold it."

The pamphlet was a map of Philadelphia, south of City Hall, extending west to the Schuylkill and east to the Delaware River. Somebody had traced a series of concentric circles to the right of Broad Street, centered on the old man's apartment and sketched in the same red color as the dust in my vision.

The old man took back the map and laid it on his lap. He traced the innermost circle. "This is the morning I noticed the wind had stilled."

He looped through two more. "This is the day you were too modern to be polite to Carlo."

He spiraled onto the fourth. "This is the day you brought the boys to the market and left them with Signora Bruni."

The fifth. "This is the day you distributed my wife's needlework over the apartment."

He traced three more spirals. They tracked the pattern of red Xs Tizi had spiraled around the map tacked to the wall behind her mother's counter. With each spiral, the old man described that day's arguments and discourtesies, misunderstandings and failings, and plain old stubborn refusals.

He moved to the outermost spiral. "And this is today, the most important of days, for this is the day you again disobeyed me and returned to visit with the guaritrice."

He stopped spiraling. "How did you get in? I ringed the pharmacy with verbena, stuffed your pockets full. Where is your coat? I sewed a layer into its hem."

He'd sewed verbena into the hem of my *coat*? "I wasn't wearing my coat. It stank. Carlo has it."

"Carlo was there." The old man looked alarmed. "Is he all right? Where is he?"

"Home I suppose. He didn't stay."

The old man looked like he was undecided about that answer. "Tell me everything she said to you."

"Why do you need to ask?" I tapped under my eye. "You know everything I do. You're like my mother."

He tapped his ears. "Signora Lattanzi's is not the only wagging tongue in this neighborhood." He put out a hand. "Whatever the guaritrice gave you, give to me."

I stepped away, aware of the bags stuffed within my bodice. "She gave me nothing except advice. About Carlo. About you. That you're men and men always want to tell women what to do."

He eyed me. "You went all the way to the pharmacy for advice?"

"I went for something for the Lattanzis, for the *agita*. All the druggist could offer was Chiclets. The Lattanzis would only throw them up."

The old man pushed up from the chair, his eyes shadowed. He splayed the map across the ceiling slope, dead center, and tacked it to the wall.

"Every day I mark the map." He retraced the outermost spiral. "And here is as far as I can mark. My heart is too weak. It is now your penance to keep track. Your bubble is growing, and you need to keep a record."

"Of what?"

"Of all the might-have-beens that may never be. When your bubble collapses, many people will need help. Signora Bruni will need it first." He picked up the booklet and shoved it back into my hands. "You should check on the Lattanzis."

Everything collapses, buildings, roads, mountains, even people. It is the way of the world. Stronger structures take longer, but eventually, everything falls apart.

I no longer had to knock. I'd found one of Signora Lattanzi's spare keys in the finial atop the newel post. So I surprised the boys, Fipo eating cold oatmeal at the table, Etti out of a bowl atop a chair. Etti jumped when I entered, his food landing in a clump the consistency of mud patties. He squatted beside the mess, and lapped at it with his tongue.

Like a dog.

Thirteen

I avoided Benedetta in the days that followed the doctor handing me the booklet. I crept down stairs and peeked around corners, sponge bathed in my attic and held my pee for the Lattanzis' bathroom lest Benedetta and I crossed paths on the way to our shared toilet.

What I didn't do in all that time was read the booklet. I buried it deep into my pillowcase, as if its physical proximity to Benedetta might be enough to bring the baby on and force me into action.

Guilt is a weight that multiplies when indulged, and on the third morning after the old man showed me his map with all the concentric circles, the guilt knocked me off-balance outside Benedetta's apartment.

The floorboard creaked. The plate lidding a bowl of beans I was bringing to the Lattanzis rattled. Benedetta popped her head out of her door. "My goodness, Fiora, where have you been? I asked the don about you last night. Was beginning to wonder if you'd moved out."

"No, not at all. Just busy with the Lattanzis." I lifted the bowl of beans like I needed evidence. "Well, I guess I better get back to them."

"Don't rush. I left a loaf for them this morning." She leaned over the railing. "I don't see it, so the boys must have found it. They'll be fine for an hour. Come in, have coffee. I'm about crazy to find a way to break the tedium."

As if inspired by her invitation, the scent of her coffee wafted from the apartment, fragrant, rich, pungent with the scent of cinnamon and cloves. My mouth watered, starved for a flavor not made insipid by the increasing strength of the bubble. "Tedium?"

"Oh, dear." Her hands flew to her chest, one palm over the other. "There I go talking like I'm the only person in the world. Of course you are anything but bored, scrubbing, cooking, doing laundry all day, while I sit around, reading my books like I'm the Queen of Italy."

I peeked past her, at dough piled on the table. "It doesn't look like you're sitting around."

"I'm rolling pasta. That's what I do. I leave my parents in Italy. I roll pasta. My husband goes to war. I roll pasta. I find out I'm expecting. I roll pasta. And every day the war news. I roll pasta, roll pasta, roll pasta." She laid a hand over her bulge. "My time is here. It is past here. He kicks. He moves, but he won't come out. So I roll pasta."

Knowledge of the unread booklet weighed heavy on my tongue. I didn't want to get sucked into conversation, afraid I'd blurt out the wrong thing. I also didn't want to appear rude. "You also bake bread."

"Only when I'm not rolling pasta." She laid a finger over her lips. "The don said I should set up a stall in the market. What do you think?"

What did it matter what I thought? The don had already spoken. "I think you would be very successful."

She threw her hands into the air. "Oh my, I wish this baby would come. Caged in here, everybody convinced if I step one foot outside this apartment, the sickness will find me. At least the baby would give me something different to do."

In the bubble's unrelenting pressure, we were all caged. Still . . . "You never wanted to do anything else?"

"You mean other than rolling pasta?"

"No, I mean . . ." My gaze dropped to her belly.

"Oh." Benedetta stiffened. It was like the air around her went brittle, and a cool breeze blew through the cracks. "You mean because this is America. Only modern thinking."

"No. Of course not. That's not what I meant at all." That was exactly what I meant. She was so pretty, so bright, so interested in what happened around her. "What I meant was, a baby is a lot of work." All poop and piss and puke. Kind of like what I'd been doing with the Lattanzis. Except for years and years. "You know, like that's all you'll be able to do."

"Signora Lattanzi does plenty. She has a shop. Your mother, too. She worked hard. I can have a baby and do something else. Besides." She put a supportive hand on her back. "It's a little late for me to be thinking about that now, don't you think?"

The hole I was digging was only getting deeper and wider. So, of course, I threw away the trowel and went at it with a shovel. "I'm sure the baby will come when it's ready. What does the doctor say?"

"*Pfft*. He hasn't been around for days. Said to send for him when my time comes. Said often the date calculations are not accurate. Is the signora feeling any better? I was counting on her to get me through this."

Finally, something I could answer with a degree of safety. "Sometimes she looks pretty good. I read somewhere that if the sickness is bad, it's bad quickly." I stopped myself, not wanting to remember, not wanting to think.

I kind of expected Benedetta to understand how maybe she'd stepped where she shouldn't, as I just had. Expected her to say something like, "And there I go again, reminding you of something sad. Come, take a few minutes. Let's talk of happy things."

She didn't. Her face went worried, brows scrunched, mouth pulled to the side. To see her like that, nervous and unsure, made me even more nervous and unsure. Of course, I asked probably the worst thing I could think of at the moment. "Does Nicco have any ideas?"

Her brows scrunched more. Her mouth pulled even farther to the side. "I haven't heard from him either." She looked past me, then to the ceiling, and to the floor. "I'm so worried. Worried the bell will ring and I'll go downstairs to answer and it will be one of those messengers. A telegraph boy. You've seen them, with the peaked caps."

I had. In the neighborhood. I thought of the lady now living in my old apartment, the lady who'd had Mamma's curtain. Maybe she'd worried about the same. Maybe the day I knocked, that was what she expected. A telegraph boy with bad news of her husband. And I'd purposely scared her. For fun.

Should I have told Benedetta it would be all right? Not to worry? I couldn't. The air around her had taken a dark turn, going gray to match the rest of the bubble film.

Benedetta shook herself. "I'm acting like I'm all alone. Like there's not a person in the world who can help me."

Dread, deep and distracting, pulled at my skirt, begging me to get out now, take the beans and run, before Benedetta asked me to do the unthinkable regarding the birth of her baby.

She didn't. She leaned against her jamb, arms crossed over her abdomen. "I could telephone my aunt, have her come down and give me a hand. She could bring my niece. Or maybe find somebody up there to keep an eye on her for a little. I was thinking I'd go up there anyway after the baby is born. Stay with her until Nicco returns. She writes to me, says the influenza is not so bad there as here and at times like these . . . well, Signora Lattanzi is right. It's always better to be with family."

Benedetta had what she needed. A husband. A baby she could call her own, one who would be hers alone to adore. And there'd likely be others. Many, probably. I'd be off typewriting someplace, maybe spending a lonely weekend sitting on an Atlantic City beach, eating fried claims out of a paper holder.

Tears sprang, surprising, and unbidden. Over what? A life I didn't want. One I steadfastly planned to avoid. Even more than I planned to avoid helping Benedetta birth her baby. I ducked my head, hoping it looked like I was only nodding my agreement. "That sounds sensible. Well, I better get these beans down to the boys. Maybe we could have coffee later. Tomorrow. Or the day after."

I said other stuff, equally awkward. It all sounded hollow to my ears. Benedetta answered. I said something pretty polite back.

I didn't know what was wrong with me. I had a friend, or the real possibility of a friend. And all that friend talked about was taking herself and her baby off to Coatesville to live a life of which I'd never be part. And I was doing and saying everything that might help that friend leave.

Sometimes . . . life is stupid.

Fourteen

The next day, or maybe the day after, or maybe the day after that, I woke to church bells playing the *Angelus* in air so dense it crushed my chest. The bells resonated through Mamma's curtain, reminding me of a world where breezes blew unfettered, the sun shined unmeasured, and time progressed without obstruction. I reached for Mamma's Big Ben, wound and rewound it, but the clock's dulsatory *tick . . . tick . . . tick* refused to catch up with the bells.

My heart slowed, the beats grew faint, my fingers numb, like my blood only sloshed as far as the second knuckle, gave up, turned around, and started its return journey. I longed to inhale, to fill my lungs to their limit, drive the heaviness to the dark places, and rejoin the outside world.

A sluggish half hour passed. The sky grew no lighter. Street lamps, weak and ineffective in the constant night fog rising from the cobbles, cast a murky glow. I braided my hair without brushing it, gathered it into a bundle at the nape of my neck, and wrapped a scarf at the crown to hide the tangles and wisps. I crept downstairs, tiptoed around the old man's snoring, lit a burner, and set the kettle to boil, expecting with each clink and clank to hear the old man stir, but he slumbered on, cocooned in the heavy sleep the bubble encouraged.

I checked the old man's roof garden, as I did most days, longing for freshness, color, new growth, a bit of life not sapped by the bubble. The old man's candles were still there, turning the world under the windowpanes warm enough to grow a jungle, yet the tomatoes remained green, the peppers were still hard little knobs, and the strawberries . . . oh, the strawberries, looked about the same as the first time the old man showed me.

Back to the kitchen for tea instead, hot and scented of lavender which layered like a cushion, steeped in what I needed most. Mamma, warm and welcoming, Poppa, strong and certain. In dreams remembrance became real. The table filled with comfort, inviting me to sit, do nothing. *Later is always fine since later is not now and now never ends, so relax, drink tea, and do not worry. About anything.*

My head thumped to the table. I blinked. Sunlight shone in subdued shadows through panes which always looked dingy, no matter how often I washed them. The old man, dressed and shaven, stood beside me, flowered teapot in hand. "Where is the rest?"

"Of what?"

"The guaritrice's mix."

"That was the last of it." A sample, a promise of more to come.

"You told me all she gave you was advice."

"I didn't want you to take this from me. Didn't want you to take it from the Lattanzis."

The old man rummaged on the shelves and showed me the bag. "This is not tea mixed with herbs. This is what we call a vector. A means to an end." He pulled a handkerchief from his pocket. Wrapped it around his hand and shook out the dregs. He shoved it under my nose. "Smell it. Breathe deep. Feel all your worries disappear. All your fears."

The world went fuzzy. The old man's ire no longer bothered me. He was a nice old man, but given to worry.

The old man went to the window and pulled down its clump of verbena. He shook it over my head. My eyes watered. My nose stung. My skin came alive, aware of every movement across its surface. I hopped up from my seat, shook out my skirt, brushed the verbena away. "What are you doing?"

He scraped his handkerchief into the sink, poured what was left in the teapot down the drain. "You must stop lying to me, Fiora Vincente.

You must stop lying to yourself. If you do not, all you are, all you hope to be will disappear. Anything the guaritrice suggests, you will follow. Your ideas will not be your own. Think, Fiora, who profits from this bubble?"

The guaritrice. But the old man would never understand. The guaritrice only did what she must to protect herself. To feed her daughter. Her teas helped the nausea, cleared the nose, reduced the fever. And even if they didn't do any of that, the teas made people believe that they did.

The guaritrice offered nostalgia to the bereft, hope to the hopeless, consolation to the forlorn. Maybe that's all any of us who were like the guaritrice could offer. In the modern world of the time, a world unable to offer the suffering little more than aspirin, weren't those reassurances worth a few dollars?

Temper took hold of my tongue. "The tailor and his wife will die without the guaritrice's tea. Their lips are blue. But for my bubble, their skin would follow. Just like my parents. You don't know how it is downstairs. You don't care. You send me, day after day. Tell me to cook and clean and scrub, but you never come to see for yourself. Never ask how you can help. You sit up here and repair luggage handles, change out the worn sections of belts, replace shoe soles. You tell me what to do. You tell me what I can't do. But you do not tell me how to bear it."

The old man shoved the bag which had contained the tea into the burner. He opened the window to let out the smoke, his movements precise, and pronounced, and overflowing with conviction. "Whatever that curtain shows you, up there in the dark, you are not the Almighty, Fiora Vicente. You cannot make such statements."

All that curtain showed me was the world five minutes into the future. Whatever happened, for whatever reason, if I were going to see it, it had to happen on the street in front of the stoop, and I'd have five minutes to change it. "I don't need to peer into the dark to know the Lattanzis will die. I have two good eyes."

"And what of your heart? Can you make no room in your certainty for miracles?"

"Miracles are for the faithful. The faithful have no room for me. You heard the doctor. This sickness overwhelms. There's no time to fight it. There has to be time enough for things and all I'm doing is giving everybody time. Time to build—what does he call it?—resistance."

"You haven't given us time. You've delayed what must be. And while we exist, in this time, in this place, none of us are living."

"I'm trying to fix it. Trying to figure out how to collapse the bubble. Without killing everything I'm trying to save."

"You can't figure out anything until you are willing to see beyond your own small needs. I did not ask you to do this for me. If I go, you will not be alone."

"So long as I marry Carlo." Became dependent on him as I was on the old man.

"Would that be such a terrible thing? Here, take this." He threw something at me.

I picked it out of my hair. "What should I do with a shoelace?"

"Tie it around your finger. To remind yourself. You gave me your trust. Now you take it back. Because of that, we are all prisoners."

Downstairs, on our stoop, I took off my scarf. I hadn't worn it because I needed it; I'd worn it for convention, because the calendar in the old man's apartment, the one advertising castor oil, showed a date in the middle of October. And Carlo still had my coat.

Filth covered the cobbles, uncollected for days. Stalls were closed. Signs tacked to several stated: NOT OPENING TODAY. NOTHING TO SELL. Carts and horses, trolleys and wagons, the lifeblood of the market, moving people and goods where they needed to be, were scarce, the market quiet, its pulse muted.

Somebody tugged at my skirt.

"You're too old to suck your thumb, Etti."

He wiped it on his jacket, then picked up his ball, which had rolled into the corner, and bounced it. "I don't want to stay inside. Can I come with you?"

I closed the door behind us. "I'm going to the grocer's. That's one hundred and seven steps. You do the counting."

"I can only count to eleven."

"Count to eleven ten times. Use your ball to keep your rhythm." I put out my hand. "Ready?"

We did fine for the first two rounds, then Etti's ball bounced haywire, moving in a slow, exaggerated arc. Etti's fingers grazed mine, then slid away. He darted after the ball, his exuberance too much for the bubble. I went after him, hoisting myself across cobbles which seemed to clutch at my shoes. A cart trundled onto the street, and in that same instinctive way I'd known on Parade Day I had time to grab the girl before she crossed her cart's path, I knew I wouldn't be there in time to catch Etti.

The seconds slowed to a near standstill. My feet stuttered in my shock. Waiting, waiting, waiting, for that moment to move to the next, when the wheel would turn, and crush Etti.

The moment did not come. A hand shot out from nowhere, a body crossed our paths, diverting Etti, and catching the ball.

Carlo.

I crumpled to the cobbles, caught between a sob and a scream, my relief painful. I think I bruised a knee, maybe an elbow. I didn't know. I didn't care. Etti was alive. The cart had moved on. And if time never moved another moment beyond that one, if I were forced to spend eternity in that exact place, experiencing that exact emotion, I'd be happy.

Carlo had other ideas. He grabbed my hand and lifted me up. He handed Etti the ball. "Is it all right if I borrow Signorina Vicente?"

"What are you going to do with her?"

"Give her back her coat for one. Fresh smelling and clean."

I took it from him. It smelled of lilacs. "How did you do that?"

"Magic." He put a finger to his lips. "But don't tell anybody."

Etti smiled. He held up a finger. "That's one thing. What else did you want from Signorina Vicente?"

"A walk." He offered me his arm. "If she'll let me."

The relief had faded. My elbow ached, my knee throbbed, and my scalp felt itchy under my headscarf. "Tomorrow might be better."

"And so might today."

Inside there were dishes to do, laundry to soak, and floors to mop. Inside was Benedetta, rolling out pasta, maybe as bored as Etti, as eager to walk as Carlo. My life had choices; there were still decisions I could make. "I'm not going to marry you, Carlo."

"Good. Excellent. I'm not going to marry you, either. Not today. Not even tomorrow. Now that we have that clear, may I please show you something?"

"What?"

He put out a hand. "All the world has to offer."

His tone, light and encouraging, had the effect of a breeze at my back. "Go see Signora Bruni, Etti. She may have a fresh loaf for you." I took Carlo's hand, then took a step. Into a world of light and color.

He walked me one block, then two, heading east. We went one more block, stopping in front of a storefront dressed with a banner far too blue for the insipid colors inside the bubble.

Carlo swept an arm. "This is where I live."

"In a shoe repair shop?"

"No, over it. I work in the shop. The owner is often not here. His children have settled in Wilmington, and he wants to join them. When he does, this will be mine."

"You're taking over his lease."

"No, Fiora Vicente. I am purchasing the whole building. Top to bottom."

At the time, I had no idea of his age, but guessed he couldn't have been more than twenty. "I thought you worked for Signor Minora."

His eyes moved down and to the right, like he'd forgotten an item on a list, then he bounced his finger off his forehead. "Oh. You mean that day outside his shop. I was only picking up supplies for Don Sebastiano. He keeps me moving."

Light dawned. "You're the one who keeps delivering all the mending."

He nodded. "Don Sebastiano has negotiated very good rates for your work."

Rates. It hadn't occurred to me I'd actually get paid, despite the terms dictated by the old man. I'd presumed it his way to keep me busy and part of my duty to the signora, for plucking me out of the rain and planting me in his apartment. "The work is not coming through the Lattanzis?"

"How? The Lattanzis are so ill. The current work comes from seamstresses in the neighborhood. With so many sick, you would think the work would diminish, but the war department has taken over all normal industry. Work for everyday people is piling up."

My face went hot. "Those seamstresses would not hire me."

"People can be shortsighted. Do not take it to heart. You have great ambition, I see that." He slid his cap off his head again. Held it in both his hands. "Well, I have great ambition, also."

Typewriting school was an idea, a dream, a place my mind went when Mamma complained my gravy was too thin, or my pasta too thick, a place removed from tradition, from expectation, from Life's. Awful. Dailyness. "I always wanted to escape who I am, become something better. And now, everything I do is the same."

He took my hand, closed his fingers over mine, and the dread which followed me like an unwelcome relative disintegrated. "Right now, the world seems dark, but the darkness will end. I brought you here so you would see I have a future."

My gaze met his, that beautiful, dark-rimmed, light blue pool of possibilities. "But only if you marry me."

I backed away, then turned and sprinted toward the market, or what could pass for sprinting along a street which grabbed at the soles of my shoes harder than cleats.

Carlo sprinted beside. "Signorina, I am not trying to marry you. I'm only trying to get to know you."

"Why?"

"Because Don Sebastiano never makes a suggestion without reason."

"Do you do everything Don Sebastiano suggests?"

"Only those things which make sense."

"Only because you don't want to wait for your inheritance."

He snagged me by the elbow, forced me to stop. "Is that what Don Sebastiano told you?"

"Yes. No. Not exactly." Not at all.

"Then may I know exactly what he *did* say?"

Maybe the time I stood there was minutes in the outside world. Maybe it was hours. To me, it was an eternity, leading to a place I couldn't avoid, and which hadn't, until that point, served me well.

The truth. "He didn't say anything."

To say Carlo looked confused would be correct, but not accurate. The undersides of his eyes moved up, the insides of his eyebrows inched inward. His lips pressed together in a twist, and he peered at me, ear cocked in my direction, like he wasn't quite sure what I'd just said was what he'd heard, and was running through all the other possibilities for those syllables in case he maybe should have heard something else. "Don Sebastiano didn't say anything?"

"No."

"Nothing?"

"Yes."

"Yes, he said nothing? Or yes, he said something?"

"Yes, he said nothing. He said nothing at all. The only time he talks about you is to tell me you've delivered something, or you're coming to deliver something, or you forgot to deliver something. I thought you were one of the neighbor kids."

Carlo scratched his head. "Then why do you think I'm trying to marry you?"

"Because everybody says you are." I started to feel kind of stupid. "You mean you're not?"

"I don't even know you. Do you want to marry a man you don't even know?"

I didn't. I didn't even want to marry a man I did know. I didn't want to marry a man. They were big, and coarse, and scratched at body parts I didn't want to think about.

He let go of my elbow. "The don's inheritance will be very nice, but my negotiation with the building is the work of years. Every penny, every day, ever since I can remember."

Oh.

He slid his cap back onto his head. "This was fun. Very enlightening. May we walk again tomorrow?"

Fifteen

Mamma used to tell me the dog barks, but the caravan moves on. Wise words for normal times. But in the bubble world my caravan was parked, its wheels dismantled, its axles broken. Day in, day out, my dog barked, sometimes louder, sometimes softer, about any food bits left on the dishes, how poorly I'd scoured the pots, the stains I couldn't get out of the laundry. Two days after my walk with Carlo, my dog did not like the soup. "A light hand with the garlic invites colds. Ask the don, he will tell you I'm correct."

Whether to go into business. Who should marry whom. Soup. The don sure had a lot to say about everything. "I think we are past that worry, Signora Lattanzi."

Her hands were shaky, her voice shrill. "These are things you need to know, or people will think you do not care."

We sat at the table, during a rare time when she felt able. I took the bowl from her. "Not care about what?"

"Your house, your home. Your life will be easier if you do not call attention to yourself. Carlo works so hard. He deserves a clean table-cloth at dinner."

She wasn't talking about laundry. "Is this what you always wanted, signora? The life you planned when you were young?"

"It's a good life. I'm content."

"But are you happy?"

"Life requires care and constant attention. Happiness is not so important when there are other considerations."

Care and constant attention. The nuns at my school would have loved Signora Lattanzi. "What considerations?"

"Helping your husband, raising good children, being a friend, a neighbor, doing what is right even if it feels wrong."

"Like taking in a stray you think will curse you?"

The question sloshed between us, growing tepid in the bubble's overly humid warmth.

The signora smacked her spoon to the table. "You resent taking help from somebody you think doesn't like you, Fiora Vicente. We are the same. I have no choice who helps me now because without help, my sheets do not get washed, my floors do not get swept, and my children do not eat."

My face went hot, intolerable in the bubble. My fists clenched. I opened one window, then another, smashing the sashes to their lintels and speaking much too loud. "You don't want me here. I don't want to be here. Maybe soon we will both get our wish."

"I don't want you here because of what you've done."

Two ladies passed by the window. Two ladies in white masks with market baskets in their hands. I didn't care. "What have I done, signora, to earn your permanent and unwavering distrust? I bathe you and feed you, clean up your messes and care for your children. Yet you treat me like a shameful cousin."

"I brought you to live here. Under my roof. And now, my children will be orphaned."

I stormed out of the kitchen. Fipo followed. "Are you coming back?"

I clutched him by the collar, much as I'd clutched the little boy in the street, the one I'd caught fighting for a sausage. "I'm coming back. Soon as your mamma cools down. I'm tired. So is she. Keep an eye on your brother. I left a bowl for your father. Make sure he eats. And stay away from the stove."

I released him, thinking I'd go upstairs, wash my face, have a good cry. Benedetta met me on the landing. "The boys should come to live with me. There's room for their cot. Carlo will carry it up if we ask."

Oh how I wanted to take her suggestion, to sweep in and let Fipo and Etti know they wouldn't have to time their days around rushes to the basin for their parents, or in bringing fresh hankies. "Awful as it sounds, they need to be there. Either that, or I have to move in with the Lattanzis." I looked upstairs. "And I could, but the old man is not as strong as he was."

"The world is so topsy-turvy. Children caring for parents. The don took you in. Now he needs your help. I'll bring the children some dinner. Don't worry. I'll leave it outside their door. You get some rest."

Rest. Yes. That's what I needed. Great buckets of it under clean blankets and fresh breezes. And a cup of tea. With plenty of sugar. I thought of the deadline for typewriting school, which, despite the lethargy of the bubble time, approached in giant steps. "Maybe I'll do a little more on the pile of mending."

To think that mending, which had once seemed more onerous than death, should provide relief from my worries stopped me on the tread. The same thought must have occurred to Benedetta because she smiled with me. Then we laughed, our hands clutched to the railing, doubled over and loud enough to chase all the heaviness to the corners.

A screech, a thud, and a scream halted us both. "Poppa."

I rushed down the stairs, plunging against air that thickened with my resistance.

"Poppa, Poppa, Poppa."

I turned the handle on the Lattanzis' door, but it felt nailed into place. I pounded. "Fipo. Etti. Open up."

Was Benedetta behind me? She must have been, but in those long, torturous seconds, I felt alone, a girl pounding on her apartment door because she forgot the key. Because she'd gone to the roof to look at the stars. Because she was tired of cleaning piss, and puke. Because she wanted it all to be *over*.

Benedetta pushed me aside. She opened the door. Etti stood in the kitchen, thumb in mouth, blanket clutched in his hand. Benedetta hurried to him, held him tight to her skirt. She waved me toward the bedroom. "Etti, come with me, I'm baking cookies."

She swept him away and out the door, seeming to suck all possibility of hope after. I approached the bedroom, hand to mouth, ears ringing, near screeching myself, terrified of what I might find.

And came upon the strong, strong aroma of onions.

The signora sat up in her bed, Fipo curled beside her. She stroked his hair. "There now, it's only soup. Go with the signorina. I think I heard Signora Bruni say something about cookies."

The signore knelt on the floor on the other side of the mattress, mopping at the floor. "My apologies. It slipped from my hand."

Fipo took the towel from him. "Signorina Vicente is here, now, Poppa. She'll clean it. Go back to bed."

The next hours were spent scrubbing and washing and imagining what might have happened had Fipo's father dropped the soup on Fipo instead, if Fipo had brought the soup down on himself when he climbed to the stove. I'd turned off the burner, but left the pot bubbling, trusting an admonishment to be enough.

I went upstairs, pausing outside Benedetta's apartment. Happy voices sounded from the other side, Fipo's followed by Etti's.

Pettiness smacked me on the nose, jealous at my inability to elicit such a response. She was so kind, so beautiful, so able. And so past her time. The baby needed to be born, but so long as the bubble persisted, it wouldn't.

Was that possible? How long could we stay here, stuck in the perpetual pressure? Another week. Two. Why not months? Years?

Outside, the war would end. The influenza would burn itself out and life would continue. New songs would be written, inventions invented, moving pictures made, and newspapers printed. The world would age, progressing around us until our neighborhood became a sideshow, like I'd read about in Mr. Barnum's circus. A sideshow peopled by the sick with their skeletal coughing, by children who hid in corners and moved like rats, hair tangled, clothing wild. Visitors would come to gawk, maybe toss us food like I once tossed to the monkeys at the zoo. And one day, the coughing would finally give out.

I knocked on Benedetta's door and let the boys know their parents were sleeping and the mess cleaned up. Etti tugged on my waistband. "Dorothy didn't mean to kill anybody, either."

He arched his hands over his body, then brought them down down down until his palms rested on the crown of his head, demonstrating, I presumed, how Dorothy's house fell on the Wicked Witch of the East. But Etti kept pushing, squatting under the pressure, then blossomed his arms upward, like a flower, and stood straight. He gave me the sweetest of smiles, and ran back to rejoin Benedetta's reading circle.

Etti understood the change in the atmosphere. Maybe he thought I'd cast the bubble that first morning when I stood before him and his brother and waved my arms, threatening a spell, the morning the old man puzzled in his rooftop garden because the breeze had stopped blowing. Etti understood the pressure, understood the inevitable end of the process.

The red circles on the old man's map marked the bubble's edge, each ring stretched thinner than the previous. So did the guaritrice's spiral of red Xs. I compared both side by side in my mind's eye. No longer maps. Targets. Aimed at a nexus, a spot of clear white, at the tornado's eye.

Mamma's curtain.

Sixteen

Dawn came, gritty and gloomy, the sun hidden behind a despair so profound, even the humid malaise creeping over the attic sash felt chill.

I missed Mamma. Missed her palm on my forehead when she woke me. Missed her talking while she worked. Missed watching her needle pierce the fabric in confident, practiced stitches. I missed Poppa, smelling of soap and peppermint. I missed his suspenders. Missed watching him button them to his knickerbockers when he dressed in the morning. Missed the careful way he combed his hair, the time he took to trim his mustache, how he rolled his shirtsleeves while he worked.

I wanted to go back. Wanted it all to unwind. Wanted to be like Dorothy in the Oz book and wish myself home, back before the bubble, before the sickness. Back when Fiora Vicente was just a girl, in the market, walking with her mamma and arguing over what would be best for her future. I wanted to redo that conversation. Change the outcome. Go on to live my life as everybody did. Ordinary.

I guess the curtain heard me. It let itself off its hook and settled over the window. The room fell into darkness, then brightened, revealing an upside-down market which flickered across the attic slope like the movies of the time. A market washed-out and pale, forlorn in streets near emptied by the sickness. One day, we'd grind to a halt, the pressure so great, we'd be tacked to the ground. Eventually, it all had to crack.

I slipped out of bed, shut the window, and settled into the curtain's soft folds, secure, wishing I could hide there forever. "Five minutes, Mamma."

Five minutes to pretend none of this had ever happened. Five minutes when she and Poppa could still be alive. Five minutes unburdened by boys underfoot, responsibilities overhead, the constant worry, the constant work, the constant wondering what would happen next.

I'd taken a road unintended. I intended to turn it back. Make all that had happened, unhappen.

The room grew snug. Mamma's Big Ben slowed, the time between one tick and the next, infinite.

Behind the curtain, the sun stalled. People in the process of getting up, or getting dressed, or getting breakfast, stilled. Time unwound, wrapped around me, flipped me onto my head.

And rolled me into the curtain world.

Time rolled with me, backward and bulky, weighted with every nasty word I could not unsay, every selfish act I could not undo, every unkind thought I could not unthink. My chest collapsed, my heart failed, my spirit flattened.

The past is cruel. It welcomes no visitor, tolerates no intrusion, gives not a whit for the ramifications of what has gone before. The past is dark. It is dense. It is dangerous. Worst of all, the past is impossible to change.

The projection tumbled me back to the present in a lump, heartsore, and bruised, and clumsy as clay, my lungs squeezed, my bones all but broken. I wanted to be brave. I was Fiora Vicente, Rosina Vicente's daughter.

It didn't matter. Nothing mattered. Mamma warned me. I hadn't listened. "You can't stop the future, Fiora. You can't change the past. Nobody can."

"Then of what purpose is the curtain?"

The minutes ticked by, the curtain's upside-down market flickering five minutes into the future. Silent.

But for hooves. Those damned hooves. Clip-clopping over the

cobbles, pulling a wagon piled high with bodies destined to lie, unattended, in the basements of overwhelmed undertakers. Because the city had run out of coffins and there was nobody to dig all the graves.

Or so I imagined. My eyes were closed.

I sat up. Straight. So was the window.

So how could I hear all that clip-clopping?

In the market projection, the wagon moved upside-down along the inverted cobbles of the curtain world, entering stage left. Not piled with bodies, piled with crates. Of apples, and carrots, potatoes and more. Last of the harvest, and heading toward the grocers, soon to be ready for sale.

I shook out my skirt, buttoned my shirtwaist, pulled on stockings and shoes, my plan to be first in line. I stopped. The hooves weren't part of some imagined vision. They were real, audible, part of the projection, and they were still five minutes into the future.

Fancy that.

I got up close to the curtain. My whole imagining changed from watching, to being, from observing, to participating. The smells of the market rose around me. Damp paper and wood, stone and sweat. And the horses. The horses. Hay and deep earth and leather and straw.

Without effort, I was there, able to go door to door, and pass through the windows, unfettered by the bubble's weight. I stood in corners and watched hungry children paw through yesterday's pot, looking for a scrap, a morsel, a bite to quiet their stomachs. The piles of dishes and dirty laundry, vomit-stained sheets and blood-tinged handkerchiefs smelled so strong my eyes watered, my stomach heaved.

I pulled back from the scene, settled my spirit on my own stoop, then passed through the door, and checked in on the boys. They knelt under the kitchen table, playing dropsies with their marbles. The constant clack-clack must be driving their parents to madness. Etti looked toward the door, and I wondered if he saw me, a spirit girl, likely floating head down and feet up. I even waved, but Etti returned to his play.

The aroma of oregano and basil filled the air, drifting me up the stairs. A pot simmered on Benedetta's stove. Benedetta emerged from behind the curtain which concealed her sleeping space, swollen and ripe, her belly button stretched tight over the life within. She pulled a dress over her head and buttoned it from the bottom up.

My cheeks flamed. I squeezed past the crack in the doorframe and stood on the landing.

Should I go upstairs? Glide past the old man, still snoring on his cot, and on up to the attic to see myself, staring into a projection, my back turned to me.

Oh yes.

A boundary, more profound than the bubble's, stopped me at the attic doorway. Okay, fine. I knocked.

And heard nothing in the attic, at least, not from my side. That knock was five minutes into the future, and I thought it would be about the most interesting thing I did that day to wait around to hear it. I might even go down and answer the door before the knock landed.

That thought removed me from participation in the projection. I again became an observer, watching the little girl with the tangled hair enter stage right, her doll dragging in the street.

Grazia.

She walked slowly, head down, sneaking glances from one side to the next. She stopped a little short of the grocer's.

A cart waited before the grocer's stand, horses docile. The delivery-man unloaded. Crate after crate. The street children moved in, from one corner to the next. They lounged against lampposts, bounced balls against walls. The deliveryman moved a crate into the store; the grocer took another. Both men disappeared inside the building, leaving the other crates piled by the cart.

The children swarmed. A bunch of carrots, a couple of potatoes, a hunk of cheese. Disappearing under coats, up sleeves, beneath caps. The little girl rushed in, too. She ducked under the cart, doll's head bouncing on the cobbles.

The grocer and deliveryman exited, with much waving of hands. The children scattered. The horse shuffled, back, then forth, then back again. The little girl disappeared beneath the cart wheel. I didn't need the sound to know her scream rose above the commotion.

Somebody knocked on the attic door.

Five minutes.

Five whole minutes.

Less than five minutes because I wasted time taking in what I'd seen.

However that amount of time translated in the bubble's strange slugabed world.

The future was not the past. Every decision that needed to happen had not yet happened. Every action that could possibly happen was still in the mind.

I could change it, I could. And I would, just as soon as my curtain world self, the projection I'd had so much fun with a few minutes earlier, stopped standing on the other side of the attic door.

Because I couldn't leave until my curtain world self left. Because time didn't allow me to meet her. Because my actions of the previous five minutes couldn't be changed. So I had to wait, letting my curtain world self do all she had been doing up until the point she showed up at my attic door. And knocked.

Yes. Confusing. And too frustrating to think about as I toe-tapped the seconds, pegged into place, and unable to avoid the upside-down scene continuing to unfold on the attic wall. The fear, the frenzy. The blood.

In my world, the real world happening at that moment, the little girl was alive and breathing and walking toward her doom. I was delayed because I thought it would be funny to see how far I could make the curtain world loop back on itself.

The old man's Big Ben continued its dispassionate rhythm, uninterested in the panic pressing on my breastbone. I tried to move after five seconds, then ten, and again at twelve. Finally, finally, there was a thud and a great heaving crack, one which caught me about the ankles and sent me to the floor. I scrabbled up, elbow bleeding, and moved like a crab, down my stairs, and clawed at the knob, turning and shoving and turning again. The door wouldn't budge.

I pounded. "Don Sebastiano. Please."

He opened for me, his perpetual calm draining from his features. "What's wrong? What happened?"

I barreled past him, taking longer to descend the stairs than I ever had, my every footfall seeming to land in quicksand. This was not the bubble. It was not the curtain and it was not the projection. Something else stalled my progress. Something deep. Something malevolent. Something determined I should fail.

The seconds ticked away.

"Mamma," I whimpered. "Help me."

"*Stop fighting yourself. Time is not your master, it's your servant. What was good is still good.*"

In the bubble, nothing happened, yet all things were possible. In the bubble, time followed no rules. In the bubble, the only moment over which I had any control was Now.

I took a breath and thought of good things. Clear light, fresh breezes, children laughing in the sunshine. I released my breath, and the power which held me relaxed its grip. I moved. Fast. Across the landing. Down the stairs. And over the stoop.

The children already swarmed the grocer's crates. I took one more breath, then took every one of those one hundred and seven steps three at a time, arms waving, heart pumping. And shouting shouting shouting. "No. Stay away. Get out from under the cart."

The children stopped swarming. They looked up. Beneath the cart little Grazia turned, her doll clutched in her hand. The grocer and the deliveryman exited the building, hands waving as I'd already seen in the projection, and with cries of alarm I hadn't been able to hear.

I swooped in, like I'd seen a player do in a long-ago baseball game, grabbed Grazia by her skirt, and pulled. Hard.

The horses startled, the wheels moved back, but Grazia was safe in my arms. Crumpled with me in a ball beside.

The grocer hauled me up. He took Grazia and held her like a precious package, smoothing and resmoothing her hair. "What were you doing? Are you all right?"

"I'm fine." I smoothed my own hair, and my skirt. "I was doing what anybody would do."

The deliveryman held the horses by their bridles, his face white. He slid his cap off his head. Held it over his heart. "Thank you."

I put out my arms—"I'll take her."—and looked at a crate of potatoes. "And I'll take those potatoes. Six large ones." I hefted the little girl onto my hip—"Do you like potato stew?"—then dug into my bodice, meaning to retrieve the handkerchief hanging there and untwist it. "How much?"

"No. No." The grocer put the potatoes in a sack. He added a bunch of carrots and a couple of onions. "Take them. No charge. Do you need help getting her home?"

The deliveryman spoke up. "I'll take them." He took the bag.

A strong set of arms swept the bag away from him. "Thank you, signore, but deliveries are my specialty."

Carlo.

He looked past me. "Are you the Pied Piper?"

Carlo said "Pied Piper" like a regular American. He would do fine when he took his test for citizenship. I turned and saw children, three wide and half a dozen deep. Dirty. Disheveled. Their hair tangled, their expressions determined.

A path, and a purpose, opened before me.

I grabbed a crate off the grocer's stack and held my hand up to Carlo, palm out. "Wait." I dashed back to the house, heart light, my way unencumbered. I passed the old man, stepped up our stoop, then through the street door, beelined across the vestibule, up the stairs and onto Benedetta's landing.

I pounded on the door. "Benedetta. Open up."

I pounded again. "Benedetta."

She answered, hair messy, eyes shadowed, face drawn. "What is it?"

"Have you flour?"

She yawned. "Yes."

"Good. I need you to bake. Ten loaves. No. Twenty." I handed her the crate. "Whatever you have in your kitchen now, pack in here. The parents are sick. Children are roaming the streets, fighting for food, and nobody is paying any attention. We can't do anything about the sickness. Nothing at all. But we can make ourselves useful. We have to help them. We have to help all of them."

Benedetta set the crate on her table. "Is it all right if I pee first?"

Depth of Field

Seventeen

Yes, of course. Help the children. Help them all.
Easier said than done.

Door, to door, to door. Like the times I'd looked for a job. I tossed another piece of mending onto the pile growing at my feet. "Their parents do not trust me. They never will. They would rather choke on their own vomit than allow the fortune-teller's daughter to hold the basin."

Carlo looked up from his shoe form. "Only because you have not been properly introduced to them. Or their basins. Tomorrow, we will go together."

Together, like we sat then, like the three of us sat every night those first few evenings, at Benedetta's table, the aroma of baking bread thicker than the air.

My back ached. My feet hurt. And I'd twisted my wrist. It ballooned in shades of purple and yellow. I reached across Benedetta's table for the next item. A shirt that was more rips than fabric. I pawed through a collection of swatches from my attic, seeking a suitable match. "For the Corini boy. Looks like he got dressed from the rag pile. He must have sold his other clothes to buy food."

Carlo twisted a grommet into place. "What's the little boy wearing now?"

"My camisole." The heat rose under my collar. Stupid. It's not like undergarments were secret. They had a whole department on display at Lit Brothers, and Sears Roebuck carried illustrations of them for pages. Still, at that time, at that age, to say it out loud . . .

I snuck a glance at Benedetta.

But Carlo laughed. "I've got a set of underdrawers to contribute to the cause."

I pulled another stitch. "Don't offer what you're not willing to give." I held up a piece of burlap, the words, PILLSBURY FLOUR, clearly imprinted. "Benedetta stole this. Tucked it under her waistband."

Benedetta wrapped her apron around her hand, opened the oven door, and pulled out another loaf. "I should have stolen the flour, too. The baker's prices are ridiculous. He claims he's giving me a discount, but he's giving himself one first."

Carlo set his work aside. He turned his chair around and straddled it, leaning his chin on its high back. "We have to convince the grocer, the baker, the others to give donations. The seamstresses, houses where people are not sick, all can donate a little something. A sheet, a towel, a pot of soup." He pointed to my pile of mending. "A shirt that is not in rags." He wiped his hand on his pant leg. "Soap."

Benedetta upended the bread onto the marble, the loaf landed with a satisfying thump. "Let's ask the priest to ask them."

"Or maybe Don Sebastiano." Carlo flipped the shoe he'd been working on and caught it. A child's shoe. "There. Three bad shoes make two good. I found the hatmaker's son in stocking feet." Carlo patted his pockets.

I thought he was looking for money. That made me think of the handkerchief twisted between my breasts. Which, I guess, had me glancing down to them. Carlo saw me, so he looked at my breasts, too. The heat again gathered under my collar.

Not because Carlo was looking at my breasts. Because Carlo was looking at me look at my breasts in front of Benedetta. And while neither of them had a clue I had a handkerchief filled with tuition money resting between them, the fact of its existence, while we discussed stealing burlap sacks, the price of flour, and making use of worn-out shoes, made me feel like a liar, like my decision to help the neighborhood children had strings, like, like . . .

"I don't suppose you have a shoelace?" Carlo patted another pocket. "For these shoes. I only have one."

Shoelace. Not breasts.

Well, why was he looking at them then if he only wanted a shoelace? I dug into my pocket, for the shoelace Don Sebastiano had tossed at me the day he wanted to remind me of my obligations. I tossed it at Carlo. "Here."

He picked it up. "Know what, Fiora Vicente? I'm thinking you would be wasted being a typewriter girl. You always have what is needed. You'd be better as a nurse."

Nurse. Ha. Like because I'd put in weeks cleaning snot, I'd want to spend the rest of my life cleaning snot. "And look at you, talking everybody into giving you their money while you take credit for helping the neighborhood. Your time spent shoemaking is likewise wasted. Better you run for councilman."

He tossed the shoelace at Benedetta. "Only if being councilman means I can get free meals at your restaurant."

Benedetta tossed the shoelace back at him. "I don't want a restaurant." She peeked, corner to corner, like maybe the Fates would hear. She leaned in, her attitude conspiratorial. "I want a bakery. Not like those tiny pastries selling across the street. My bakery would only produce the best. *Cucidati* big as your fist. Filled with the freshest of figs. Honeyed nuts like I remember from my nonna's kitchen. The most tender, most delicately flavored, most irresistible of *spongata*, with layers so flaky you're tempted to peel them away and eat them, one by one."

She threw back her head and laughed. "I'd eat at least three of those every day. Before dinner." She pinched a cheek and dropped her voice. "Don't tell the doctor."

"We won't, signora, but a bakery is not enough. It's not near enough. You are like Our Lord Jesus Christ in this kitchen, feeding the masses with loaves and manicotti." Carlo kissed his fingers up to heaven. "And so deliciously. No. A restaurant is your true heart's desire. A restaurant is what you get. I feel it."

"You can't feel anything, Carlo Lelii. You are not like our Fiora. Look what happened with that little girl. How she saved her. Fiora knows things." Benedetta tapped her temple. "Despite all her modern thinking."

Carlo turned to me. "Is that true, Fiora Vicente? Do you know things? Are you truly your mother's daughter?"

His face was friendly, his tone respectful. Like being my mother's daughter was a matter of pride, not pain. "Sometimes, I know something. Not often. I can touch things, in the right moment. I sometimes get an impression. I am nothing like my mother. Not . . . talented."

Carlo appeared to take my words seriously. "You are talented. You are still untried. Keep practicing. Someday, when you most need them, your talents will see you through."

I didn't want to argue with him. Not with the three of us so cozy. But the conversation made me sad, reminded me of all I could no longer take for granted. I went back to my mending.

Benedetta turned another loaf out onto the table. "I know, let's do something fun. We are all working too hard. Who has an idea?"

Carlo squared his shoulders. "Let us put our hands together and make a solemn oath. We shall each never fail the other. In word or deed. We will always be there to help, no matter what the other needs. And when times are good, we will remember to celebrate. With Signora Bruni's delectable pastries if at all possible." He stretched his hand over the table, and I knew he meant for me to take it.

There are those moments in our lives we count as the time before, and the time after. Carlo stood there, palm out, the expectation I'd finally put mine in his, live in the world of the normal, the conventional, so electric the air sparked.

The moment passed. I took Benedetta's hand, and placed it in Carlo's.

Benedetta's hand fluttered, resting uneasy. She was married. Carlo was not. This was not done. I put my hands over both, covered them top and bottom, making a circle of trust. "Like the Three Musketeers."

They looked to each other, then to me, the color going high in their cheeks. "Like in the story," I added.

The awkwardness passed. Carlo straightened. "Yes. Of course. The Three Musketeers." He raised his hand, lifted all of ours with his. "Carlo."

Benedetta did the same. "Benedetta."

And me. "Fiora."

We held our handclasp high between us, reaching until we couldn't reach anymore, myself on tiptoes, and Benedetta steadying herself against the table's edge. Up, up, up. Our hopes, our dreams, our certainty of the future.

"To Carlo's shop."

"And Benedetta's bakery."

"And Fiora, the best typewriter in the world."

Our hand clasp broke, and I imagined our wishes like butterflies.

Carlo spotted Benedetta's camera, the Brownie, on its shelf. "We should commemorate this great moment. All of us. Together. United by snot."

Benedetta stepped to the side. "You and Fiora should." She lay a hand over the baby bulge. "Nicco wouldn't like it."

Carlo stopped his examination of the camera. "Why wouldn't Nicco like it?"

I answered for her. "Nicco thinks it would be bad luck to take a photograph of the baby before he is born."

"Ah. Then we won't. You and I will stand in front of Benedetta and she can look between our shoulders. Then Nicco and every superstition will get its due." He turned to Benedetta. "All right?"

She nodded, her smile blossoming ear to ear.

Carlo set the camera on the table and paged through the instruction manual, sounding out the English when he got stumped. "Depth of field." He looked up. "What is that?"

"Nicco told me it means the camera requires a certain distance to be in focus." Benedetta touched a finger to the end of her nose and extended her arm, like she was measuring a yard of fabric. "Longer than this I think. Or the photograph will be blurred."

Carlo tapped a finger to the table. "We need the proper tool. Something we can use to flip the lever and expose the film from a distance. What can we use? Everybody think."

Benedetta handed over her longest wooden spoon. Carlo contributed his buttonhook, and I grabbed the lace I'd given him for the shoe off the table. It took us a few minutes, a couple of false starts, but finally we had an apparatus that would work—a shoelace dangled from the end of the spoon and tied on its opposite end to the buttonhook. Next we got the hook under the lever, dumped the verbena out of all those iron rings the old man had hung around Benedetta's apartment, and used the rings to weight the camera and prevent it from shifting. The spoon would extend Carlo's reach, and once we were all arranged, he could lift the spoon, drawing the shoelace taut, which would pull on the buttonhook and move the lever.

We were a team, a group, united in purpose. The sickness would end. The war would be over. My brothers would return, along with Benedetta's husband, wearing their medals, back from fighting the Kaiser. We would feed them beautiful meals, and the men would go off together, leaving Benedetta and me to picnic in the park, the baby on a blanket between us. The old man would be well, his hair halolike in the sunshine. Even the Lattanzis could come, the signora unable to be a sourpuss over the soup because Benedetta had taught me to make it with plenty of garlic. Then the boys would launch their airplane. Farther and faster and high as they wanted.

We turned on every light in Benedetta's apartment. We removed every shade. We created day where there was none, providing our own sun to arrow through the aperture, and ourselves, hands clasped triumphantly over our heads, Benedetta looking between my and Carlo's shoulders, to project on the film.

With love, with faith, with the promise of tomorrow.

Click.

Followed by *knock-knock-knock.* "Signora Bruni. Signora."

Etti. At the door.

He stood in his nightshirt, wide-eyed and trembling, and pointing toward the stair.

The newfound energy our celebration had released steam-engined me down the steps. I hit the lobby with barely a thud and flew through the Lattanzis' open doorway, Carlo close behind.

The next moments happened in stop action, much as the upside-down market flickered in my attic. Bits and pieces of remembrance that to this day sometimes visit me in order, sometimes helter-skelter.

Fipo. On the floor. Curled in on himself. Writhing.

The teakettle overturned in the sink. The stove's burner hissing. Stench of singed hair. Matches scattered across the floor.

A tableau I did not need to be sensitive to understand, did not need my mother's talent to figure out. "He's burned."

Turn on the tap. Splash of cold water.

Carlo. Strong. Steady. Fipo in his arms.

Me. Turning off the gas, throwing open the sash, setting the kettle upright.

But what comes back to me most profound about those first moments, and the next minute, was the silence. Especially from Fipo, clenched and clawing. The scene turned surreal, seeming like one of the curtain's projections, but instead of the projection being splashed across the wall in my attic, this projection splashed across the Lattanzis' kitchen. A kitchen I'd left clean and orderly two hours before. Any moment the credits would roll, the lights would come up. Fipo would return to his sleep, and the rest of us to our fun.

Benedetta broke through my isolation. She rushed to Fipo. Ran a hand over his forehead, a finger across his cheek, then checked his arm. "This doesn't look too bad. You're a lucky guy. Next time, don't touch the stove."

Next time. "What were you doing?"

Fipo slumped forward, teeth chattering.

Carlo indicated the kettle. "Making tea, I think." He looked over Benedetta's head at me. "I can take him now. You should stay with the signore and signora."

The silence frothed like a pot coming to boil. All this fuss and not a word from the bedroom. Not a sneeze, not a cough, not the tiniest complaint. I turned toward their door, the distance to it seeming to double and triple. "Fipo." His name came out plain, raked clear of emotion. "Why were you making tea?"

He let out a wail, choked and chilling and dripping with grief. "To make Mamma feel better."

The film finally sprocketed through its reel, the end of the celluloid flip-flip-flipping.

No.

Eighteen

The hours that followed the Lattanzis' deaths wandered one into the next, wearying and weak. There was the old man and Carlo and other strong men, with blankets and stretchers, and paperwork none of us knew who should sign. The doctor took charge, speaking with them in the corner. He slathered Fipo's arm with ointments and salves, asking over and over, "Why did you leave them alone?"

They were fed and nightshirted, tucked into their beds. The stove was cold, the nightstands set with water, and hankies, medicine, and tea. All was well when I left. The boys already sleeping. They were none of them alone. Why did I need to be there?

I stopped answering the doctor's questions. He didn't stay long anyway. I returned to what I knew. I washed dishes and did laundry, worried the furnace might go out, that the gas bill needed to be paid, not wanting the boys to return to blood or snot or the lingering stink of death.

"Carlo will go with the Lattanzis to the undertakers." The old man spoke to me as if from a great distance, as if I listened at the door, ear pressed to the wood as I had the first night I'd met him, cold and hungry and uncertain as hell.

He pulled the Lattanzis' medicine bottle from my lips, replaced the cork, and slipped it into his pocket. "Do not worry. Carlo will make sure they are seen to. We will arrange for a service later."

It didn't matter. I didn't care. The Lattanzis were nothing to me. Neighbors for a few weeks. Reminders of all I was not, all I did not have, how little I'd been left. Obligated by their grudging charity. And responsible for their prolonged suffering.

I gathered the market basket. We needed potatoes. And lentils. Whatever the market might have. I needed to get out, breathe air on the other side of the walls of the Lattanzis' apartment. Air that was a little less thick, a little less oppressive, a little less a reminder of all I never should have done.

But the people in the market had returned to suspicion, with head tilts and glances, and poorly hidden gestures. They half-whispered, one after the other, variations on a theme. "First the DiGirolamos, now the Lattanzis."

I returned to the apartment, defeated. My short-lived victory, withered. I crawled up to my attic, curled on the bed, and watched the upside-down market proceed in its five-minute forwardedness. A forwardedness which may as well have been ten minutes before, or three days hence, because . . . "Nothing changes, because nothing changes."

I wound the Big Bens and fell asleep.

The next morning, the old man knocked on the attic door. "Carlo is waiting for you."

To place cool compresses, apply poultices, do dishes, clean laundry, scrub floors. "Tell him to go ahead. I'll join him later."

Of course, I didn't. Not that day. Not the next day. Not the day after. The market moved along as it lately did, listless and lackadaisical, and like it didn't much like having to keep putting up the pretense.

The door to my attic opened, sending light from the old man's part of the apartment up the stairs. The upside-down market bleached. The door closed. The market returned. Steps approached. I presumed the old man. I wiped a tear-filled wad of self-reproach from under my nose, pulled the covers over my head, and pretended to be asleep.

The old man pulled the covers off me. "Get up, Fiora. No hearing person could possibly sleep with all that clock ticking."

Not the old man. Benedetta. Blinking the way the old man did until he got used to the level of light.

I shoved the Big Bens under my pillow and sat up. Straightened bedcovers. Shoved hankies under the mattress. Embarrassed by the piled collections the old man had stored in every available space, collections I'd never bothered to arrange. "What are you doing here?"

"I've been leaving the door to my landing open. You haven't passed once to use the bathroom, so I came upstairs because I have to know. Are you peeing in a cup?"

I stopped trying to make my attic resemble Benedetta's homey surrounds. "I hold it until I figure you're asleep."

She put her hands on her hips. "Does it hurt to do that?"

A little. "I don't drink a lot of water."

That statement seemed to amuse her. She gazed at the projection, then walked to the inverted rooftops, ran a high finger along the topsy-turvy trolley tracks. She turned. The pie lady upended a basket of squash on the swell of Benedetta's belly. "Why is everything upside-down?"

I explained. "Like your camera."

Benedetta raised her arms over her head and out to the sides, circumscribing her own bubble. She pointed to the curtain, to its single open aperture. "All this . . . illumination, comes from that?"

The curtain bent light in ways, in those days, I had no vocabulary to describe. Sent it into the future. Trapped it in the past. Until Benedetta's question, I'd never thought of the curtain as producing light. To me, it more redirected the dark. "Yes," I told her.

"But it only shows you what you see every day. Go outside, stand on your head. It would be the same. How do you tell fortunes looking at what you can see from your window?" She walked to the curtain, examined the embroidery. "So beautiful. But what makes it magical?"

Tell her? Not tell her? Would the curtain care? "The projection is not what is happening now. It is what will happen five minutes from now."

"Five minutes?"

"Yes." I wound the old man's Big Ben next to Mamma's. They *tick-tick-ticked* at the same pace, five minutes apart.

"I don't understand. Just set them to the same time."

"I've tried. No matter what time I select, my mother's Big Ben is always five minutes ahead of the don's."

Benedetta peeked behind the curtain and out the window. She put the curtain back into place and looked at the projection. She peeked out. Looked back. Peeked out.

Looked back. "It all looks the same."

"It's more obvious when people are on the street."

Benedetta took a few seconds, hands folded over her bulge and lips pressed together, like she didn't want the wrong words to slip past. "I don't have big ambitions, no big plans to leave the neighborhood, go to Atlantic City on my own. But I'm not a simple village girl. I read. I think more than you. I keep up on the news of the world, and the happenings in the blocks around us. You don't have to tell me fables."

"It's no fable. The curtain is special. I don't know how it works, exactly. I mean, I've been learning but not a whole lot and there's still so much I don't know, but it can manipulate things."

"Things?"

"Space. The air around us. Time. Scrunch it up, or make it longer. Like how it's been feeling. You know. Humid and . . . heavy. Too warm." I explained a little more, waving my arms and wondering if making an illustration might help. "Etti has noticed it, too."

"Etti and you are blaming the curtain for the weather."

"No. Yes. I mean. The curtain . . . does stuff."

"What kind of stuff?"

"I know it sounds impossible, but watch. See, I undo a second flap, and the market goes away. Like opening photograph film to the light." I undid a third flap and a fourth. Spiraling outward until all the flaps were undone. Then I stepped away and turned toward the ceiling slope. "Watch."

To Benedetta's credit, she did watch, for a full minute in that elongated world. Mamma's Big Ben *tick-tick-ticked* away. The old man's did, too. Fairy lights played across the far wall, as they had when I first hung the curtain. Benedetta squinted. She jutted her head forward. "Is that a map?"

It was.

"Of the neighborhood?"

Yes.

"And what are all those circles? Isn't that our house in the middle? Right where we live? What does it mean?"

Yes, yes, yes, and, "Those are the boundaries, day to day, of that . . . bubble I was telling you about."

Meanwhile, the curtain did not refasten any flaps, did not flutter on the rod. I tugged on it. It stayed as it had been. Did not move. Did not adjust. Did not do a thing to prove itself to Benedetta.

Benedetta stretched her neck, moving it to one side, then the other. "Carlo is in my apartment, helping the boys roll pasta. Brush your hair, wash your face. Join us."

"But—"

"But nothing. The Lattanzis were sick. They died. Lots of people have died from this sickness. You want to believe they lasted so long because of your . . . bubble, fine. I understand. I think they came so close to recovery because you took such good care of them." She put up a hand. "Enough. I have ten loaves ready and another two in the oven. My back aches, my feet hurt. Two musketeers can't do the work of three. So pull yourself together, Fiora Vicente, because Carlo and I can't—"

A fairy light winked out. Then another. And another. The room darkened. Benedetta turned, gaze glued to Mamma's curtain. One flap, then the next, covered over its grommet, moved by an unseen force. Electricity filled the air, the hairs lifted on the back of my neck. And the curtain again projected the market onto the ceiling slope.

I expected Benedetta to scream, or to cry, or maybe to do like I did the first time I saw the curtain show its bag of tricks and make a dash for the stairs. But all Benedetta did was point to the projection.

Two upside-down women crossed the market, one tall and thin, the other short and thick. Dressed in solemn suits and sensible shoes, they looked respectable enough to hand out Votes for Women pamphlets. They wore pins in their lapels and one carried a briefcase; the only item missing was a sign tacked to their foreheads, OFFICIAL BUSINESS ONLY.

They headed our way.

Benedetta's hand flew to her chest. "I know these ladies. They're from the Children's Bureau. I—I saw them when they came to talk to the don about you, and—"

"Wait. How did you know that?"

"People talk, Fiora. My goodness, who needs a fortune-teller? Everybody knows everything about everybody. And one of them must have contacted the Children's Bureau about the boys." She grabbed my arm. "You said five minutes, correct?"

Yes. Five minutes. To move the boys, make up a reason why they weren't here, and another to convince the bureau they didn't need to return. Five minutes. Five elongated, bubble-length minutes.

I glanced to Mamma's clock, tick-ticking away. Four minutes now.

Nineteen

"Carlo. Carlo, Carlo, Carlo."

We pounded on Benedetta's door. The boys were elbow deep in flour.

We dusted them off. "Quick. Hats and coats for the boys." Rapid explanations.

And Carlo keeping an eye out the window. "How can you know the Children's Bureau is coming when they are nowhere to be found?"

My every instinct grasped for some explanation that would be reasonable. And found none.

Benedetta wiped at jam on the edge of Etti's mouth. "Carlo. She's a fortune-teller."

Bless her. "Take them to the park maybe. Anywhere." I shoved bread into Carlo's pocket. "In case they get hungry. Where's the old man?"

"Gone for a walk."

"The doctor told him to stay put."

"He feels confined." Carlo waved a hand. "Everything is so . . . compressed."

"Like when Mamma keeps the lid on the soup." Etti piped up from the depth of his scarf. "Do I have to wear this? It's hot."

Carlo rewrapped the scarf, a little looser. "Keep it around your mouth and nose, little man. Your mamma would want you to. We are going out in disguise. Do you know what a disguise is?"

Etti nodded. He looked around the room. "Can Mamma see us?"

Fipo wound his scarf so tight, it should have cut off his breath. But . . . no such luck. "Mamma can't see us. She's dead. So is Poppa. We have to leave, or we can't stay with Signora Bruni."

I thought Etti would cry. Thought he would crumble into a ball, wrap himself away from the rawness of Fipo's truth. He didn't. He took Fipo's hand. "All right."

Carlo headed for the door. "How long should I keep them?"

"An hour, maybe two. I don't know."

Benedetta shooed them down the stairs. "If the door is ajar, stay away. I'll close and lock it after the ladies leave." She peered across the market. "Go. Go."

Carlo stepped off the stoop.

I put my hands on his shoulders and turned him around. "The other way."

They were gone.

Benedetta and I closed the door after them. We locked it. We held hands, backing up one step, then another, the front door transformed to every monster we'd ever feared. We ticked down the seconds. Waiting.

Somebody knocked. A polite, but officious *ratta-tat-tat*, the kind of sound the Reverend Mother made when she wanted to get our attention.

I don't know what I'd expected. Maybe a deep and ominous thud, one that echoed off the walls and resonated down my spine. A thud weighty enough to match the drama of the last five minutes.

I smacked my forehead. "Don't answer. The boys' things. What if they check the apartment?" I ducked into the Lattanzis' and went through the boys' clothes. Nightshirts, socks, shirts, and caps. Books and toys, and the rubber band–propelled airplane. Into a box.

The knock came again.

I left the apartment and scooted across the landing, box in hand.

The knock came a third time.

Benedetta gave me a hurry-up-hurry-up wave. I pulled open the door to the basement.

And kicked the box into its murky depths.

I turned . . .

. . . and caught the cuff of my shirtwaist, the cuff I hadn't bothered to button while alone in my attic, the cuff that flapped as I moved, in the deadbolt.

I twisted, wrangling my wrist back and forth, up and down and around, keeping an ear for Benedetta.

"Hello, may I help you?" Muffled words from somebody on the outside. I imagined Benedetta holding the door open as had the landlord, so only the smallest rectangle showed, and doing her best to keep the sound of my efforts to liberate my sleeve from being heard. Then Benedetta spoke in Italian, fast and loud enough for me to hear. "Fiora Vicente? She left a few days ago. Our neighbor died and she was distraught." She switched to English and repeated herself. I peeked from under the stairwell, as had the boys, the first day I met them, the day they left their airplane on the bottom tread of the stairs and told me they planned to fly their airplane to Oz.

Benedetta waved her hand behind her back, a silent and emphatic *Go. Hide.* I shrank back to the basement steps. Closed the door. And pressed my ear to the keyhole.

The latch clicked.

"Yes, of course. Please. Come in. I don't understand, why would anybody make a report? Signorina Vicente has been doing well. Very busy in the neighborhood. People love her."

One of the Children's Bureau ladies spoke. I had no idea which, but I imagined it was the thin one, her voice high and tense, like a clothesline in the wind. I didn't catch the words, but Benedetta's answer, again loud enough for me to hear, filled in the blanks. "Oh no, the boy's injury was not serious. He is already recovered, from what I understand. They went to live with their aunt. In Coatesville."

More talking, this time I presumed from the short and thick one. Her voice was even quieter, with rounded syllables that made English sound smooth and refined.

Then Benedetta. "The boys will be fine. I plan to take them myself.

I'm their cousin. We are all from the same village, but, as you can see I will be . . . how do you say? Indisposed. So just until things settle here. Then I will get them and fill out all the proper paperwork."

"She's in there. Go upstairs and search." A fresh voice spoke from a farther distance, harsh and hateful. "Go on. Find the little witch and take her to the orphanage. She can help you there. Here, she is nothing but trouble. We will not—"

"Which of you called the Children's Bureau?" Benedetta cut through the troublemaker. "Which of you has been so ungenerous toward a house of grief?"

Silence.

"I see how brave you are when you have to own up to your actions. Please, feel free to wait on our stoop. Don Sebastiano will be back later. Perhaps he will have questions, and perhaps you will not be so quick with your comments."

I could see her in my mind's eye, standing straight, and valiant, staring down the crowd, unafraid.

One of the Children's Bureau ladies spoke. I think the tall, thin one, a long stream of which I understood nothing except, ". . . police."

I clutched the stair rail, blind to the discussion not twenty feet away, wishing, when Benedetta waved me away, I'd gone up to my attic, instead of down to the basement. I could be watching from Mamma's curtain, would already know what would happen five minutes hence. Maybe I could have entered the curtain world, made my way to the back edge of the crowd, deflected their attention, drawn them off.

I felt for the tread and sat.

And kicked the box, the box with the boys' things, the box I'd tossed down the stairs seconds after the third knock on the door, the box which, I realized after I kicked it, I hadn't tossed all the way down the stairs. Because when I kicked the box just that moment, there, in the dark, the box tumbled the rest of the way.

It bumped. It thumped. It rattled. It clattered. It shook and it shimmied. It clanged and it banged.

For what felt like forever.

I hung on to the rail, ready to run, ready to do battle, ready to go stand with Benedetta and dare the Children's Bureau, dare the crowd to make me go anywhere, make me do anything, make me feel bad about my mother, my station, my life. I was Fiora Vicente, Rosina Vicente's daughter. And I did not scare easily.

The door to the basement opened. A figure blocked the light. Maybe the short and thick Children's Bureau lady with the melodious voice, and an official paper that would send me to an orphanage.

I screeched.

The figure blocking the light jumped, and I saw she wasn't the short, thick lady from the orphanage. She was Benedetta, hand clapped over her heart. "What are you hollering for? What's the matter?"

"What's the matter? I've been here in the dark. I thought the Children's Bureau lady said something about the police."

"Oh. That." She swept her hand downward. "I drew this for them."

She pulled a paper from under her waistband, written over in Italian. Some kind of chart with boxes and arrows.

I examined the chart. "This says I'm your cousin on your mother's mother's side. And Signora Lattanzi's niece on your father's side." I didn't actually know anything about my ancestry, and this would explain even more Signora Lattanzi's willingness to help me. "Am I? Related, I mean."

She giggled. "Not at all. But the Children's Bureau thinks you are. And that's enough for them for now."

"What if they come back?"

"They won't. They think you're in Coatesville with the boys. Good thing my aunt has a lot of bedrooms. It's getting pretty crowded up there."

"So now what? I walk around with my scarf wrapped around my head, too?"

"Yes. No. I don't know." She took hold of my hand and crushed my fingers, every angle of her face crowding toward its center.

Pain, crampy and complete, took a direct route from her fist and clutched at my midsection. "Oh no. Oh no no no. You're not. Not now, I mean."

"Shut up. Be calm. We have to think. Because this baby is finally coming."

Twenty

The booklet. The *booklet*. What did I do with the doctor's booklet? I upended boxes, shoved fabric piles aside, scrabbled in every corner of the old man's attic.

Think. Think. What did it say? But all that came to me were the illustrations, exaggerated in panicked impossibleness—the woman, trussed up like a bird on the spit and the baby inside, expanded by my frenzy to the size of a six-year-old.

I hadn't read the booklet. Not really, but for one set of words flashing past during the time I'd paged through it with the old man. "Be calm. Childbirth is a natural phenomenon and if you approach it in a rational manner, there is no reason to presume you or the baby will come to harm."

Harm.

Harm.

I was so stupid to tell Benedetta about the bubble, stupid to think it'd be fine. Stupid to feel safe, to feel happy. My own rising spirits had brought this on. Relaxed the bubble enough to let the baby progress, started his outward path. I needed help, needed reassurance, needed somebody, anybody to tell me everything I did in the next seconds, and minutes, and hours, would be the right thing.

I dropped to my knees.

And looked under the bed.

The booklet. Covered in dust bunnies.

Thank you, Jesus.

I dragged the booklet out and paged through, reading by the light cast by the projection.

Another sentence surfaced. "While many women deliver healthy babies in the home, with modern scientific methods hospital delivery is safest and best."

Relief took hold of my heartbeat and calmed it to a canter.

Hospital. Yes. Of course.

I'd do like the booklet said. I'd be calm. I'd . . . wait for the old man, maybe. Hope Carlo didn't decide to keep the boys all day. Once the contraction passed, Benedetta had looked all right. She'd know if it were close. Know if anything were trying to come out . . . down there.

I stared at the map, hanging on the ceiling slope, the hospital still stubbornly situated outside the last red concentric border. How fast did babies come?

Something thudded downstairs, heavy and insistent and sounding like it wanted my attention. "Fiora."

Okay. Pretty fast. Off the edge of the projection, the trolley rolled into view, heading toward its upside-down stop.

Five minutes.

I didn't wait to see if I saw myself boarding, saw myself helping Benedetta board with me. I grabbed my coat, grabbed my scarf, and headed downstairs, near somersaulting through gravity that seemed to evaporate in my eagerness.

To get Benedetta going. Get myself going with her. Make sure that baby was born safely, and securely. And anywhere but there.

Benedetta held to the doorjamb, her face white, making little panting sounds. I put on my mask, then wrapped another around her head. She pulled at it. I took her hand away. "Stop. You have to wear it. They won't let you board the trolley without it."

She grabbed my collar, twining her finger through a buttonhole. "Trolley. Are you crazy? I can't go on the trolley."

"You have to. We must. Nobody is here. I don't know how to help you." I thought of her aunt, Don Sebastiano's reasons for not wanting

Benedetta to go there. "You can't give birth here, not so close to a death."

Her face went still, her lips grim. Her grip tightened, her knuckles pressing painfully on the front of my throat.

I swallowed. And did a mental countdown. "Now you listen to me, Benedetta. The trolley will be here in two minutes. We have to go."

I'd only had my own cycle five times at that point. I barely understood how a baby got inside a woman, much less how I was supposed to get one out. I pulled the booklet from my pocket and held it up. "Unless you think you can talk me through this."

She buttoned her coat, and we made a slow, lumbering progress to the trolley stop. The market was near empty, the excitement on our stoop, over. A lady sweeping her sidewalk made a harrumphing kind of sound. "I understand Coatesville is very nice this time of year." Then she walked into her house and shut the door.

Did streets echo? Before the influenza, even in the hour before dawn, I'd have said no. Life takes up space. Even when bundled into its bed at night, it perfuses the air, its pulse loud in the silence, unheard, but not unsensed.

The trolley rumbled to its stop, the car crowded. We boarded, working our way to a space by a window, yet the trolley felt empty, the passengers sapped of hope, skin-wrapped skeletons caught up in a pestilence-riddled nightmare, waiting their turn to meet the reaper.

I let go of the handhold, shaky, my impression strong. We were weeks into this sickness, the rates of infection, of death, reported in the newspaper daily, but little advice given. Public buildings were closed; businesses struggled to keep working. The war churned toward its end, working out its last bloody battles, and the government was determined nothing would slow that final push, no army, no philosophy, and certainly no germ.

I stood protectively between Benedetta and the rest of the passengers.

The trolley slowed, the wheels dragging on the rails. The pressure gathered. We were close to the edge, close to the place on the old man's map where the concentric circles grew thinner, compressed by a barrier exasperated by despair, and formidable enough to perhaps make supply trucks move a block onward, take a different route for their delivery, find a more convenient way around, a subtle circumscription, unnoticed in the chaos caused by the influenza.

Benedetta's face grew red. Sweat broke on her brow. She clamped a handhold, eyes squeezed shut, and moaned. "I can't."

I stood straighter. *Can't?* "Can't what?"

Benedetta groped for the rope, signaled a stop. "Let me off. Move. I don't want to stay here anymore."

I went after her, implored her to stay, to maybe find a seat, hang on a little longer. I thought the baby was coming then. I thought I'd be pushing everybody aside, telling them to make room, and then I'd . . . what?

I had no idea. I hadn't read the booklet and I wasn't going to read it then. It lay, an accusatory crackle in my pocket, and there it would stay. I tried to tell Benedetta that, but she didn't listen.

We stood by the tracks, and watched the trolley cross the boundary without us.

"Benedetta? What are we doing?"

She lurched toward the sidewalk, and headed down an alley. "I can't. I just can't. I can't have this baby. Can't be a mother."

I followed after. "Of course you can. I mean you have to. This baby is coming. You said so yourself. You don't have a choice." I ran ahead and got in front of her, spurred by a hopeful thought. "Do you?"

I didn't know. Maybe the bubble would kick in again. Make it all stop. Send the baby back from wherever it was coming.

Benedetta made a tight little sound, halfway between a sob and a laugh. "I don't know anything, haven't been anywhere. I have no idea what I'm doing."

Well neither did I.

She carried on a while longer, moving deeper into the alley. I pulled on her sleeve, tried to move her toward the street, but she clawed along the building bricks, a mouse caught in a maze.

My Benedetta was a practical, cheerful young woman. She kept her house neat, and her conscience clean, and knew exactly the right thing to say to everybody. I didn't know the Benedetta who ignored my pleas, blubbering and flustered and sobbing so much her eyeballs must have been ready to slide out of their sockets. She was a changeling, a substitute, a stopgap sent to suffer for the real Benedetta. The woman who'd crocheted every article a baby could possibly want with love and with kindness could not possibly cower in a doorway, choking and tearful and declaring louder than was wise. "I do not want this baby."

I clapped a hand over her mouth. Not quite over her mouth, over her mask which was still over her mouth. "Watch your words. You don't know who might be listening."

I looked up the alley. I looked down. I looked harder. I knew the place. I'd been there before. The side door to the pharmacy. The door from which the guaritrice had let me exit when I'd gone to the pharmacy with Carlo.

The guaritrice was a midwife.

She could help.

All the reasons I shouldn't battled with all the reasons I should.

Benedetta let out another whimper. She clutched at the underside of her belly with the dazed expression of someone who'd been given a gift they didn't much like, then looked up, the distress in her eyes real. "I'm going to die, aren't I?"

Anger, blistering and volatile, steamed beneath my skull. The doctor was crazy. How did he expect me to help my friend? I'd done enough nursing with the flu to understand pain, but I didn't understand what to do about it if there was a baby attached.

My mouth, always on a short fuse, exploded. "Shut up, Benedetta. Nobody's going to die. Not today. Stop bawling. You're making it impossible to think."

The sky darkened. The air grew stifling and impossibly hot.

Benedetta unbuttoned her coat, then removed it, then flapped the collar of her shirtwaist. "I can't stand it. I need air. Is this because of the bubble?"

I shouldn't have told her. The bubble was my burden to bear. It belonged to no other. I unbuttoned my own coat and pounded on the entrance. "My friend is having a baby. Please, you must help."

A clump of something, stalks and leaves cascaded to the cobbles. Benedetta scooped it up. "Verbena?"

From the iron ring over the door. Placed there by the old man. To keep things in. Or keep them out.

What in the world were we doing there?

I nudged Benedetta, poking her shoulder. "Get up, Benedetta. We have to go."

"Go where?"

Anywhere. Anywhere at all. Just not there.

From behind the door came a shuffling, and a growl. Fear tendriled around Benedetta like smoke. "Is that a dog?"

The shuffling sound from the other side of the door got louder; the growl transformed to a howl. Something skittered in the shadows. A mouse. Or a rat. Burrowing in the trash piles.

I hauled Benedetta off the cobbles. Put my back to hers. We had to get out of that alley. Had to get back to the street. Had to find a house with occupants. Maybe a telephone.

Benedetta pointed. "Fiora." Her voice sounded happy. "We are saved."

A patch of brightness broke on the edges of my vision. I heard my name. "Who is that?"

The patch grew stronger. Every bit of Benedetta relaxed. She leaned against the jamb, her features stopped angling every which way and fell into their normal pleasant proportions. She shaded her eyes, her relief patent in the easy way she draped her fingers over her brow. "It's Carlo."

The noises stopped, the shadows fled. We were good. We were fine. We were going to get Benedetta to the hospital.

The door behind us, the door which I'd once exited as the side door to the pharmacy, opened. A set of strong hands pulled Benedetta and me through the entrance.

I saw Carlo advancing. He was right there, his face white-masked like ours. Then the door slammed shut. Leaving Benedetta and I in darkness darker than the darkness that happens when I close my eyes.

The shuffling returned, scraping and scratchy. Other sounds followed. Metal on metal. The click of a door bolt sliding into place. And the striking of a match.

A light flared. Benedetta held my hand. She squeezed tight. I blinked and blinked again. A shadow, fuzzy-edged and female-shaped, coalesced before me.

Tizi.

Holding an oil lamp.

Hand on hip, mask gone, her features cold and calculating and not in the least welcoming. "Mamma said you'd come."

Twenty-one

I'd pounded on the guaritrice's door because Benedetta got off the trolley. She got off the trolley because I made her get on. Because she was in labor and I hadn't read the doctor's booklet. Because the guaritrice told me she knew about how to bring children into the world. Because I'd been talking to her about Benedetta. Because Benedetta was worried she was long past her due date. Because I'd used Mamma's curtain to make a bubble of stagnant time. Because I'd wanted to save the old man's life. Because I didn't want to marry a man I didn't know to avoid an orphanage. Because my parents died.

Both of them.

Rapidly, without appeal and without guidance as to what I was supposed to do next.

Mamma used to tell me every moment is the sum of the moments before. Like an arithmetic problem, except instead of three plus five making eight, the sum of my becauses brought me here, trapped me on the wrong side of the guaritrice's door from Carlo.

Because Tizi closed the door on him. Within steps of his crossing the threshold.

Because whatever the reason Tizi's mamma said Benedetta and I would come, Carlo wasn't part of her plans.

I pounded on the door again. Not to be let in, to be let out.

Benedetta pounded with me—"Carlo. Carlo!"—for what felt like minutes, hours, days.

Yes. Days. In the bubble world, all time felt like the same time, and possessed of infinite possibility.

The guaritrice stopped us, appearing out of the shadows and shoving Tizi to the side, her maskless smile so full of teeth, she looked like—

"—the Cheshire cat." Benedetta whispered the words through motionless lips, her gaze fixed on the guaritrice. "Like in Mr. Carroll's story."

Tizi ran her palm over her tummy, expression bemused, then reached a finger and traced along Benedetta's. "How did it get inside you?"

The guaritrice pulled Tizi's hand away. "Don't. Some things are personal."

Tizi's palm flew to her cheek. Like she'd been slapped. The air got electric, snappy and spiked. Tizi tucked her chin and raised grumpy eyes to her mother, lips tight and tensed for battle. "Why can't I know?"

"You will, my sweet. When the time is right." The guaritrice held up a vial and shook a drop onto her forefingers, first one, then the other, then rubbed across both our foreheads. Lavender. And cinnamon. The scents enveloped me, raising memories of comfort, of warmth, of safety in a world that had always been certain and would always remain. The electricity subsided, my tension drained away.

The guaritrice touched my chin. "Everything is fine, little one. It is late. We do not want to wake the house."

Yes, yes. It was late. That's why the sky had grown so dark. People were sleeping. The druggist above the store. Maybe another neighbor on the floor above him. There had been the growling, the shuffling. No doubt his dog already scampered back to him, once it saw Benedetta and I were not a threat.

The door pounding started again, the sound distant. "Fiora, Benedetta. Open up."

Benedetta fumbled at the knob. "We should answer that."

Tizi picked up her lamp. "Why? He can't do anything to help."

The guaritrice wrapped an arm around Benedetta's shoulder.

"Besides, we are closed. Whoever it is will come back tomorrow." She drew Benedetta down the passage. "Tizi, why don't you get Fiora some tea?"

My ears rang, my insides flip-flopped. Carlo's knocking fell off to the dullest of concussions, like wood striking wool and echoing from some disconnected place. Benedetta was gone, walled off from me as the guaritrice had walled off Carlo.

Call it instinct, memory from my traumatic encounters with the curtain world, but some deep part of me didn't want to go somewhere from which I couldn't exit. I unwound my scarf and pulled at the crochet. I bit at the end knot, gave it a pull, then tied the yarn to the doorknob. Tizi watched me, a finger playing along a birthmark in the hollow of her cheek, a mark dark and familiar, a mark much like the old man's.

Maybe she liked strawberries. I didn't know where the idea came from. At the time, I thought the notion sprang from my conversation with my strawberry-loving friend. That could be it. Maybe the guaritrice loved strawberries and touched her face while she was expecting.

Tizi raised the lamp high. "Let's go. Mamma has a new blend." She disappeared down the hall, the lamp glow receding with her.

I followed after, the way twisty and turny and much too dark, the scarf unraveling as I went. Marking my place, marking my path, marking my way back.

The passage seemed longer than last time, the bends sharper. Hollows opened at regular intervals, unremembered and mysterious, narrower than the main passage, offering breaths of breeze, and tantalizing smells. Gravy. And sausage. And the almond nougat Mamma made at Christmas. I detoured into one, took three steps, then six, then stumbled, my shoe slipping in something crunchy and crackly and, oddly, a little bit slimy.

Something scurried over my foot, then scrabbled near my ear. I scrambled to my feet, followed the thread back to the passage. I was good. I was fine. The yarn hadn't snapped; my ankle hadn't twisted. I continued, hand to wall, heart fluttering in my throat, slow and cautious. I listened for Tizi's footfalls, strained for Benedetta's voice, very sorry I hadn't thought to count the turns, count my steps, create one solid reference from which I could tick off my progress.

The pharmacy was a storefront, a shop, like so many other shops on the street. Big enough for business, a few displays, but it seemed I walked miles, the scarf unraveling to the size of a tea towel, then a napkin. I always turned to the right in what my sense of direction told me was a giant spiral. Like the curtain, like the old man's map, like the guaritrice's illustration. A spiral connected crossways by the hollows, spokes in a wheel. Narrowing from an arm span, to an arm's length, until there was no more than a hand span between me and the wall. Drawing me in, leading me to a center.

Like a web.

"Help me, Mamma." My voice sounded whispery and wistful. "I'm right here."

The passage stopped its inward collapse, and pushed me through the guaritrice's familiar beaded curtain. But instead of opening into the guaritrice's alcove, the beads opened into a wide area, with carpet which looked like soft grass dotted with scarlet poppies. The walls were edged by pillars which resembled giant tree trunks, and the ceiling a sky of deepening purple. Here and there a bright spot peeked out from behind the painted cloud cover, like stars. I wished upon one, then the other, the way Mamma used to, fancying I saw them twinkle.

Tizi swept in from wherever she'd been and grabbed my hand. "Took you long enough." She pulled me to a chair at the room's center, backless and covered in velvet. The chair's base was mushroom-colored, its top red with spots, and the longer I stared at it the more it looked like a toadstool. Tizi pushed me toward Benedetta, perched along its rim. "She won't let Mamma do anything without you."

Benedetta clutched at her stomach, her white mask hanging loose and useless. Her face went pale, then red, then purple. She lurched toward me, threw her arms around my neck, and for an insane moment I imagined she and I were under a real purple twilight, dancing to a tune beautiful and deep and only for us. I even wrapped my arms around her, happy for the bubble's elongation, wanting to linger. For a minute, maybe two, maybe forever.

Benedetta's breath blew hot and accusing on my ear. "Help me."

The imagining broke. I wasn't in a woodland glade. I was in the darkest recesses of the pharmacy, and Benedetta was caught in a full-blown contraction. I looked over her shoulder at the guaritrice, her smile grown to impossible proportions. "Help her."

The guaritrice went to a cupboard, opened it, and selected a vial from a selection of many. She pulled the cork and handed it to Benedetta. "Drink this."

I grabbed it away. "Wait. What is it?"

The guaritrice smiled all the harder, her form seeming to fade around it. Like the cat. "It is only a little medicine. Something harmless that will take away your friend's contraction. Dull the pain."

"Keep the baby from coming?" Benedetta's words exited in stutters and strains. "Fiora. Shut up. Give me the medicine."

"But—"

Benedetta pitched toward me. She swiped the vial from my grip, put it to her lips, gulped the contents, then crumpled to the poppy-covered carpet, curled like a roly-poly.

I turned on the guaritrice, my fear spitting fire. "What did you do to her?"

"Your friend is having a baby. Having a baby hurts. Did your mother never tell you? It is prolonged and tedious with pain that can make you wish you'd never been born." She recited the words with the calmness of reading a list from a dictionary, her face neutral and her demeanor unconcerned.

Benedetta clawed her fingernails into the carpet pile, her breaths coming in bursts. I raced to the guaritrice's cabinet, rattled my way through the vials and bags. "You must be able to dull the pain. Maybe you didn't give her enough."

"I gave her plenty. It doesn't always work. She is very emotional."

"Then give her something else."

The guaritrice clapped her hands. Tizi ducked behind the beads.

The beads I remembered from my previous visits. I squinted. The counter was there also. And the map. Hidden beneath the impression of forests and flowers.

Benedetta pulled herself across the floor, her sounds mewling and mousy. I crawled along with her. "Benedetta. Listen to me. You're all right. You're fine. The guaritrice can help. But you have to help, too. You have to relax." I thought of Mamma, what she used to say to me when I got to be too much. "Stop fighting yourself."

Another contraction took hold. The guaritrice held Benedetta's hand and rubbed at her forehead. "Breathe through it. It will ease. You were going to tell me the baby's name."

"Nicco. For my husband."

"But what if it's a girl?"

Benedetta traced a curlicue along the top of her bulge. "How could it be a girl? Nicco wants a boy."

"Men always want a boy. And boys can be . . . useful." The guaritrice let go of Benedetta and picked the vial off the carpet. She returned it to the cupboard. "Without them, there'd be no babies at all."

"No, it has to be a boy. For Nicco. He's in the war."

"Ah. You are alone then."

"No. There's an aunt. In Coatesville."

"An aunt. How nice." The guaritrice licked at her lips. "Especially after the loss of the Lattanzis. Such a good soul, the signora, so kind. Always thinking of others. But now she's gone and your husband is in the war. Men, they are never there when we need them, are they? Always off to fight. Women are so much smarter. We find better ways to get what we want."

"Nicco gets what he wants. He signed up and left. Expected there to be a son here when he returned. A wife and a son. Waiting." The last word slipped past Benedetta's lips with a fistful of complaint bundled under its coat.

The guaritrice turned, hands clasped under her chin, her face taking on the animation of an adolescent. "And you thought it would be funny to have a girl instead. How very clever, my pretty."

Benedetta screeched. I grabbed at the guaritrice, at her sleeve, pulled it like a child begging for a treat. "You said you could help. She's getting worse."

The guaritrice's face went sharp, like chipped flint. She shook me off. "You didn't bring the curtain. Always you want something from me, never do you bring what I need. I am powerful. I want to help. But without the proper tools, I cannot properly do my work."

Everything constrained within me let loose. "What tools? What work? What do you do here? You make tea. Expensive, expensive tea. That you sell to people with choking children, feverish wives or husbands. How would my mother's curtain help you with that? Help you help Benedetta?"

"You are a stupid, silly girl. Your friend is in trouble. Her pains won't stop, but the baby is not progressing. It is stuck, like everything else in your stinking stagnant bubble. I can save your friend. I can save the baby, but I must have the curtain."

"The curtain is at Don Sebastiano's. Hanging in his attic. I can't just produce it for you."

"Are you sure, little one? Have you ever had the curtain, then not had it?

I had, once.

"Then try."

Try. Sure. "How?"

"You must imagine. Must think of all the reasons you want the curtain. Call to it, and it will appear."

Eyes squeezed shut, fingertips to my temples, I imagined the curtain hanging at its window, the upside-down market moving inexorably on the wall. I imagined the curtain here, in my hands.

Nothing.

I popped my eyes open. "You do it."

"I can't, little one. The curtain has one master, the bearer of the burden. When your mamma left you, she passed that burden to you. You must try harder."

Something about her description niggled at me. But there was

Benedetta writhing on the floor, whimpery moans escaping her lips and so like Fipo when he burned himself after his parents' death. I couldn't think, couldn't argue, couldn't consider anything much beyond my nose. So I tried again. Harder.

And imagined the feel of the velvet, the soft comfort of the fabric, how it smelled of Mamma, of life, of the lavender she folded into her linens, of happy dinners around the table. I dreamed of all the curtain meant, of my disappointment in its constant five-minute forwardness, of my life now gone, the impossibility of its retrieval. Of what use was looking into the past, if nothing could be changed.

I wasn't sure what to do after that. Twitch of a wrist. Flick of a finger. Arms extended, the curtain resting across them in my mind's eye. Would magic words help? "Abracadabra."

My arms remained empty.

I stood taller, got hold of my attitude. "Alakazam."

Tizi popped in from behind the curtain, two steaming mugs in her hand. She handed me one. "Alakazam? That's ridiculous. What are you doing?"

Nothing. I was doing nothing. But I wasn't ready to admit that. I sipped at the tea, luscious and calming, unwilling to give up, not ready to give in. With no idea how to proceed.

I put down the cup. Once more. I could try once more. Third time the charm and all. "Open . . . sesame."

I'd expected nothing. I got nothing. Because I'd done nothing and the only thing that comes from nothing is nothing.

The guaritrice's face went icier than a puddle in winter. "Do you think this is funny, little one? A joke? You can create whole worlds inside the curtain. But for each thing you wish, you must pay a price. And if you do not imagine properly, you will not get the results you want. You do not have the curtain because you do not want to have it."

Mamma used to say a lie is the truth shrouded by fear. Fear of betrayal, of discovery, of being lost, of being found, of finding one's dream, or seeing one's dream destroyed. Of being together.

Or alone.

I didn't want to give the guaritrice the curtain, didn't want to let it go, didn't want to sacrifice what little I had left of my mother, even if the sacrifice meant another could live. Not really, because I only believed in the price as one believes in God, as an abstract, a possibility, which was how I thought of Benedetta, and her baby. Because they belonged to Nicco, away at his war. Belonged to an aunt, living up in Coatesville. Even belonged to the old man, to the Lattanzis, to Fipo, and Etti, and Carlo. Glued by a shared history, a village they remembered, and a sense of family I began to doubt I'd ever had.

The guaritrice clapped her hands. "Tizi, bring me the tea."

Tizi lifted the saucer carefully from the tray. She placed her hand along the side of the cup. "I should warm this, Mamma. It's grown cold. It won't take a minute."

"I'm sure it's fine. Our time is growing short."

"But—"

The guaritrice held out her hand. "Now."

Tizi brought her mother the cup, her steps slow and measured.

The guaritrice took the tea. She waved Tizi away and turned her back on her. Tizi took a half step back. Then another. She looked to me, something in her face. A plea, a petition . . .

The guaritrice handed the cup to Benedetta. "We will get that baby out of you somehow, my pretty. Drink."

. . . a warning.

"No!" Tizi lunged for the cup and knocked it from Benedetta's hand. The spray arced into the air, broke apart, and descended in droplets, landing on Benedetta in pinpricks so small, they almost looked like dust. Red dust. Head to toe and everywhere in between.

I'd drunk that tea. Almost half a cup. The red covered me also. Inside.

I stuck my fingers down my throat and retched. Over the chair, over the carpet, over the guaritrice's shoes, then I pulled my hanky from my pocket, still stuffed with verbena, went to Benedetta and scrubbed, scrubbed, scrubbed. At her hair, her face, her hands.

The guaritrice balled her fist and punched Tizi across the face. "Look what you did, you little troublemaker."

Tizi stumbled back, tears streaming. "Take her, Fiora. Go. Now."

The guaritrice's face changed, in a shimmer, going from angry and arrogant to agreeable and kind. "No. Don't take her. Here, she can have a fine and healthy baby. Outside the bubble, who knows what will happen. Go home. Get the curtain. I will wait. The curtain for a healthy baby. A healthy baby is all we want. Do not go to the hospital. She cannot wait, do you hear me? If you take her, you will kill her."

Benedetta pulled away from me, her eyes going vacant. "Perhaps she's right. I can't get all that way. The bubble is safer. See, the pains have stopped and we're already here. I'll wait in the chair. You get the curtain. Bring it here. Let her have her way. You said yourself, it's only a piece of fabric."

"Yes, of course." The guaritrice again put her arm around Benedetta's shoulder. She gave it a squeeze. "See now? All friendly. And Tizi does not truly want you to go. The tea was special. A new blend, crafted especially for your friend. It takes time to brew. Tizi's disappointed she has to redo her work. Isn't that right, Tizi?"

Tizi cowered by the counter, tea snot glistening across her mouth and her cheek already swelling. She ran her sleeve across it, stood up, and straightened her shoulders. "Yes, Mamma. That's right."

I got in between the guaritrice and Benedetta, cranked my hip to the side, and barreled it into the guaritrice's so hard, she fell sideways. I grabbed Benedetta, hustled her to the passage, found the end of my yarn. And ran.

Twenty-Two

We didn't actually run. We more cantered in an awkward hobble, my arm around Benedetta's waist.

The guaritrice's voice barreled after us, disjointed and desperate. "Get them, Tizi. Bring them back."

I hustled Benedetta faster, turning corner after corner in the darkening passage and gathering the yarn trail I'd left on my way in. Benedetta stumbled. I held on, got her steady. She sank against the sidewall. "I can't."

"Sure you can."

"Leave me. I'm a terrible mother. Awful. Ready to trade my child for a piece of fabric."

"It's not a child yet. It starts as a baby. All you have to do now is give birth to it." I pried her off the wall. "Then you'll figure out the rest."

I dragged her along, turn after turn after turn, spiraling inner to outer, the passage feeling increasingly uphill, our collective will slackening. The passage widened, the cross-passages, webbing the labyrinth, grew broader. I gathered skein after skein, the yarn a hopeless tangle, circling our arms, clinging to my coat buttons, twining about my skirt. I struggled with the tendrils.

Beside me, Benedetta thrashed. "Help me, Fiora. I can't get it loose."

I felt for her waist, patted down along her hips and down her legs, feeling for the threads. I unwound, and yanked, using my teeth to bite through the fibers, my thoughts wild. I needed a knife, a machete. I was in a dream. No. A nightmare. Brought on by anxiety. And exhaustion. And the . . .

I stopped my struggle. "Benedetta, listen to me. You must be calm. None of this is real. It's the guaritrice's tea, her medicine. It made us go to sleep. Not for real." I tapped my temple. "In here."

"In where?"

It was dark, pitch, she couldn't see my movement. "In our heads. All of what we think is happening is in our heads." I grabbed her hand, touched it to either side of the hollow. "Can you feel that? What do you think?"

"For a way out?"

"Yes." A shortcut, a direct route. "There's no thread, nothing entangling us. Believe me. Take a step. You will see."

She tightened her grip. And stepped with me.

The yarn fell away. I felt the lines untie, then slither down my coat, and slide off my stockings.

Benedetta squeezed my hand. "Fiora. It's working."

We took another step, then two more, keeping our palms to the wall. A breeze fell fresh on my face, the sound of traffic rumbled in underfoot, a message from the outside. We were going to make it, to a world of sunshine, and blue skies, and a reason to continue.

Something moved, shuffley, then skittery.

Benedetta pull me back. "What . . . is that?"

Something dark. Something hungry. Something unaccustomed to being challenged.

Keeping us in. Keeping us from getting out.

I stuck my hands into my coat pockets and pulled out wads of verbena and held them over my head. I didn't know why. All I knew was the old man put it in my pocket because I'd never know when it was needed. I directed my attention to what waited, and spoke in the most deep and menacing voice I could muster. "Stay back. I'm warning you."

"Fiora?" A voice, pitiful and plaintive echoed from the hollow. "Help me. I lost my lamp and the passage is so dark."

Benedetta let out a sigh, long and whooshy and full of relief. "It's only Tizi."

I held her back, a dreadful certainty gathering in my gut.

She pulled forward. "We have to help her. She helped us."

"Benedetta, stop. That's not Tizi."

The verbena warmed in my palms. The skitter-shuffle grew closer. I strained to see, strained to know what lay in my path, what prevented me from my purpose. The image filled my mind's eye, then resolved.

Eyes. Too large to be human, globular and glowing and galvanized on us.

I cranked back and catapulted the verbena forward. It spread out in tiny glimmers and coated the menace, revealing a bulk, bizarre and buglike, which sparked at each point of contact. Like fairy lights.

A hiss, spitting and spiteful, faded into the shadows.

Benedetta gasped.

I got hold of her shoulder and hauled her back, out of the hollow, back into the passage. I groped along the floor, seeking the yarn. We were close, we were always close, we were never as far as we thought we'd been. I just needed something to guide me.

Or someone.

Thud. Thud. Thud. "Fiora. Benedetta. Open up."

Carlo.

Just ahead, another ten feet, maybe twenty. On the other side of the door.

We followed his voice and made a dash for it. I put a hand on the knob, turned it, and gave the door a heave.

And ducked with Benedetta to avoid Carlo's fist, already descending to land another blow to the freshly opened door.

I pushed past him, Benedetta in tow.

"Fiora. Don't leave me." Not Carlo. The Tizi Voice.

I turned. "Carlo. Let's go."

He gazed through the open doorway.

The Tizi Voice's plea came again.

I grabbed him, grabbed Benedetta, and heaved. "I. Said. Go."

Like a cork popped from a bottle, we cannonballed to the corner.

The Tizi Voice came again, whining and wailing. "Pleeeeeaassse."

Carlo stopped us. "We must go back. Can't you hear that?"

I took his collar. "You must not. None of us should. If you do, it will be the last thing you do."

"That sounds pretty final." He hesitated, but I guess something in my face told him I meant it. He pried my fingers off his collar and tossed Benedetta's coat about her shoulders. "Here. I found this outside the door. What are all those red stains? You were only inside a minute."

We'd been there for hours. Days. Maybe years. We'd been in a bubble inside the bubble. A bubble created by the guaritrice, meant to confuse, to entrap. We were out of it, we'd escaped. And now we had to leave mine. Had to get on a trolley and cross the barrier. Because . . . "Benedetta's having the baby." I adjusted her mask back over her mouth and nose. "We gotta go."

I don't know why I was in such a hurry. We got to the hospital, the doors were shut, and a line snaked around the building.

"There's no room," a tired-looking man in a white mask told us.

Carlo spoke up. "We're not sick. The signora is having a baby. What should we do?"

The man checked Benedetta's eyes. He felt her forehead. He made her put her tongue out. "Take her to the Holy Sisters. They're set up for people who do not have the influenza. It's just a little farther."

A little farther. Benedetta looked ready to drop.

"The exercise will help her progress. Is this her first?" the man asked.

I nodded.

"Then she has plenty of time." He turned his back on us, moving to the next person in line.

Outside the bubble, a little farther wasn't far. With a pregnant woman in the midst of another contraction, it was an eternity. Carlo scooped Benedetta into his arms and carried her.

The white-masked sister put a pen to her clipboard. "How far apart are the pains?"

I didn't know. A minute, an hour, never-ending. I'd done my part. I'd gotten Benedetta there. The professionals could take over.

The nurse sat Benedetta in a wheelchair. Carlo and I headed toward a room with a makeshift sign labeled FAMILIES.

"Young lady?" The sister's voice followed me. "We're going to need your help."

I turned. "But—"

"We're understaffed. Somebody has to stay with her."

Carlo knocked on the jamb. The jamb edging the door to the room marked for families. The room where I could sit quietly while people who knew what they were doing did what they were supposed to do. He flicked his head toward the sister. "Go ahead. Come get me when you're finished." He tapped me under the chin. "Don't forget I'm here."

Stay with her. Keep her company. Help her into the hospital gown. Hold her hand.

Sure, I could do that. I'd heard it could take a long time to have a baby. One of Mamma's clients once complained she was in labor for two days.

Maybe I should have brought a snack.

The nuns assigned us a curtained space, with a bed and a chair. The space was one of six in a large room which was really a schoolroom, with a chalkboard on which somebody had listed the stages of labor, complete with illustrations. A pencil sharpener was screwed to the wall beside the heavy wood door.

On the other side of Benedetta's privacy drapes, people grumbled and adjusted, snored and sniffled. I wondered if they were here to have babies, or tonsils removed, or maybe get a broken bone fixed.

Benedetta and I should be quiet. Speak in low, polite voices, about topics suitable for public display. I perched on the edge of the chair. "So. How are you feeling?"

Benedetta bent over the mattress, her belly hanging under her, and let loose a cry. Squawky and scratchy. Like a parrot at the zoo.

The sister rushed in, bearing a tray of instruments. "Sounds like we're getting close. Into the stirrups, young lady." She nodded to me, now glued to my place. "Stay there."

Another nurse bustled in. She thrust her hand between Benedetta's open knees. "All right now, dearie, deep breath."

I couldn't imagine, would never have guessed. Benedetta clasped my hand throughout, the touch neither gentle, nor soft, nor even particularly friendly. She held tight, near crushing my bones while the nurses poked and prodded and told Benedetta it would all be over soon, if she'd only just breathe.

This was what it meant to be with a man. It was ludicrous. Why would anybody put themselves in that position willingly? I imagined Carlo and I together, the actual mechanics of love fuzzy, and fanciful and, I was convinced, painful. I clamped on Benedetta's hand as hard as she clamped on mine, unable to watch those instruments disappearing beneath the sheet the nurses had draped across Benedetta's knees. Benedetta writhed beside me, eyes crazed. "I'm going to die, Fiora Vicente. I feel it."

"Don't be ridiculous," I told her. "Nobody is dying today. You're having a baby." Then I remembered something Mamma told me once. "It's all perfectly natural."

If natural meant rearing like a whipped horse, eyes bulged and all the neck veins stretched like piano strings. Sweat poured down Benedetta's face. She pressed her lips together and arched, her eyes rolling into the back of her head. "She's not dying, is she?" I asked the nurse.

"Hush," she told me. Then to Benedetta: "Get your breath, young lady. I'm going to need you to push."

Benedetta didn't respond. She was too busy panting.

"She speaks English, doesn't she?" the nurse asked.

I nodded, repeating the instructions in Italian anyway and adding, "Don't frown, or the baby will come out frowning, too."

"I don't care." Benedetta grabbed my waistband. "If I die, tell Nicco I am never ever doing this for him again. Do you understand me? Tell him, just like that. Never."

"Shhh, relax. Tell Nicco yourself. You're not going to die." I gazed at the chalkboard illustration, at the chalk-drawn baby, grown to the size of a porpoise sliding down a passage expanded enough to accommodate it. I thought of my own anatomy, with which I only had a passing acquaintance. The illustration went blurry.

"You." The sister's voice came out of the fuzz. "If you are going to faint. Leave the room."

Leave the room? Oh how I wanted to follow that instruction. And if I did, it likely would be the only instruction I ever followed willingly in my life. I even took a step in the direction of the door.

Benedetta ripped off her mask and plucked at my sleeve. "Don't you leave me, Fiora Vicente. Do you hear? Don't you dare leave. Please."

I looked in her eyes, dark and deep and rich as hot chocolate, without worry she'd think I was casting her a curse. For the first and only time in my life.

Please stay. Please don't leave. Please help me because I'm scared. I'm panicked. I'm frightened.

And more than that.

Please make sure my baby is all right. Care for him. Feed him. Give him a warm place to sleep. Keep him safe for the day you can hand him to his father.

"Benedetta," I whispered. "You will be all right."

The nun looked up from between Benedetta's knees. "Ready, young lady? Deep breath and push."

I had no expectation of this last part. No more than I'd had for the first part. Or for anything that happened in the middle. Benedetta took the biggest breath I'd ever imagined, a breath like I'd wished I could take in the bubble, a breath like what must have happened at the creation of the world, a breath like what would happen at the world's ending. A breath like no other. Filled with faith, filled with hope, filled with the promise of tomorrow.

Then she hollered.

Long and loud. Really, really loud. I'm pretty sure the window-panes rattled.

Then her holler cut off, ending in a great whoosh, her face red, body trembling. I heard a cry, wet and lusty and oh so indignant coming from a purplish lump smeared with what looked to me like fruit *mostarda*.

The nurses wrapped the lump quickly, and I grabbed my friend's shoulder. "You have a girl, Benedetta." My excitement edged out every other emotion. Every emotion I'd ever had. Every emotion I thought I would ever have. "A girl. A sloppy, sticky, full of mozzarella girl."

This was life, how it should be, squalling and flailing, then wrapped into a bundle and placed in my arms. Well, Benedetta's arms.

The sister smiled, or so I presumed from the way her cheeks lifted under her mask. "Say hello to her, Mamma."

Benedetta leaned over the baby, touching each tiny finger. "Une, due, tres . . ."

"We already counted," the sister told her. "She's perfect. Now relax. We need a few more minutes."

The nurses could have removed Benedetta's tonsils at that moment, and I doubt she would have noticed.

Not so for me. Every image, every movement, every uncomfortable and embarrassing aspect of the experience was to be forever seared in my soul. Again the hands and the instruments went diving under the bedsheet. "What are you doing?"

"The afterbirth, sweetheart. It comes after the baby. Then we must clean your friend up. She will stay here a few days. Then you or her husband must come to collect her."

"Oh that's not her husband waiting out there. Her husband is away in the war."

"You then. And him, if you like." The nurses brought out a giant needle and thread, and I all but lost my knees.

"I'll be back," I mumbled and was out the door and down the hall past the room marked FAMILIES, seeking out the water fountain. I splashed handful after handful onto my face, unconcerned most of it ended up on my shoes. Carlo found me there. He soaked a handkerchief and laid it on the back of my neck. I slumped against the wall and imagined how the next weeks and months would go.

Benedetta holding the baby while I made soup in her kitchen. Benedetta, Carlo, and I walking the baby to the park. Perhaps Carlo would hold the baby on his shoulders the way he'd held Etti the other day.

Hmmm. The baby would have to be older for that. I waved Carlo away, to let him know I was fine. Then told him about the baby. "She's beautiful. Perfect. She has a lot of hair."

"Because your friend was so overdue." One of the sisters stood beside me. "You did a fine job in there. You'd make a fine nurse."

I waited for the trailing remark, the sideways glance that really said, "I'm saying that to be polite. You are the daughter of the fortune-teller. No nursing school would ever consider letting you attend."

But the comment didn't come. The sister stood before me, her eyes as open and honest as Carlo's.

"I almost fell over," I told her.

"But you didn't. You were brave. Very, very brave. You got her to the hospital all the way from your house. You kept her as safe and comfortable as you could. Childbirth can be dangerous, but because of you, this child has been brought safely into this world. Be proud of that and proud of yourself."

"Is she all right?"

"She's fine. Just exhausted. She's asking for you. Come back when your stomach's settled." She turned. "And comb your hair. It's a mess."

I watched her go, my heart light, then followed on angel wings. Benedetta was already cleaned up, on fresh sheets, and nursing. She put out her hand. "Come, see our baby."

A new set of imaginings replaced the others: How happy Nicco would be when he came home from the war. How proud Benedetta would be to place their daughter in his arms. How she would put an arm about my shoulders. "And this is my best friend, Fiora Vicente. She helped bring our baby into this world, so I want her to be godmother."

And I would become a permanent part of the scene because that would make Benedetta and me family. I took her hand, felt the blush creep up my neck.

The bubble must go. Life must be allowed to continue. The guaritrice was wrong. Benedetta was fine. The baby was fine. They were outside the bubble and they were fine. I hadn't killed her, hadn't hurt her baby. The guaritrice was wrong, and I was never going to listen to the guaritrice again.

I leaned over, took Benedetta's face between my palms, drew her toward me.

And kissed her.

Twenty-Three

kissed her. Kissed Benedetta. Not the kiss I'd give a friend, or my mother, or my father, or my brother. Not prim and sweet and safely on the cheek.

Oh no.

I kissed Benedetta like I didn't know a girl could kiss another girl. Like I didn't know I could kiss anyone. Full on the lips, mouth open, aware of her breath, her scent, how her hair tickled my forehead, how her face fit my hands. I kissed Benedetta and little pricklies rose—on the back of my neck, in the back of my throat, directly below my sternum. I kissed Benedetta and came away hungry, came away searching, came away longing for more. I kissed Benedetta with all my heart, with all my soul, with sudden knowledge a kiss like that happened only once because it happened first, so could never happen again. Not like that. Not with her. Accidentally intimate. Unintentionally intriguing. And not at all chaste.

It was the rush, the excitement, the sense that, in helping Benedetta bring her baby into the world, in all that horrible time since my parents died, I'd finally done something right.

And it was exactly the wrong thing to do.

Benedetta didn't like it. She jerked her head back, her expression befuddled. She wiped her hand across her mouth. "What are you doing?"

I didn't know, hadn't meant anything bad. She was so beautiful, so triumphant, her baby in her arms. *Our baby* she'd called her. Like we were . . .

together. One. My imaginings of the last few minutes and hours. My imaginings in the days and weeks of our friendship. Coffee and cookies and picnics at the seashore. She and I alone. She and I with the baby. My brothers come home. All of us together, around a table. Family.

Crumbled.

"I . . . I just wanted to wish you congratulations."

She kept her gaze on mine, the accusation clear, but I wasn't certain of what I was being accused. Exactly what I'd done. My action made no sense to me. I had no stitch with which it could be circumscribed, no piece of cloth to which it could be attached. I was free-floating, my act raw between us, flapping in an ill wind.

"May I also congratulate the new mother?" Carlo peeked in. Smiling, but somber. The light in his eye as focused as the day the Lattanzis died. "*Brava*! Benedetta. Your baby is beautiful. God bless her." He put out a hand. "Fiora. Come. We should go."

"Go?" The suggestion was welcome, a fix to my predicament. Yet, I bristled. "Why should we go?"

"We have work to do. The families in the neighborhood still need us. And now we're one musketeer shy. Let our friend rest. We will return and collect her in a few days."

Yes. We'd leave. Return in a few days. Give things time to settle. Let everything go back to as it had been. I followed Carlo out the door.

Had he seen me kiss Benedetta?

I didn't ask, and Carlo didn't say. He behaved as he always did on the way home, didn't seem to notice when we were sucked back into the bubble. His step barely slowed, his mood barely faltered.

I slept that night in fits and starts, the air too dense, bothered by images of Benedetta. In her bathrobe on her landing. Twisting my braid into a bun. The feel of her hand in mine, her touch on my elbow, the way bits of her hair were always escaping her pins. My bedcovers were too close, my mood too heavy, my attitude sour, and my way forward not clear. I woke cranky and confused and in no mood to deal with the old man.

I didn't have to. He'd left me a note: "Downstairs with the boys."

Good. I packed up my rags and soaps, hoped Carlo had charmed something out of the grocer and left, my gaze lingering longingly on Benedetta's door. She'd be home soon enough. And so busy with the baby, she wouldn't have time to think about what had happened at the school turned infirmary. We'd start fresh.

I continued to street level and tiptoed past the Lattanzis', past the sound of the boys playing, the old man speaking over them, his voice sonorous and steady.

It was really too bad he'd lost his children.

I let myself out the street door.

The sheet was sopping and still soapy. I fed it through the wringer, two rollers attached to a tub we fed laundry through to get out the worst of the moisture. We'd crank the handle, the rollers compressed, and the water squeezed into the tub. Like a pasta maker, but for fabric.

Carlo pulled the sheet out the other side. I should have rinsed it better, put a little more time in on the stains, but Carlo and I were only at our third house on the street and already my knees ached, my fingers were pruned, and the memory of my incomprehensible behavior with Benedetta nibbled at me like a goat.

Carlo shook out the sheet. "So you look at the upside-down projection and everything you see is what will happen in five minutes?"

"Yes." I took the sheet from him and put it through the wringer again.

Carlo again pulled it out the other side. "And that's how you knew to get Grazia . . ." he glanced to the little girl, silent at the table, her hair washed and braided, her dress clean and ironed, her eyes watchful, a tiny figure in a kitchen long unoccupied by either of her parents. Her doll, likewise washed and braided, sat silent on the seat beside her. Carlo lowered his voice. "That's how you knew she was in danger, knew to get her out of the way of the horse's hooves."

"And how I knew the Children's Bureau was coming. Benedetta saw them first. Saw them crossing the market and knew we had five minutes until they arrived." I left him to hang the sheet and went to stir the soup. I picked up Grazia's bowl. "I'll get you more."

After so many hours outside, in the regular world, the bubble's warm compactness had settled in my chest. It stuffed my nose, fuzzed my thinking, and caught in my every crevice and pore. I pushed a streak of hair off my forehead, ladled up the soup, and placed it in front of Grazia. Then I placed another bowl before her brother. Then I went to check on her parents, coughing and hacking and too weak to eat.

I made them drink a little water, laid cool compresses across their foreheads, and returned to the kitchen.

The bulb burned dimly in the bubble's ever-present gloom. Carlo made shadow animals with his fingers for the children. They laughed. I moved the soup pot off the burners and onto the table. I lifted Grazia's chin, made sure she was paying attention. "Eat the soup cold the next time you're hungry. I'll stop by tomorrow to check on you. If you need something that can't wait, come knock on my door. You know where. The tailor's shop. Ring the top bell. The top bell for the top apartment. All right?"

She nodded. Carlo and I let ourselves out.

We went to the next house. Washed, and mopped, cooked and laundered. Weighted by my responsibility and sweating in the artificial summer.

Carlo gathered the signore's and signora's basins, holding them high to avoid the stench and zigzagging through the children to get to the bathroom. He returned, expression thoughtful. "But anybody can see the projection, correct? You said Benedetta could, and the don. And myself, if I went up to your attic and looked."

His suggestion, while holding the emptied basins, felt too familiar. As did his every glance, his every touch, his every probing remark. When he looked too long at me, I blushed. When he passed too close, I trembled. When he made a suggestion, I wanted to argue. When he agreed with me, I asked what was wrong. I was sorry I'd tried to explain about the curtain. Sorry I hadn't let him think I had magical powers. I wished I had enough talent to read his mind, enough under-standing to read his emotions, enough confidence to convince myself the answer to my single, overwhelming question didn't matter—had he seen me kiss Benedetta?

I went back to washing dishes. "If what you're asking is whether you have to be able to tell fortunes to tell what will happen in the market five minutes from now, the answer is *no*. You don't have to be anybody special or do anything special to see five minutes into the future. But people don't have to know that. And so long as nobody is interested in knowing what will happen six minutes or further into the future, I can make enough money to go to ten typewriting schools."

"I didn't say anything about typewriting school."

"I didn't say you did." I threw my scrub brush into the bucket. "Grazia's parents will die. Just like the Lattanzis. The Children's Bureau will come, and there isn't a thing I can do. Even if I see them coming."

"You don't know that. Not for sure. And there may be a relative."

"You mean an aunt. In Coatesville." I rung out a rag and went to work on the counter. Carlo brought the basins back to the bed-room. I sliced bread and spooned beans and sat the kids at the table. We ate with them. "We could get married. Adopt Grazia. And her brother."

Carlo dropped his fork. The children looked up from their bowls, eyes round.

I kept going. "Benedetta is taking Fipo and Etti, and she's by herself. That's all the Children's Bureau cares about. If you're married. If you have a place to live."

Carlo picked up his fork and put it into the sink. He turned on the tap and ran the suds. He looked to the children. "Help me get the meal cleared, little ones, and I'll tell you all a story before I leave."

We had time to see to a fifth house and a sixth. And a seventh. We went to an eighth, then called it a day. We headed back across the market. "Listen to me, Fiora. Children are orphaned all the time. We cannot adopt them all. We could get married and the Children's Bureau may not let us have Grazia and her brother, anyway. Then what do you do? Married to somebody you don't love."

I stopped in front of the fishmonger's. "I like you fine."

"Like is not the same as love."

"You love *me*. That's enough."

"Where did you get that idea?"

"You're always around. Always running into me. You must have liked me at first, or you wouldn't keep coming back. Besides." I crossed my arms. "Don Sebastiano suggested it."

"Then of course we should marry and make each other miserable for the rest of our lives. And why are you going on and on? You don't even like children."

I'd been cooking and mending and cleaning up messes I didn't want to think what they were for weeks. Children were fine, when they belonged to somebody else. And didn't get in my way. But I wasn't about to admit that to Carlo. "What do you mean I don't like children?"

He walked off. I chased after. Past the barbershop, the baker's, and the lady who crocheted the pretty lace collars. I don't know why. I think now I was trying to prove something to myself, something I wasn't even sure I needed to prove. "That's it? Please. I feel responsible for her parents. For them being sick."

He pulled up short. "How could you be responsible? They caught a disease. They might die. That has nothing to do with you."

One thing to explain about seeing five minutes into the future, another to admit to trapping everybody inside a bubble of time. "Can't you at least think about it?"

"There's nothing to think about. You don't love me. You don't even like me much. Except as a friend. Somebody who can help you with your work. Because you feel responsible for what's happened, because of what happened with your mother. But you don't need to feel ashamed if you don't feel for me like a woman might feel for a man. That's how it is with some people. They are not like everybody else. That doesn't make them bad. It just makes them different."

Different. Because of my mother. There wasn't anything I could do about that. Surely he knew, surely Don Sebastiano had explained. "I have no idea what you're talking about."

"Don't you?" He lifted my chin, as I'd done earlier with Grazia, as Don Sebastiano had done on the first day we met. And let me look deep into his eyes. "Do you really not? It is best to be honest. Even when the truth is difficult. You don't love me, Fiora Vicente. You don't love any man. You love Benedetta."

Carlo was angry, vindictive, making up stories because I didn't fall at his feet when we met on Parade Day, didn't stay to chat when I saw him outside the leather shop, wasn't overwhelmed with appreciation when the don presented him to me as a solution to my need for citizenship, for security. No wonder Benedetta had acted so strangely. Maybe my kiss got a little carried away, but Benedetta might not have cared if Carlo hadn't been there. Somber. And silent. And watching.

Like I'd done something wrong.

I pulled a loaf of bread from the Lattanzis' oven. It was small, too dark, and much too hard. Nothing like Benedetta's. I turned to the old man, my hand on my hip. "How did Carlo know where to find us?"

The old man looked at me over his newspaper. War news and war news and war news. I'd stopped reading it. I was steeped in my own struggles, with snot and poop and piss and puke, fevers and hunger and children crying for their parents. The war was supposed to be over and it kept going. To no purpose. The Kaiser couldn't win, no matter what battles he won. Yet the Kaiser kept fighting, even though he'd already lost the war.

Because he didn't want to admit it.

The old man turned the page to the editorials. "People talk. You know how they talk. The fishmonger's wife saw you get on the trolley. I sent Carlo to the pharmacy on a hunch."

I slammed the loaf to the table. Like a hammer. Why couldn't I make those things? The recipe is straightforward—flour, water, salt, yeast. Time to rise. Time to bake. Nothing magic.

I still can't do it.

In those days, girls didn't fall in love with girls. Girls fell in love with boys. They got married, they had babies. One day those babies grew up. *Those* girls fell in love with boys, *those* boys with girls, and everything continued for another generation.

We didn't know another way. Our thinking was modern, but not yet modern enough.

Everything was my brothers' fault. Because they'd gone off to fight in the Isonzo. If it weren't for my brothers, the old man might have thought it more important to find me a job than a husband. More important to make sure I had an education, than a pile of mending. More important I followed my dreams, than everybody's expectations. If it weren't for my brothers, I wouldn't have had to make up reasons why I wasn't interested in walking with Carlo, wasn't impressed with Carlo's ability to buy a building, didn't give a fig Carlo was the old man's heir.

If my brothers hadn't been so absent, Carlo's presence wouldn't have forced me to a fact I didn't want to accept: I'd kissed Benedetta. Like a girl is supposed to kiss a boy.

And I'd liked it.

I pulled another loaf from the oven, turned it out on the table, snatched the newspaper from under the old man's nose. And tapped my temple. "You see things. Know things. You're like me. You didn't send Carlo to the pharmacy on a hunch. You sent him because you knew Benedetta and I were there. Why can't you be honest?"

"I tell that which is most true, and keep what is not necessary to myself. Maybe I don't tell you enough, but truth is true whether I tell you, or not. Why were you at the pharmacy at all? Every few days, we have this conversation. Every time, you ignore me."

Because the doctor left me with a booklet. And Signora Lattanzi died. And the old man went for a walk when he wasn't supposed to. Because I was trying my best, working my hardest, doing every little thing everybody thought I should do, and nobody telling me if I were doing any good at all. "Because Benedetta got off the trolley. I wasn't planning to go there. We got there by accident."

"With the guaritrice, nothing is an accident."

Etti picked up one of the loaves and tried to take a bite. The crust wouldn't give. He pointed to a lump projecting from its top. "Look. It has a wart."

Fipo made a whiny buzzing noise, like a top spinning out of control. "Everything she does goes bad."

His airplane whizzed over our heads and landed in the next batch of dough, rising on the back of the stove. The dough went *pfft*, and collapsed.

I pulled the airplane from the gooey mess, disturbed. There was something there. Smoke and flame, exhilaration and regret, the oddest sensation of acceptance, the understanding control is an illusion.

Not urgent, not imminent, not for years.

Maybe I could change it. "Fipo. Watch where you toss your toys."

"I won't. This was my parents' house. Now it is mine. Mine and Etti's. We were all here. We were happy. Then you come and Mamma's dead and Signora Bruni is not coming back. What did you do to them? Why didn't you like us?"

Fipo's words rolled over me like an oxcart. Lumbering, and long, and unrelenting.

The old man took the airplane from me. He gave it back to Fipo and flicked his head toward the door. "Better you and Etti play in the vestibule."

The boys clattered out. The old man folded his paper, his face thoughtful. "Signora Bruni sent a note this morning. She does not think your bubble is a safe place for the baby. She said being on the outside is like being allowed to breathe. She says she has a whole new vision. She's decided to stay with her aunt. In Coatesville."

My eyes filled, the inside of my nose stung. I took the dough off the back of the stove, slapped it to the wooden slab, and lay into it the way Benedetta would, rolling and punching and punching again. I understood why Benedetta baked so much. I wondered if she'd still feel the need, way up there in Coatesville.

"But—"

Her apartment, the tiny baby bed, all the pleats and bows and beautifully crocheted blankets.

But—

The Three Musketeers, our work in the neighborhood, our pledge to be true to one another.

But—

The old man, his garden, the strawberries he still struggled to ripen.

But me. But her. But the one topic we didn't talk about, the one topic we never would. One incident, enough to sink our friendship, separate us, cast our memories onto a sea of regret.

But—

"—Fipo and Etti."

"Signora Bruni didn't forget them. Says she can take them if the Children's Bureau come sniffing around again. Her aunt is willing. With so many orphaned, the authorities may not require strict proof the boys are related. She and I will have to talk further. There's a lot to consider. As Fipo just informed us, he and Etti own the house."

"Fipo and Etti are our landlords."

The old man looked amused. "Fipo hasn't figured out that part yet. Let's not tell him."

"How long until Signora Bruni leaves?"

"Three days. She asked that you pack up her things. Carlo can take them to her."

Carlo didn't have to take them to her. I could, along with an apology, and . . . "Do you have strawberry preserves?"

The grocer shook his head. "For Signora Bruni, I'll bet. I sold my last jar before the sickness. Strawberries are a summer fruit, the preserves best when fresh. There may be a jar hiding in the market someplace, but maybe you could bring her peach. Or apple?"

Word of how I helped Signora Bruni have her baby had spread. Because people talked. Oh how they talked. I was again in the market's good graces. I didn't know how long that grace would last, but I didn't want to squander it. "No. The preserves have to be strawberry. Maybe you could look again. I'd be willing to pay a little extra."

The grocer disappeared under his counter. He made a big show rattling jars and moving boxes.

I didn't care. I had time. Minutes, hours, days. I thought about the packing I'd already done, the underthings and hairbrushes, diapers and tiny shirts, crocheted caps and little trimmed blankets. And I had an excuse to see her. She'd be happy for the preserves. Understand all I intended was that we'd truly remain friends. She might decide Coatesville is too far. She'd rather stay where she knew.

And I'd promise. Oh how I'd promise to help as best I was able with the baby. Without a string attached.

I'd even go to a library and get out a book on how best to do that.

The grocer emerged from beneath his display, waving my quarry. Strawberry preserves. Freshly made this past summer—

He named a price.

—and impossibly expensive.

I refused. "She will be eating these preserves, not putting them in the bank."

We haggled a while, the air seeming to shimmer with the energy. I was being successful, behaving like an ordinary person, like any person in the market. Then, the grocer's face went still. It went concerned. He looked past me, eyes flicking left, then right, then left again. He put the preserves in a bag. "Take them. No charge. Send Signora Bruni my compliments."

I looked behind me for the reason for his sudden generosity and espied a messenger heading for the end of the block, one of those telegraph boys Benedetta had worried about. This one wasn't looking for an address, wasn't peering from one door to the next. This one walked quickly, eyes front, like he'd already made his delivery. I swept my gaze back. The Lattanzis' door was behind him. I took the bag from the grocer, his eyes telling me all I needed to know. The messenger had been to our house. To deliver a telegram.

Nicco. The ever-present passenger during my time with Benedetta, offering opinions, laying down rules, and making decisions.

He hadn't written, not a jot, in all the time I'd been there. Benedetta had been so worried.

And now she'd be alone.

A wisp, the tiniest little tickle poked at me. Benedetta would be alone. And I could be there to help her.

A screech, a thud, and a scream stopped my thoughts and snapped my head around. People pointed, hands to mouth. The trolley, halted shy of its stop. And a bundle of rags caught beneath its wheels. The conductor, bent over them. "I didn't see her. She ran right in front. I didn't see her."

Her. I drew closer. The conductor held up what I first thought was a baby, then realized was a doll, washed and braided. A doll I recognized. The rags resolved, now a dress. I'd ironed it the day before. And blood. So much blood.

"It's Grazia," the fishmonger's wife said, and what she said was true. She looked to me. "You said she'd get run over. God forbid. You told her mother."

I hadn't. That's not how the story went.

Fipo and Etti barreled past me. I corralled them, holding them tight to my skirt as I'd seen so many mothers hold their own children when I passed by. Fipo struggled, like the boy in the alley. "Signorina. Let me go, let me see. Did you kill her? Like you killed my mother?"

His voice rose with each accusation.

And the murmurings began. "She saved this girl last week."

"She's been caring for her family."

"Why?"

"Why?"

"Why?"

I was not brave, did not stand up, did not even go to Grazia. The conductor took off his coat. Laid it over her form.

The old man brushed past me. "Take the boys. Go upstairs. Stay there. I will be up in a minute."

I didn't fight him, didn't protest, didn't tell him I could take care of myself, handle life on my own. I didn't say any of the many things I would have said under any other circumstance to let him know I was independent, secure, able to do everything myself. The little girl was dead. I'd seen her fate. I'd saved her. And it hadn't mattered.

I needed to leave. Never return. Start again someplace nobody had ever heard of Rosina Vicente, or her daughter.

I retreated, the boys in tow. But they wouldn't go up the stairs with me, wouldn't obey my slightest instruction. They drew me into their apartment. Made me sit in the chair. Fipo pointed me to the table. To the telegram. "Read it."

"I can't, Fipo. This belongs to Signora Bruni."

He picked the telegram off the table and held it out to me. "Read it."

It was short. Brutal. Written in that abbreviated diction telegrams used to keep down their cost. "Regret to inform deaths of . . ."

It went on only long enough to say its piece. Names, ranks, date, location. Ending in "Details to follow."

A telegram. Delivered moments ago. Informing of more dead heroes. A telegram the grocer thought was meant for Benedetta, but which was addressed, inexplicably, to me.

Twenty-Four

Shut up. Shut up. Everybody needed to shut up. Carlo needed to stop seeing how I was, the old man to stop offering me things to eat, and Etti to stop asking me to read him a story. I needed their absence. I needed their indifference. I needed them to leave me alone.

I'd bemoaned my brothers' interference. They were gone. I'd wanted to help Grazia. She was dead. I'd looked the DiGirolamos in the eye, cared for the Lattanzis, fought with my father, hollered at my moth—

No, I didn't want to think about it. Wanted to leave that be. Wanted to close my mouth, close my mind, close off any possibility I'd had anything to do with anything.

People get sick. They die.

Kids run into traffic. They die.

Old men forget their medicine. They die. Unless their orphaned ward stagnates time and puts everybody in the vicinity into a bubble.

"My brothers are dead." I whispered from under my covers.

I sat on the edge of my bed, defiant. "My brothers are dead."

I pulled Mamma's curtain aside, threw up the sash, leaned out, and shouted to the market. "My brothers are dead. My brothers are dead. My brothers are dead."

Nobody looked up.

I turned. Fipo stood at the top of the stairs. "Signora Perelli says you've gone crazy."

Signora Perelli was the fishmonger's wife. "I haven't gone crazy."

"You're just angry."

I flopped into the chair and pulled on my stockings. "Yes. I'm angry. Very angry."

Men are stupid. Will fight even when they can't win. Even if they've already won. The Isonzo didn't have to happen, didn't have to continue. My brothers didn't have to die. The war would be over soon. Everybody said so. And still they fought. They fought and they fought and they fought. For one more field, one more stream, one more village full of goats. Because they were men. Stupid, stupid men.

And they ran the world.

I tightened the laces on my shoes. "Have you eaten yet?"

"The don gave us oatmeal." Fipo picked at the edge of the jamb. "I'm tired of oatmeal. Can't you make us something better?"

"Oatmeal is easy to make."

"That's what the don says. But I want something better. I want hotcakes. Can I have hotcakes?"

Fipo didn't want hotcakes. Fipo wanted to see if I'd say *yes*.

"If I make you hotcakes, will you leave me alone?"

"Yes."

Liar. "Fine. I'll make hotcakes. Now go away."

"You're not going to make hotcakes. Because you don't know how. You don't know anything. And you don't want to know anything. Except typewriting. Because you don't want to take care of us."

"And what does that matter to you? Soon you'll go to stay with Signora Bruni, and you'll have all the hotcakes you want. Now get out of here."

He stomped down the stairs, opened the door at the bottom. "I don't want to go to Signora Bruni. I want her to come here. I want everything to be like it was. Before you came."

He slammed the door after him.

I wanted everything to be like it was before I came, too. I'd tried. The curtain wouldn't allow it.

In the way the curtain sometimes sensed my thoughts, it let itself off its hook. It covered the window, and again projected the upside-down, five-minute-forward market across the wall.

I watched my neighbors do in five minutes pretty much what they were doing right now. What they would do tomorrow. What they would do the day after. There were fewer on the street than yesterday, when there'd been fewer than the day before, but the influenza had to end, just like the war. Life would go on and all that was happening now would turn into what had happened then and we'd forget about it and move on.

Because there was always another war in the making, another epidemic waiting to rise. Because life was like that, the same old thing. Buildings rose, rivers changed course, but the dailyness of every day continued. People got up and dressed and went to work and went to sleep. They ate and they drank, they peed and they pooped. The next morning, they did the same.

My brothers were dead and the world kept going. My parents died and the world did the same. The future was too large to fathom, the past too heavy to bear, the present always there and infinite, and none of it had any answers.

The curtain was my burden, but it served no purpose. And my every attempt to bend it to my will sent it full circle to kick me in the backside. The guaritrice claimed the curtain had power, claimed it could create whole worlds. But those claims were no good because every good I'd ever had in the world seemed determined to leave me.

"I hate you." I got up close to the curtain and said it again. "I hate you."

You're useless, you're wrong, you're a waste of my time. "You don't like me. Why do you stay? You were Mamma's curtain. Now you're mine, but you don't help me, you don't help anybody, you don't show me a thing I can use, don't warn me of a thing I can change."

The bubble I'd created had holes. Still vulnerable to enmity and to love, to superstition and enlightenment, to good and to bad, to joy and to sorrow. People still died, children left orphaned, babies born. The only thing the bubble had prolonged was suffering; the only thing the bubble stopped was progress. There was no world I could create whose result I could ensure, and that made the curtain dangerous.

Dangerous when used.

Dangerous when not used.

Dangerous in theory. Dangerous in reality. And dangerous because I couldn't be sure what it would do next.

The guaritrice wanted the curtain. Since the day I'd met her. Mamma hadn't warned me. Hadn't told me a thing. I'd walked right in, hurting, and hollow, and desperate for help. The guaritrice was smart, she was cunning, and if I didn't do something now, the guaritrice would get what she wanted.

What can't be used properly must be put away. What won't be put away must be destroyed. I went through the old lady's things, found a pair of shears, and I slashed at the curtain, fueled by the fury of frustration, the despondency of grief, and the unavoidable rancor of remorse. The fabric gave way, shredding in long velvet bits, the embroidery unraveling, the grommets clinking to the floor. One by one.

I gathered the pieces, the scraps and the bits and the long velvet strips. I needed something metal in which to hold them, a match with which to ignite them. I needed kerosene to make it burn hotter and I needed . . . I needed . . .

An open space to do all that.

Maybe the old man's rooftop garden, but I'd need to wait until he left, and I'd need to make sure the boys weren't around so they wouldn't get any ideas.

Fine. Maybe I'd burn it all the next day.

I fell onto the bed and threw my arm over my forehead, exhausted. Like I'd scrubbed ten houses without a break and had to push the mops all uphill. Gray bubble sunlight streamed through the attic window unencumbered, illuminating the veins on the inside of my lids, creating a world where red trees branched against a yellow sky.

I added a city, emerald green like in Fipo's book, rising in the background, and filled the fields surrounding the city with scarlet poppies. Mamma and Poppa were alive in that world, my brothers still with them. Every dream I ever had lived there, every want and wish. Men did not run things, Benedetta was again my friend, and Nicco didn't bother us too much.

Because I didn't put Nicco there. I put him somewhere here. Working maybe, or still in Italy trying to convince Benedetta's parents to emigrate. It didn't matter. Benedetta and I were again together, our baby between us, and free to go to Atlantic City whenever we wanted.

Something shifted beside me, furtive and fluttery. "Go away, Fipo. I'll make hotcakes later. Go find the don. Go for a walk. Go keep Etti occupied."

Fipo didn't answer. I opened one eye, then the other. Looked to the door, to the window, to the corners. And to the floor. To the pile of scraps, gathering and realigning, melding along the rips, the grommets inserting where they belonged. The flaps found their places; the strip of leather I'd sewed to the top reattached.

The curtain leaped to the window, whole as the day I collected it from the landlord, the top wound over the iron rod. The fairy lights reappeared, dancing along the opposite wall. And nothing was left where I'd gathered the pieces except a few stray threads and the old lady's shears.

To this day, I do not know why I stayed, do not know why I didn't grab my few possessions and charge down those stairs, set myself up on the old man's landing. But remember what my mamma said about my curiosity.

The fairy lights disappeared, one by one. As they had the first time I hung the curtain. As they had the day the curtain revealed itself to Benedetta. As happened every time I tried to make the curtain act like what it looked like, a beautiful work of embroidery meant to shelter me from the world beyond my window.

I waited, expecting the five-minute-forward market to blossom in the final aperture. But the curtain projected a different image on the opposite wall. An upside-down skyline in shades of yellow with red-branched trees growing in a poppy-filled field. In the distance rose a city. Emerald. Just like in Fipo's book.

An imagined world. Like the guaritrice said. Where my parents were alive, my brothers, too, where Benedetta waited with her baby, and my every want and wish had a home.

Somebody laughed, shrill and triumphant. And at my elbow.

The world disappeared and the attic plunged into darkness. I groped for the grommet, hope finally my friend, and unbuttoned the centermost flap. Whatever game the guaritrice was playing, I wouldn't be her partner. My world had expanded, and for the first time in a very long time, my world was awash in possibilities.

The market emerged on the opposite wall, not my red-treed, emerald-citied world. But I'd made it. I'd seen it. The colorful aspects of that world were gone, the impossible aspects, but other bits might remain, if I did now what I needed to make them true.

And what I needed was my friend. I needed Benedetta. My brothers were dead and I needed to talk to her about them, tell her how they were and what they did, and what I liked about them most.

I needed Benedetta, needed to apologize, to tell her whatever I'd done, I'd never do it again, that all that mattered was her and her baby, their health and their happiness. That I'd be there for her however she wanted and if she didn't want me to be there always, that was fine, so long as I could be there sometimes. That I understood about the bubble, that it couldn't last much longer. I'd find some way to deflate it, some way to defuse it, some way to salvage what remained, and resolve what was lost.

Somebody rang the old man's bell, tinny and high-pitched. The top bell for the top apartment.

I presumed Carlo. To pick something up, leave something off, maybe ask polite permission to get me into the open air. Ringing before he let himself in because he wanted to give a warning, a little notice, not startle me in my time of grief. Or maybe he'd just forgotten his key. I didn't care, didn't want to see him. Not today, not for a while, because despite his concern, Carlo was a reminder of how badly I'd behaved, and my cup of guilt was already overflowing.

I brushed my hair, then braided it, then coiled it at the back of my neck. I wanted to add a pretty collar, but that wouldn't be right for mourning. I wanted to tie a ribbon in the chignon, but that wouldn't have been proper either. I gave Carlo enough time to do whatever he'd come to do and leave, then headed downstairs, washed my face in the sink, gathered the market basket, and put the strawberry preserves inside. I added a loaf of my bread and a knife to slice it, and wondered if I should look for a loaf at the baker's. Something more palatable with a crust that wouldn't crack Benedetta's teeth.

The thought was what mattered, Mamma always said. I covered it all with a tea towel and added one last item. Because I didn't have the heart to tell Benedetta about my brothers out loud. The telegram.

I headed down the stairs, past the Lattanzis', opened the door to the street, and stepped out. The market looked pretty much like the projection again flickering on the wall of my attic. Except receding up the sidewalk was a messenger. A messenger like the one who'd come to tell me about my brothers. The fishmonger's wife caught my eye. She made the sign of the cross, and I knew the messenger had been the one to ring the old man's bell.

Mamma always said deaths come in threes.

She and poppa made two.

Add the DiGirolamos and their brood made nine.

The cycle started again with the Lattanzis, and ended with poor little Grazia.

And now my brothers started it again. Leaving one to make three.

One messenger to deliver the notice. To tell us of the only other possibility.

Nicco.

The bubble drank in my realization, a great, slurping pull that shrank me back through the doorway, sucked me up the stairs and into the old man's apartment. It kept me there and forced me to see what I'd missed on my way out, so concerned as I was with Benedetta and my brothers. And preserves. And my own problems.

The door to the old man's roof garden. Open. As it had been on the bubble's first morning.

And a wail, a cry, frightening from a man.

The old man was sick; he needed his pills. Nicco was somebody he cared about, a boy from his village. I dashed through the door, and there was the old man, tearing at his garden. The windowpanes were askew, soil scattered everywhere. Basil and oregano, unripe tomatoes and hard, shrunken zucchinis. The old man keened over a container, strawberry plants dripping through his fingers. "What's the use? What's the use? She's too strong. The innocent always pass on." He moaned and he wept and he held the unripe berries to his chest.

And I knew without knowing in that weird way I sometimes did. That childbirth was dangerous. That the influenza was hardest on pregnant women. That the messenger hadn't come to inform about Nicco.

He'd come with notice of Benedetta.

The Infinite Now

Twenty-Five

$\mathcal{E}$verything collapses. Buildings, trees, mountains. Everything wears away. Everything serves its purpose. Except . . .

Me. In Benedetta's apartment. Crying worse than I ever did over Mamma and Poppa. Worse than I cried for my brothers. Worse than I'd ever cried before. Worse than I'd ever cry again.

While I cried, I scrubbed. Every pot. Every plate. I swept every corner. Fluffed every pillow. Folded every tiny shirt, every lace-trimmed bonnet, every crocheted bootie. The activity filled the spaces emptied by Benedetta's absence, soothed emotions scraped raw by regret. I did things properly, the way Signora Lattanzi had taught me, the way Benedetta would have liked, and harbored some notion my work would make things easier for Nicco when the war finally released him. Like Benedetta were still there, maybe in the bathroom, possibly stepped into the market. Gone just for a little and in a little while, would return.

The boys rolled pasta with me. The old man worked at his table. We left all the interior doors open, pretended our apartments were part of one big house instead of separate living arrangements. We called back and forth like family, the aroma of the old man's pipe wafting down the stair, the tap-tap of his hammer, homey.

The boys ate enough for six, then Etti handed me Signora Bruni's book, the one with the city of emeralds, and asked me to read.

I opened to where he said. "'We dare not harm this little girl, for she is protected by the Power of Good, and that is greater than the Power of Evil.'"

Etti put a hand over the page. "Does it mean Signora Bruni's baby?"

"It means any child."

"Not Grazia."

I closed the book. "Sometimes it is hard to understand why things happen."

The boys headed to their part of the house to get ready for bed. I stood in Benedetta's orderly kitchen, head tilted, every nerve poised for her presence.

All that returned was the bubble's constant, unrelenting pressure. And the knowledge I'd been avoiding since Benedetta and I made our escape from the guaritrice.

The monsters were loosed. Hope had fled.

I needed to stop crying. I needed to make plans. I needed to find that illustration Benedetta drew for the Children's Bureau ladies. The one written in Italian, with the arrows and boxes she used to convince the women how we were related. I needed to take that illustration to the infirmary, to the Holy Sisters.

But first I needed Carlo.

Because I needed a husband.

Because I needed to get Benedetta's baby.

The sister didn't seem to understand why Carlo and I were there. She checked Benedetta's file, then looked past us, to the people milling about the hallways. The injured, the sick, the careworn. She had people to see. Live people. People she could still help. "You couldn't have known what would happen. There's nothing you could have done."

Except as the doctor asked. Read the booklet. Prepared. Helped Benedetta deliver at home. Away from germs, away from the sickness, away from the outside world. She wouldn't have needed to go on the trolley. Wouldn't have gotten off by the guaritrice. I thought of the tea, red-tinged and suspect, of how it arced through the air.

I wanted to take Benedetta's file. Wanted to rattle it under the sister's nose. Wanted to climb on her little table, kick the notice proclaiming SIGN IN HERE to the side, and confess. Loudly. "You don't understand. I killed Benedetta. I have a magical curtain and used it to imagine a world. A world peaceful and hopeful that turned on my wishes without my having to put in any work. I placed my friend there. I placed her baby there, also. I imprisoned them both, along with my dreams. Because I didn't like the world I lived in, because I couldn't face the future, because I resented my circumstances, begrudged my gifts, and disrespected my benefactors. I used the curtain improperly, and Benedetta paid the price. And if I don't get Benedetta's baby, then the last of Benedetta I might salvage will also be lost."

I didn't do or say any of that. I unfolded Benedetta's illustration and started explaining to the sister, pointing from one box to the other, tracing along one arrow, then the next and hoping the sister didn't speak Italian. "Signora Bruni's husband will be home from the war soon. And we want his daughter to be there when he returns."

The nurse looked at Carlo and my ringless fingers. "Are you married?"

Carlo took my hand. He met the sister's gaze, his open and honest. "Yes, we are."

I waited, but lightning didn't strike either of us dead. "The baby should be with family."

Relief smoothed the furrows gathering across the sister's forehead. She again checked Benedetta's file. "We were under the impression Signora Bruni's only other relative was her husband."

My mouth went dry. "Other relative?"

"An aunt. Signora Bruni's listed next of kin. She came this morning and took the baby with her. I imagine by now, they're already settled in Coatesville."

Carlo and I left the hospital empty-hearted and empty-handed. Carlo hunched into his coat. "Benedetta's aunt will take good care of her baby."

I turned up my collar, tunneled my hands into my opposite sleeves. I'd forgotten my mittens, left my scarf on its hook by the old man's door. I'd grown unaccustomed to their use, uncomfortable with their bulk, uncertain of myself in a normal world where October was chill, and bracing, and smelled of winter. "What do we do?"

"We go home."

We did. Fipo corralled us. "The don is sick. He's in Mamma and Poppa's bed."

I hiked up my skirt and ran into the room, my fear outrunning me.

The old man waved me away. "I'm fine. I was tired."

"He took a pill." Fipo held up the package. "If he's fine, why did he take a pill?"

The old man took the envelope from Fipo. "I took the pill because my heart is sad."

"For Signora Bruni." Etti stood in the doorway, flicking his suspenders, his expression curious. He went to the old man and rubbed his cheek. "Because she's with Mamma and Poppa. Are you going there, too?"

"Not today." The old man put his hand over Etti's. "I need a nap. Let's talk later."

Carlo and I shuttled the children out. I sent them to play in Benedetta's kitchen, then pondered changes to our living situation. "The first floor is safer for the don. Two flights is a long way. I could set up a place for his work in the kitchen. The boys like being near him."

Carlo didn't look convinced. "Better ask the don about that first. He has his own ideas about things."

I picked through the keys on the signora's ring and let us into the Lattanzis' shop. We inspected the bolts of cloth, the cutting table, the various bins and boxes. Carlo examined the sewing machine. "We may be able to find a tailor willing to offer a fair price. Fipo has no interest in following his father's trade. All he talks about is airplanes. He wants to learn to fly. To be an ace. Like in the war. Airplanes are the future. Fipo has ambition."

Fipo never talked to me, except to tell me how badly I did things. As his mother had. "What about Etti?"

Carlo cast his gaze to the heavens. "He loved Benedetta's stories. He wants to visit imagined worlds. I think he'll be an explorer."

I ran a finger over the clothes press the old man told me about when I first arrived. The shop was neat, well-ordered, set up with pride. Mamma and Poppa would have loved for an arrangement such as this. It seemed a shame the Lattanzis' hard work should go out the door, piecemeal. "The shop should be rented, perhaps to a tailor. We could include the equipment in the lease. The money would be enough to cover utilities, enough for groceries, whatever is necessary. Soon as the influenza passes, schools will reopen. Fipo will need pencils and paper."

I thought of him, his well-tailored knickerbockers which were already getting a little short, even in the bubble's stunted growth. Once the bubble exploded, or faded, or stopped expanding and shrank to nothingness, Fipo and his brother would shoot up so tall their heads would touch the ceiling. "How odd it will seem to Fipo for another tailor to fit his clothes."

"You're worrying about things that haven't yet happened." Carlo removed his coat. He slung it over his shoulder. "I do not understand how the weather can change so quickly. Do you feel it? Like rocks, here." He put a hand to his chest.

I didn't want to explain. The revelation had only hurt Benedetta. "Your heart is sad. Like Don Sebastiano's."

Carlo grabbed me by the shoulder and turned me to face him. "Then we must do something about that sadness. We must carry on, as if she were here. Do what we were doing. What Benedetta was doing. Nurse our neighbors, tend to their children, figure out the rest as we go along."

I didn't want to carry on. I was a refugee in a perilous and precarious world, locking and relocking the doors against an enemy more toxic than any germ, more pervasive than any gossip. An enemy both invisible and ever present and able to be carried on a thought.

Despair.

I shook myself. "I'm taking the boys for a walk."

"We'll both take them."

"I'll take them alone."

Carlo came anyway.

Etti didn't want to walk far. He lingered by a rack of newspapers and gazed at the daily posting of dead heroes. "How can they be here and not alive?"

Fipo traced an edge along one of the photographs. "They are a bit of light somebody captured on a film."

Carlo ruffled Fipo's hair. "How did you know that?"

"Signora Bruni told me." Fipo made motions like he was holding the Brownie camera. "She took pictures of us, too."

"Then I'm also a bit of light." Etti looked pleased, his smile spreading dimple to dimple. He sank, right at our feet, spreading across the sidewalk like water.

At first I thought he was playing. But Carlo bent, then knelt, then lifted him off the cobbles, alarm taking over his good humor. He shook him. "Etti. Etti."

I felt Etti's forehead, his cheeks. "His skin is cold." Mine went cold also. The doctor. We needed the doctor.

A crowd gathered.

I looked from one to the next, the street dissolving under my feet, like I were falling into a great hole. "Has anybody seen the doctor?"

"Up the street." A voice came from . . . someplace. Then, "I'll bring him," came from somebody else.

"Show me. I'll take Etti." Carlo headed after the person.

The crowd parted. Fipo and I followed, then miracle of miracles, the doctor pushed through. He checked Etti's breathing, his pulse. He flicked the ends of Etti's fingertips, and pulled the skin down under Etti's eyes. He wrapped his stethoscope around his neck, adjusted the earpieces, and listened to Etti's heart.

Etti stirred. The doctor patted his cheeks.

Etti pushed him away. "My head hurts." He vomited into the street. The crowd moved back.

The doctor put a hand to Etti's forehead. "That feels better, I'll bet."

Better? His lips were blue. "Is it the influenza?"

The doctor eyed me. "No. He's been into the don's pills." He returned his attention to Etti. "How many did you take, young man?"

Etti settled against Carlo's shoulder. "One. My heart was sad."

His statement swept me up and out of my hole and put me back on steady footing. "Oh, Etti."

The doctor clapped his hands at the crowd. "Why is everybody staring? Don't any of you have something to do? The boy will be fine."

People dispersed, and the mumbling began.

"One after the other."

"The house is unlucky."

"And after all the Lattanzis did for her."

The doctor turned his back on all of it. "Keep an eye on him. Take him home and give him something to eat. He should stay quiet for a while." He dropped his voice to a whisper. "He's young. He's resilient. He's also very lucky. Make sure the don keeps his pills where the boys can't find them." He returned his attention to Etti. "And you, young man, stay out of business that isn't yours."

He put his stethoscope into his bag.

And was gone.

Carlo carried Etti back. "We will work together. I'll tend to the street. You stay with the boys. Keep an eye on the don. Cook. Bake bread. Be like Benedetta."

Then *he* was gone.

Everything collapses. Every fabric wears thin. Every intention can be ground into dust. Especially those which are good.

I did as Carlo suggested, obeyed what the doctor directed. I kept Etti quiet, made sure the old man kept his pills where the boys wouldn't find them. Found chores for Fipo to do. I cooked and cleaned and scrubbed and chattered, in all things doing my best to be like Benedetta.

Somebody rang the bell. The higher-pitched bell, for the top apartment. The bell came again, the deeper bell for the Lattanzis'. Followed by a knock.

"Enough, Carlo." The old man's voice, deep and a little thready, came up the stairs. "Did you forget your key?"

Something tick-tocked between my ears, like I'd wound a Big Ben and set it on my head. There was a spare key under the flowerpot. Surely Carlo already knew. I turned off the burner, meaning to tell the old man, prevent him from answering, but—

"Can I help you?" The old man. Pleasant, and perplexed.

The response was muffled, and familiar, remembered from the time after the Lattanzis died. I peeked around Benedetta's jamb.

The Children's Bureau ladies.

I grabbed hold of Etti, already pushing past me to see who it was, and put my finger to my lips. I hoped Fipo would have the sense to stay in his room.

The tall, thin lady checked her clipboard. "Boys are a lot of work. We understand the older one was burned, and the younger got into your medicine."

The old man talked a while, offering explanations, assurances of our more careful care. He put a hand to the door's edge and leaned against it, running out of steam along with his arguments.

I shrank back into Benedetta's kitchen, and found her illustration where I'd saved it, under the Brownie camera. Then I checked the mirror, pinched up my cheeks, tied my apron properly, wanting to appear mature, capable, qualified.

Etti tugged on my skirt. "Signorina?"

"Stay here. Be quiet."

I descended the stairs, swallowing and swallowing again. I used my best English, in a tone both serious and serene. I went through the illustrations as Benedetta once had, reiterating the promise Benedetta meant to keep, a modern woman, able to accept the responsibilities the boys presented, and willing to do what was necessary to nurture them in their time of sorrow. "The boys were in Coatesville. Her aunt returned with them when she collected Signora Bruni's baby. We have had trying times. Many losses in the past weeks. We hope you will understand it takes a little time to adjust."

To me, my words felt right, even the part where I lied, but the expression on the ladies' faces told me they were not satisfied, did not think it enough, were not convinced in my ability. I'd been doing the work of a woman before I'd had the chance to be a girl. Yet my efforts were ignored, my motivations judged, my neighbors unable to accept my intentions were good, my actions meant to help, my only desire, hard-learned, but real, to live my life as I thought best, without hurt, nor harm. "Up and down this street children are running wild, their parents sick and no adult to care for them. Yet here you smell dinner cooking, see that our clothes are pressed, and the table set for civilized people. Why do you listen to the complaints of a few? Why do you not believe the evidence before your eyes?"

I stepped toward the short, thick lady. Stepped toward them both.

The old man stepped beside me. "Fiora. Get the boys."

Impossible. No. I must have heard wrong. "But—"

I can help. I can fix this. I can make it all go away. I can keep the boys safe, the old man comfortable, the neighbor kids under control. Give me time. A week, a day, an hour, a moment. To get settled, get organized, figure out how to go on.

The old man put a hand on my hair. "Fiora. Please."

Everything collapses. Everybody leaves. Every good thought can be turned bad.

Without careful and constant attention.

Twenty-Six

The Children's Bureau ladies took the boys. Etti was silent, thumb in mouth, Signora Bruni's Emerald City book under his arm. Fipo went out fighting. "This is my house. Mine and Etti's. Mamma wants us to stay. Poppa." He threw his satchel to the ground and pointed to me. "Make *her* leave."

The old man went down on one knee, spoke to Fipo on his level. "For now. Only for now. Behave well." Then he spoke in Fipo's ear, his voice low, rapid, intense.

Whatever he said, Fipo calmed. His shoulders relaxed, the anger fell out of his face. He nodded to the old man, picked up his bundle, took Etti's hand, and headed down the stoop. I watched them go, watched while they waited for the trolley, neighbors watching with me. I wondered which one had notified the Bureau, which ones were feeling sad with me, and which worried what would happen to their own children should they fall sick.

Etti looked back once. I waved. The trolley arrived, they got on, and were gone.

The old man closed the door, then sagged against it.

I planted myself in front of him. "Why didn't you talk to them longer? How could you let the boys go?"

"Inside, we are caged. Outside is safer. If I had the strength, I would take them myself."

"Benedetta died outside."

"The Lattanzis passed inside. We will retrieve the boys when the time is right."

"You mean when the bubble collapses."

"I mean when the time is right."

Fine. I could make the time right right then. Without a moment's delay. The curtain made the bubble and the curtain could unmake it. I ran upstairs, to do the one thing I hadn't yet tried. Ask the curtain nicely.

"The bubble was a mistake. I was nervous, uncertain. I wasn't thinking clearly."

I stopped talking.

The curtain hung much as it had when I entered the room, five minutes earlier. The market moved as it typically did, five minutes ahead.

I started in again. "None of this is your fault. You were reacting to my nerves, trying to help, but all I wanted to do was keep the old man safe, keep bad things from happening. It isn't working, so . . . you can let the bubble go now."

The curtain kept hanging. The market kept flickering.

And I was talking to a piece of fabric. A fabric stitched to my past, that had changed my future, imprisoned my present, and scattered all I'd come to embrace as important. A piece of fabric which thus far had not served me, one I could not destroy, could not get rid of, could not let go. A piece of fabric that had headed me down a path I had not intended, a path which appeared fruitless, unless . . .

A spark, a flare, a flame ignited a corner of my mind.

. . . unless the path I'd been following were not my own. Maybe the path I followed belonged to the curtain.

A grommet unfolded, then another. The upside-down market disappeared, replaced by the fairy lights.

The landlord had tossed me out without warning. I'd left the curtain without thinking. Maybe not by accident, maybe by design. Because the curtain didn't want to be taken. Because it had some task unfinished, some purpose not yet fulfilled.

Unrelated to me. Unrelated to anything that had happened.

Another grommet unfolded. Another fairy light appeared.

All this time I thought the curtain was holding me hostage. Maybe I'd been holding the curtain. Maybe the curtain chose the window in the old man's attic because I'd set it on a path it hadn't intended. Maybe it cast the bubble to keep me from taking it farther, then stayed firmly five minutes forward to leave me a trail, like the yarn I used at the guaritrice's, a path back on which we could both return. Not in time, like I'd already tried. In place. And once there, maybe the curtain would show me the best way forward.

The curtain fluttered. The grommets unfolded, one after the other in quick succession, the fairy lights cascading across the opposite wall. Then the curtain slid from its iron rod. It folded itself as I'd folded it when I tried to take it to the guaritrice, tucked in and tidy.

I picked up the bundle. It curled neatly into my arm, like a cat finding its place. I ran a finger along the velvet, feeling ridiculous. "Do you want to go home?"

Home looked dejected. The windows unwashed, the stoop unscrubbed, the potted evergreen beside the door unwatered, its needles dry and falling. I climbed the steps, and examined the sign beside the buzzer: TWO LONG RINGS FOR UPSTAIRS, THREE SHORT FOR GROUND FLOOR.

My old home, the landlord. I hovered a finger, undecided.

The curtain slipped from my grasp, fell in its neat little bundle to the mat.

I retrieved it. It fell again. I retrieved it a third time and it leaped from my fingers, landing in the plant pot. I picked up the curtain. It caught on the evergreen's brittle branches, and held on.

I looked around. "What is it?" Something about the buzzer. The stoop.

Or maybe the pot.

I'd forgotten about the key. Buried in the dirt like Signora Lattanzi hid hers. A last link. A last connection. A last remembrance of the life I'd lived here. And a way to get into the house without buzzing.

I slipped the key in the lock, and entered.

Dust piled into the corners, newspapers by the door. The air was still and stale, like everywhere in the bubble, but the conditions here spoke of neglect, of decay, of the bubble's infinite time dedicated to other matters.

Even the street was deserted.

The curtain weighed heavy in my hands, brooding and dreadful. It dragged me across the vestibule and past the landlord's door. I went by on tiptoe, then climbed the steps, one at a time, as I never had, imagining the replacement signora in Mamma's kitchen, busy with dinner, her table set with no plate at its head. The curtain grew more ponderous with each tread.

I didn't want to stay, didn't want to know where my quest would lead. The curtain didn't want me to go, didn't want me to leave until it showed me what I needed to see. I stood on the landing, outside the door, afraid to knock, afraid not to, and wishing I didn't have to keep making decisions.

Somebody rang the buzzer. Two long rings. Impatient, imperative, and for this apartment.

The door opened, cautiously. I stepped back, aware I had no idea what I should say. A little girl peeked around the edge, clean and pressed and looking confused. "Are you here for the landlord?"

The girl was older than the children I'd seen when I first visited. She opened the door wider. I looked past her into an orderly space like Mamma used to keep. The two younger children sat at the table before a plate of sliced apples, a baby slept on a pallet beside. I returned my attention to the girl. "I'm not here for the landlord. I . . . I wanted to leave something for your mother."

The buzzer rang a second time. Three short. The landlord's door opened. The landlord didn't exit. The signora did. The signora from whom I'd collected my mother's curtain and whom I'd expected to answer her own door.

The little girl went to the top of the stairs. "Mamma?"

I shrank into the corner of the landing, still and silent, reminded of my time in the curtain world, there, but invisible, able to observe, but not partake.

The signora unlocked the street door, spoke to whomever was there, then stood aside. She glanced upstairs, her expression distracted and distressed. "I told you to be quiet, be respectful."

"I know, Mamma. Somebody's here."

Men shuffled behind the signora. Men in work clothes and caps and carrying things I couldn't identify from my vantage.

"Of course somebody's here. Go. See to your sisters. Close the door."

"But Mamma—"

But Mamma was busy. Directing the men into the landlord's apartment and speaking to them from the entrance. "I tried to clean up. They have relatives in New Jersey. I didn't want to upset them, didn't want them to see." She hesitated. "It's just, they suffered so. First the children, then the parents. I nursed them but there was nothing, no medicine. Tea and hopeful words were all we had to offer. And prayer. Plenty of prayer."

Children. Parents. Tea. Nursed. My ears buzzed, my heart skipped across my chest. I knew who those men were. I'd seen men like them before. Men in work clothes and caps who came to collect my mamma and poppa, came for the Lattanzis. One of them probably carried a clipboard.

The curtain grew leaden. It dropped to the floor, landing solid enough to leave indents.

The signora stopped her patter. She looked to her entryway. "What's going on up there?" Her voice was mamma-stern and directed at her daughter, hands planted firmly on hips.

The little girl cupped her hands around her mouth. "Mamma. Someone wants to see you."

I didn't want to see her mamma. Wasn't in the least certain why I'd come. I'd leave the curtain. Let the signora have it. Tell her I'd teased her. It wasn't magical, wasn't magical at all. It really did go with the apartment, and my taking it was the same as stealing and I was sorry. I was so, so sorry.

About everything. About it all. How I'd worried her unnecessarily about her husband. How I'd threatened the landlord. My glee to see his humiliation with the guaritrice. Explain I hadn't meant to hurt anybody, never meant to cause harm. I'd only acted that way because my grief had been fresh. I was angry. I was resentful. Because the signora had what I'd lost, a family, a home, the right to remain in the place where all my memories were housed.

I didn't get a chance. The signora dashed up the stairs. She scooped her daughter into her arms, shielded her eyes from mine, then cowered in her doorway. "Don't hurt me. Don't hurt my children. I prayed for you. Prayed for your parents. Please. Don't hurt my husband."

Everything collapses. Not every broken thing can be fixed.

I held my tongue. What I said wouldn't matter. I picked up the curtain, now light and easy to handle. I'd seen what it wanted me to see. The result of my anger, the result of my resentment, the result of my mistaken assumption that because I hurt, everybody else should hurt, also.

Something invisible laughed between us. Jarring, jangling, screechy with scorn.

The guaritrice.

I didn't know if the signora heard her, didn't wait to find out. I backed down the stairs, backed out the door to the street, gaze averted from the men in the work clothes and caps, with their stretchers and clipboards and instructions as to where they were taking the landlord and his family. I asked God to have mercy on the landlord's soul. Then I begged Him to have mercy on mine.

The guaritrice's laughter followed me into the succeeding minutes. Those minutes stretched into hours, folding over and doubling on themselves, then doubling again. All I wanted to do was curl on my bed, hands over my ears. The second hand on the Big Ben refused to sweep, moving along at a pace so lifeless, it seemed my own heart would stop.

The curtain found its own way back to the window in the old man's attic, untucking and unfolding, gliding up and over the rod in a way I'd have found wondrous the day before, or the day before that, or the day before that. But wonder had ceased in the unceasing drumbeat pounding between my temples.

It's my fault, my fault, my fault.

I'd cursed the landlord, drawn delight in his distress. His family passed, one after the other, wife, then children. I knew without knowing, the landlord went last.

But I had no time for mourning, nor the luxury of recrimination. There was bread to be baked, beans to be boiled, floors to scrub, laundry to soak, the cycle of service and solicitude that became my bulwark against the silent accusation of my thoughts.

Along with Carlo, sitting at the old man's table, replacing soles on the street children's shoes while the old man napped downstairs at the Lattanzis'. "The landlord and his family got sick. They died. Many families are sick. Will you also take responsibility for what time the sun rises, or the moon sets?"

Five minutes forward on a magical curtain is easy enough to prove. Wait five minutes. But to convince somebody I'd stagnated time in an entire neighborhood . . .

"You feel it. You said it yourself. Like rocks." I touched my chest, then clapped a hand to my head. "Stop pounding that nail."

Carlo put down his hammer and touched a finger to his temple. "Belief is a house for which the mind provides the mortar. You look for meaning where there is none, invent a bubble, decide you've trapped us all there, and now you are looking for a way out. But we live in a real world, and it moves from day into night whether we wish it or not, whether we notice or not. This bubble exists only in your mind. And when you decide it is finished, it is finished."

Men. Able to make the true untrue with a declaration.

Carlo stood. He stowed the shoes into his satchel, threw the satchel over his shoulder, then smacked his forehead. "You have me so turned around with talk of magic bubbles, it's a miracle I remember my own name." He dug into his pocket and pulled out a packet. He laid it on the table. "The don's pills. The druggist said you forgot to take them with you on the day you picked them up."

"Don't be ridiculous. Of course I took them with me." I rummaged among the awls and punches. Looked beneath cartons, shook canisters, upended baskets, until I found them, torn between relief and annoyance that once again, the old man had left them far from where he might need them. I held the envelope out to Carlo. "See?"

Carlo examined both packets. "The dates are the same. The druggist is very busy. He must have forgotten."

Reasonable. Hardly worthy of consideration. But Carlo's explanation refused to settle into its slot. I snatched back both packets and opened them. The pills were white as they should be, round as I remembered, the envelopes square and brown, with instructions on the outside written in a clear hand, in every respect the same. Yet, Carlo's packet presented as good, proper. The one I'd just found deep among the cinnamon sticks had an ominous feel, off-center, out of balance. Just. Not. Right.

My gut got crampy, my chest tight. Something pricked at my thumbs, and in my mind's eye, the packet I'd picked up on Parade Day suddenly glowed red, toxic and threatening. I dropped it. The pills scattered across the floor, the way my apples had scattered across the cobbles on the day I first met Carlo. Like that day, Carlo dove after them.

I dove after Carlo. "No. Leave them. Don't touch them."

He reached to where I held him by the shoulder, covered my hand with his. "What is it, signorina?"

I sank to my knees. "I've been so stupid. What have I done? No wonder the old man is so sick. It's not his heart. It's his pills. They come from the guaritrice."

Twenty-Seven

I doubled over on the floor beside the old man's table, wanting to crawl under it, wanting to lose myself amid the baskets and boxes, leather scraps and dust bunnies. "I was so focused on the tea, so lost in the guaritrice's kindness. The old man warned me. He figured it out right away, but he never thought to question the pills, and I didn't believe the danger."

Carlo dragged me out and stood me up. "Who is the guaritrice?"

I explained and I explained. Carlo listened, his gaze growing cloudier as I went. Finally, he threw up his hands. "Magical tea to go with magical pills because of your magical curtain."

"Her *mother's* magical curtain."

Carlo whipped around. "Don Sebastiano."

The old man stood in the doorway. "There is plenty in this world you understand, Carlo, and plenty you don't need to. Signorina Vicente is worried about the pills she brought me from the pharmacy a month ago. I'd like you to go to the Children's Bureau and check on the boys. Check on Etti. He got very sick from one of those pills."

"All due respect, Don Sebastiano, I don't think you should encourage the signorina's notions."

"Then humor an old man and visit the boys because you miss them."

Carlo's face went tight and stormy, like he still had plenty to say. Whatever it was, he kept to himself. He turned on his heel, stomped out of the old man's apartment and on down the stairs.

Carlo's departure didn't stop me. I grabbed his satchel, headed onto the old man's landing, and let every thought still roiling under my surface explode in an exasperated and steaming eruption, emphasized with plenty of finger-pointing. "You *met* the guaritrice. You *know* who she is. You *spoke* with her. But you don't *remember* because she made her *daughter* brew you some *tea*."

Carlo slammed the street door after him.

I opened the satchel and sprinkled the contents over the banister. "And. You. Forgot. Your. Shoes."

The old man yanked me back into his apartment. "The guaritrice can't have a daughter."

"Of course she can." Couldn't she? "The guaritrice suggested we become friends."

"No." He dug his nails into my wrist. "A child is good. A gift from God. The guaritrice is death. She is destruction. No good can come to one such as her. Whoever that girl is, she is no daughter of the guaritrice."

The way the guaritrice told her what to do, how to act, what to say. The way Tizi only obeyed when the guaritrice was around. "She sure acts like the guaritrice is her mamma."

"Because the guaritrice sensed that is the relationship with which you would be most comfortable. Because the guaritrice wants your trust. Because she wants the curtain. Guard your heart, Fiora Vicente. Guard your tongue." He looked to the windows. "Because you do not know who might be listening."

"What the neighbors don't overhear, they make up anyway."

"I mean the guaritrice."

"Even less. The curtain does what it wants, doesn't care who it hurts, and try as I might, I cannot bend it to my will."

"Of course you can't. You bear the curtain's burden, but you are not the curtain's master. You keep it safe, keep it secure, keep it from falling into the wrong hands, but you cannot command the curtain. The curtain belongs to me."

The old man still had me by the wrist. Good thing, or I might have fallen down.

I started babbling. "How come Mamma had it? How come it's my burden if the curtain belongs to you?" And, most importantly. "Why didn't you tell me?"

The old man released me. He pulled the box off the shelf, the one where he'd put away the letter from my brothers giving permission for the old man to be my guardian. He pulled papers from it, some wrapped in ribbon, others heavy with official seals. "It is all here, a wasted life, now without meaning because I've lost the ones I loved. I cursed the day that curtain left and would have cursed the day it returned. But for her." He pushed a photograph toward me, dog-eared, and worn.

A girl sitting on a bench against a painted backdrop of flowers and forests popular in those days. She was serious, and somber, and looked just like me. "Mamma?"

The old man nodded. "She was about your age. Arrived at our door, my wife's and mine, much the way you did. Cold. Wet. Hungry. Brought by the guaritrice. She said she worried about contagion."

My mother. Like me. I couldn't imagine her in that way. To me she was so capable, so sure. "Contagion?"

"Cholera. The guaritrice arrived with her cures and her teas and her promises of help. Our community was isolated, superstitious, and very, very scared. So the village embraced her, allowed her into their homes, their lives. But not my wife, not me. We remained wary. So the guaritrice sent us your mother."

My mother. The guaritrice. "I don't understand."

"They were sisters, or so the guaritrice claimed. Your mother was so young, the guaritrice working day and night with the sick, or so she appeared. She told us she did not want your mother with her."

My knees went wobbly, my hands shaky, my head got floaty, and the pit of my stomach hollowed out. "The guaritrice is my aunt?"

"The guaritrice is nobody's aunt. Nor cousin. Nor sibling. Nobody's daughter, nobody's mother. The guaritrice is a parasite. She arrives with sickness, and feeds off its fruits, sucking at the stricken, the hopeless, the poor in spirit. Then she leaves, devastation in her wake, latent until her next opportunity to thrive."

"The guaritrice is young. She is beautiful."

"The guaritrice is whatever will serve her. She is old as fable, and fresh as an open wound, and she will exploit any weakness, any dent in your defense. She sent your mother to us to play on my wife's tender feelings, to make us more kindly disposed toward her. The guaritrice used your mother, as she uses everything, everyone, for her own gain, her own purposes."

The old man settled onto his bench. "In a land such as ours, traditions run deep. My grandmother was the village wise woman, as was her grandmother before her, and her grandmother before that. In my generation, there were no girls, so the curtain came to me. It clung to my window, sometimes offering insight, mostly regulating the light. People presumed because I had it, I knew something, so asked my advice on everything, from herding sheep to pastry making, and no matter what I told them, silly or serious, the curtain made it turn out all right." He set his elbow on the table and his cheek on his palm. "Ridiculous when you take the time to think about it."

Mending, starting businesses, who Carlo should marry. Soup. "So you're not magical."

"No more than you. My sons took sick and left. No supplication I uttered, no promise I made, no sacrifice I offered brought them back. My wife was expecting. Very near her time. The guaritrice made an offer, my grandmother's curtain for a healthy baby. My wife agreed. She gave the guaritrice the curtain, but your mother brought the curtain back. I didn't know, didn't know any of it. I was away helping at a farm in the hills. By the time I returned, my baby was lost, the guaritrice was gone, and my wife's fever raging to such a height I feared I'd lose her, too.

Every belief I'd ever had for any moment of my life swept me up and off my feet. They cast me into the maelstrom, and landed me in a strange, exotic world. "You're saying my mother killed your baby."

"No." The old man packed so much conviction behind the word, I had no doubt it and every word that followed would be the truth. "Your mother was a good and a kind girl. But misguided. She'd been with the guaritrice for as long as she could remember, had grown a harsh and brittle shell. Living with us changed her. My wife was kind. She was caring. She developed a true fondness for your mother. So when your mother saw her opportunity, she retrieved the curtain and escaped the guaritrice, then offered the curtain to my wife as the price of her protection."

The old man's voice was strident, defiant, brimming with emotion. "Had I been there, had I known, I'd never have taken the curtain back. My wife had struck a bargain. Return of the curtain broke that bargain. My child paid the price. After my wife recovered, I never wanted to see the curtain again. I did not want to see your mother again. Your mother accepted her responsibility and took on the curtain's burden. She worked as a seamstress and lived a quiet life on the other side of the village. Finally, she married. She had a family. She emigrated with the rest of us, and made sure to live far enough away that she and I would not run into each other on a daily basis. But our burdens are not so easily shed. The influenza swept into town, your parents were lost, and here you are. Along with the curtain."

No wonder everybody treated me so oddly. They knew the old man was distant and after what happened . . .

I stopped. I didn't have to think about it. Not then. Not ever. What was done was done. I couldn't go back. Couldn't change a thing. I'd learned that much from my time with the curtain.

The old man shuffled through the cards and letters, documents and memories, his movements agitated, then calm, angry, then sad. A photograph fell from the fray. The old man picked it up, his expression wistful. He handed it to me. "This is my wife."

The photo showed a girl dressed in traditional clothes, delicate and overdecorated and decades out of date. My mouth went dry. I knew this girl, knew the gently sloping brows, how they always made her look so sad. I knew her in two ways. In a vision in the old man's garden, the day I picked the strawberries, with wrinkles and age spots superimposed on this girl's fresh-faced curves.

And at the guaritrice's. Her expression sometimes open and honest like in this photo, other times closed off and cranky.

I looked like my mamma. Yet Tizi looked nothing like the guaritrice. Was it possible? Hadn't the old man just told me? Tizi looked nothing like the guaritrice because the guaritrice was not her mother.

The truth slammed into me with the force of a trolley. I looked to the old man's face, to the mark on his cheek near lost to his age spots. Tizi had a mark just like that. I'd only seen it the one time I saw her without her mask, the time she knocked the red-tinged tea out of Benedetta's hand and saved Benedetta. I looked to the old man's pinky and ring finger, the way they crooked, like Tizi's. I looked into the old man's eyes, blue-gray and stern, and understood why Tizi's always felt so familiar.

It couldn't be. I hopped up and pulled the photograph from behind the stove. The photo I'd hidden the day the old man interrupted me redecorating his apartment. The photo of his children's funerals. I showed it to the old man.

He touched the smallest cross. "I never saw the body. They burned her along with all the cholera's victims."

No body. This spark of clarity made inaction intolerable. I couldn't tell the old man. His heart might not be able to take it. Whatever I did, I had to do on my own.

Like . . . explain it all to Tizi. Bring her back with me. Maybe . . . let her live in the old man's attic. I imagined the scene in my mind's eye. Imagined my reaction to be told my mother wasn't my mother and some old man I'd never met was my father.

But maybe Tizi already knew. Maybe she knew and didn't care. Maybe she knew and hated the old man for leaving her with the guaritrice.

Maybe I had no idea about anything. I sank back into my seat. "I don't understand. The curtain chooses the window, yet belongs to you. How could my mother keep it? How can I?"

"The curtain stayed in your apartment from a force of will. Your mother's force of will. She didn't want to pass the burden to you. You didn't have it with you when you arrived. So I presumed your mother was successful."

"How could you know I didn't have it with me?"

The old man looked at me the way the nuns looked at a pupil who doesn't quite get the equation. "Distance does not matter with the curtain. I always know where it is. It goes nowhere without my permission." He plucked a verbena sprig off the table and handed it to me. "You, on the other hand, are more difficult for me to perceive."

And that was why I was unable to bring the curtain across the trolley tracks the time I tried to bring it to the guaritrice and get her help figuring out how to make it work for me, the reason the curtain disappeared from my hands when I persisted. I again looked at the photo of the old man's wife. "But the curtain doesn't tell you everything. The curtain keeps its secrets."

He gathered the photos. Put them back in the wooden box. "Curtains reveal, they conceal. They let in the light, or cast a room into darkness. Your mother's curtain is no different except it shows you the world from an angle you may not have considered. And now I sense a reckoning, a convergence of all the angles my brain is not bright enough to perceive, and I do not believe I have the strength to face it."

Unfortunate. Because I doubted I had the courage.

The doorbell rang. The top bell for the top apartment.

The bell came again.

I hurried downstairs to answer, released from the bubble's pull by the force of my emotion.

A messenger in a peaked cap, clipboard in hand, was at the door. He inquired after the don. He handed me an envelope, made me sign that I'd received it, then tipped his cap to me, and hurried on his way.

I stared at the envelope. I didn't want to open it, didn't want to bring it to the old man. Whatever news it contained would be bad, whatever resulted would be worse, and at that moment, I'd have been content to never receive another bit of news from anybody about anything for as long as I lived.

The old man was not such a coward. He descended the stairs, took the envelope from me, pulled out the message, put on his glasses, then held the message at arm's length to read. His face grew serious. "It's from Benedetta's aunt. In Coatesville. She wants you to meet her at the train station on Thursday."

My heart shrank, collapsing into a cold, hard lump the size of a walnut. "The baby is dead."

"No. Her aunt wants you to meet her at the train station because she wants you to bring her the baby. She says Nicco's instructed that he would feel better if the aunt cared for the baby until his return."

Relief washed in on a warm, welcome wave. It swept out again on a tide of confusion. "She already has Benedetta's baby. How can she ask that I bring Benedetta's baby to her?"

The old man folded the telegram. He slid the telegram back into its envelope, then slid the envelope into his pocket, his stance resolute, his expression unflinching. "Because she doesn't have Benedetta's baby. She thinks Benedetta's baby is here."

Twenty-Eight

I needed to take the curtain to the guaritrice. Because she had Benedetta's baby. Because she'd already made it clear she'd be willing to trade the baby for the curtain.

I should have done so at first, instead of at last. Made the offer, instead of being forced to do it. Should have embraced the present, let go the past, admitted I couldn't control my future. But I couldn't get the damned thing to fold. I threw it to the ground and looked to the old man. "Why won't it cooperate?"

"The curtain senses your confusion." He picked the fabric off the floor, his face gray, his hands trembly. He stuffed it into Carlo's satchel. "Everything you need is already provided. You just have to find it. Be clear regarding your path, certain in your resolve, or you will be lost and the guaritrice will consume you."

"You always say *lost*, or *passed*, or *left*. Never *die*."

"The curtain is a lens onto another world. It shifts your focus. I see death the same, a shift in focus. I say *lost* because those who pass through that lens can never be retrieved, they can only be found. Only at the end of our lives and only if we are very, very blessed."

The satchel twitched in the old man's lap, a bit of the curtain's velvet spilled out the top. The old man held that bit to his chest. He ran a finger over the fabric, murmured a few words, like he was praying, then buckled the top of the satchel over it. "That girl. The one you met at the guaritrice's."

"What about her?"

He handed me the satchel. "I don't know if it will be possible. Don't know if the girl could even be convinced, but . . ."

The old man knew. He had to know. He probably knew the moment I looked at the photo he gave me, the one of his wife. Maybe he knew the moment it happened, the moment the guaritrice took her, all those years ago. Maybe that's why he kept my mother close. Maybe he thought she would lead him back to his daughter.

Or maybe Tizi was an unknown girl to him. A person the old man thought of as something I hadn't. A victim. Somebody who, unlike Benedetta, could still be saved.

I hoisted Carlo's satchel onto my shoulder. "If the girl can be convinced, I will convince her."

Then I went to retrieve Benedetta's baby.

The entrance on the alley was locked of course. It was dusty, and rusty, and looked like it hadn't been used in years. I jiggled the handle. This way, then that. Twisting and turning and rattling and cursing. I flung Carlo's satchel at it, flailing and frustrated, then crossed my arms, slid down the door, sat on the threshold, and smacked my forehead to my palm, finished before I'd even started.

The latch gave way, the door swung open. I fell backward, tumbling into gloom, head over heel, scraping knees and elbows and landing with the strangest and softest of bounces.

I scrambled to my feet, ready to run, but there was nothing there. Not a wall, nor a window, a stick of furniture, or even an echo. Nothing.

Except Mamma's curtain, now spilling from Carlo's satchel, its embroidery glowing in the gathering gray. Patterns traced along it I'd never seen before, bends and curves I did not recognize. I moved to the left, the embroidery faded. I stepped to the right, the embroidery brightened. A path unspooled along the fabric, chain-stitched in bright yellow. An arrow appliquéd above the path pointed to the proper direction.

I walked through darkness illuminated just enough for me to get by, my gaze fixed to the fabric. Every time I strayed from the path, the curtain faded. Every time I adjusted my course, the light strengthened. I turned corners, followed curves, doubled back, and looped around again. I descended gentle slopes, negotiated soft rises, my sense the edges of the passage were a little beyond my reach, a world away from anyplace I'd ever imagined, and enrobed in a constant and infinite Now.

A baby cried.

The curtain quivered. It wrapped around my wrists and spiraled me toward the sound, through the doorway behind the guaritrice's counter and into the heart of the guaritrice's lair, the room pillared with fake trees, carpeted in scarlet poppies, and roofed by the ceiling's painted stars. The guaritrice's counter was still there, as was the map with the spiraling red Xs. But the chair that reminded me of a toadstool was gone, replaced by a flower-wrapped bower hung from a rafter and swaying gently in the curtain's soft glow.

A light switched on behind the beaded doorway. The glow from Mamma's curtain extinguished. I shoved it back into the satchel, and buttoned the satchel under my coat. Tizi came through the beads, her hair haloed in the glow, a blanket-wrapped bundle in her arms.

She jumped when she saw me, the slope of her sad-looking eyebrows going steep and surprised. Her cheek was swollen, bruised purple and yellow where the guaritrice had punched her. "You shouldn't be here. The pharmacy is closed. Did you come to see my little sister?"

Sister. Cold creeped between us. "Yes, that's exactly who I came to see." I put out my arms. "May I hold her?"

Tizi clutched the bundle tighter to her chest. A tiny fist thrashed, the fringe of a baby bonnet moved, and a cry, plaintive and piercing, filled the room. "Mamma wouldn't like that. She says when she is gone I'm in charge. She is working hard, you know. A mother must. Especially with another mouth to feed."

I stuck out my abdomen and patted where I'd hidden the satchel. "Do you remember the Signora Bruni? The size of her stomach?"

Tizi nodded.

"That's where babies grow." I stepped closer. "That baby cannot be your mother's baby. Your mother has always been so slim."

The cries got louder. Tizi dumped the baby into the bower like she'd dump a pile of rags and gave the bower a nudge. "Like the fairy tale. When the bough breaks."

The baby will fall. Benedetta's baby.

I bolted for the bower, my steps elongated and abnormal. The scent of cinnamon filled the air. A hand landed on my shoulder. A breath blew past my ear. "Of course it is not my baby, little one. It's not a baby at all. It is only a cat, crying for its supper."

The guaritrice.

I shrugged her off, stood on my toes, and tipped the bower's edge toward me, the cinnamon scent strong enough to be sickening. What I'd thought was a tiny fist became a paw, what I'd thought was a baby bonnet became two soft, triangular ears.

Tizi giggled.

The guaritrice snapped her fingers. "Tizi, enough. It is not kind to tease our friend. Find that creature some milk before it gets so loud we can't think."

Tizi's good mood shriveled. She skittered behind the counter and rummaged among the boxes and bits, a stage prop given her cue.

The guaritrice returned her attention to me. She clasped her hands in a worried way. "I do apologize. Tizi is getting too old for dolls, so I got her the cat, but she pretends it is a doll, so my efforts are wrong."

Dolls. Cats. If Tizi were the old man's daughter she should have left dolls behind years ago. My head filled with cotton. "I thought . . . I thought . . ."

"You thought I'd taken Signora Bruni's baby. You thought I went to the infirmary, picked her up, and brought her back here." Every muscle in the guaritrice's face went downcast, her voice sorrowful. "So hard to be accused of something you did not do, is it not, little one? So bitter. Makes you feel frustrated, hemmed in, powerless to forge the future you think you deserve. Makes you come to me, to a place where you have only been shown kindness and do the same. Accuse. Finger-point. Over tea. Harmless, soul-soothing tea."

The cotton cleared. "Your tea is not harmless. It hurts people. It makes people sick."

"The influenza makes people sick. A germ you cannot see unless you look through a lens." The guaritrice looped her thumb and forefinger before her eye, the way I had when I first measured the window in the old man's attic. "My tea is nothing. It provides a small hallucinatory effect. It makes people forget their pain, forget their failings, forget their fears of the future. This is why you made your bubble, no? To keep yourself safe, prevent uncomfortable changes. But your bubble is not effective. So sad about your brothers, and the old man is so sick."

She spread her arms. "Imagine a world like mine, where every day is as we please, for as long as we please, a world where nobody can dictate what we must do. Join Tizi and me. Help us with our work. Be among people who understand your unique gifts."

Her voice was smooth and suggestive and cozy as cookies. Yes. We could be family. We could make teas to help people and provide for ourselves. And when we had helped all we could, there would be another town, then another. An infinite number of towns, an infinite number of people.

Tizi flew from behind the counter and flung herself between us. "Why does Fiora have to come? I found myself a sister. We don't need her."

The scent of cinnamon turned to dung. My head reeled. My stomach heaved. I looked to the bower, to how close I'd come to accepting the guaritrice's fairy tale. "Tizi, listen to me. You cannot keep that baby. She belongs to Signora Bruni."

Tizi moved to the bower, her gaze steady and direct and just like the old man's. "This baby belongs to no one. Her mother left her."

"Her mother did not leave her. Her mother died. This baby has a father who loves her and cares for her. Please." I kept my voice level, my demeanor calm. I reached out my arms. "Let me bring her back to where she belongs."

The guaritrice stepped between me and Tizi. "Signor Bruni is away at the war. War is capricious. So much might still happen. Come, little one. It is ridiculous for us to argue. We are three women united in one purpose. The care of this baby, the nurture of each other."

Care. Nurture. A core of cold welled from my center. "You called her a thing. A creature. You have no interest in this baby. You have no interest in any baby. Except how you can use them, how they can serve you. The way you use Tizi." I again charged the bower.

This time the guaritrice caught me by my braid. "And what have you used, little one? Improperly and alone? You come here with plenty to say, unwilling to pay the price."

She yanked me back. The satchel fell from under my coat, landing to the floor with the quietest of thuds. The guaritrice scooped it up. "What have we here? Are you going on a trip, little one?"

My turn to make a grab for things. I didn't have to answer the guaritrice's stupid questions. I caught hold of the leather strap. The guaritrice held on. The top came loose and the curtain fell free. It cascaded to the floor. The guaritrice reached for it, plucked at an edge. The fabric sparked, and a smell like a burned-out electrical circuit filled the room.

The guaritrice sucked at her fingertips, like they'd been singed. "Tizi. Quick. Grab it."

But Tizi didn't. She scooped the baby out of the bower. "Mamma. No. You said I could keep her. Said she could be mine. Because you—I mean, because I hurt my cheek."

"I said we would see. Your cheek will heal. We can find other babies."

"But *this* baby's mother left her. She did not do what she must. You don't need that curtain, Mamma. Don't need anything. You have me."

Tizi sounded so lost, looked so . . . alone. And she was holding Benedetta's baby. "You can come with me, too, Tizi. You don't have to stay. You're not a child. You can think for yourself. There's a whole world out there. Filled with sunlight and fresh breezes." I smacked a fist to one of the pillars. "With real trees." I kicked the carpet. "Real flowers. In every color of the rainbow."

The guaritrice pointed to Tizi, the gesture final. "Tizi. Pick up that curtain. Now."

I stomped my foot. "Ask your mother where you came from. Go ahead. Ask her how she got you, what she demanded in return. Or don't ask. It doesn't matter. You can come with me. We can bring Signora Bruni's baby home together."

Tizi whipped around. "Why would I take her anywhere? I went through a lot of trouble to get her. Crossed streets, took the trolley, stood for hours waiting for one of the sisters to see me. This is not my mother's baby. This baby is mine."

Tizi had found her. My head reeled. Tizi was a near child, still in braids. The sisters were so stern. "Why would they even consider you?"

Tizi showed me why. Her figure filled out. Her face lost its roundness, her affect its innocence. The bruises on her cheek faded. She transformed to a woman, serious and serene enough to fool the sisters into believing she were Benedetta's widowed aunt. Mature. Capable. Able to accept the responsibilities Benedetta's baby presented, willing to do what was necessary until the baby's father came home from war to make his claim. "You don't know how it is, Fiora. I am here every day. I work so hard. Day and night. Mamma never lets me stop. I'm not like you—Rosina Vicente's daughter. I'm just Mamma's, and I do what she tells me."

Her tone changed mid-sentence, high, then low, defiant, then humble. She was a singer, searching for the right note, the right pitch, uncertain which mood to take, which attitude would elicit the most advantageous response from me.

Whoever Tizi had been meant to be, she was now the guaritrice's tool, strong enough to cross the verbena, brave enough to face an unfamiliar city, outspoken enough to state what she wanted. Able to appear as a youngster, or a woman, to charm, or cajole. And maybe Tizi's desire for Benedetta's baby went beyond loneliness. Tizi appeared unaware of how men and women were supposed to be together, but the day would no doubt come when the guaritrice would use her in a more base way to achieve her goals. The day when the babies would no longer be stolen, but produced by Tizi.

Tizi had learned to become what was needed to get what she wanted. I needed to become what was wanted to do what was best. "The guaritrice stole you, Tizi. You don't belong to her. You can't belong to her. You are good, and good can never come from evil."

Tizi's bruises brightened, the swelling on her cheek returned. She winced and put her palm over the injury. "What are you talking about? If I don't belong to Mamma, who do I belong to?"

"You belong to Don Sebastiano."

Tizi whirled on her mother, her expression angry and accusing.

The guaritrice laughed. "Do not listen to this foolish, foolish girl, my pet. She only tells you what she thinks will make you give up your prize. She accuses us of hurting people. Us, with our harmless little teas, yet *she* murdered her mother."

She put out her hands, thumbs pinched against their opposite fingers. She waggled them back and forth, the way somebody does when they're going to tell you what's what. "I heard what you said. We *all* heard what you said. 'You and Poppa live in an old world, with old rules. I will not spend my life sewing, spend it caring for children, worrying what the neighbors think. This is America. A modern world, filled with modern thinking. If you and Poppa will not let me follow my ambitions, then I will find a way to follow them on my own.'"

The guaritrice's imitation was perfect, right down to the way I'd planted my hands on my hips, and jutted my chin at my mother. The response of a girl frustrated with her parents, raging and rebellious because she wanted to do more than everybody expected, see more than anybody imagined, a girl caught in a whirlwind of emotion who hurled her accusations without thought. Accusations that landed loud and clear and in the middle of the market.

And then the girl's parents died.

My resolve went boneless and sank me to the floor. "Please don't take Signora Bruni's baby, Tizi. She has a place, people who love her. She does not have to be like us."

"Do not listen to her, Tizi. Fiora is just like her mother. Do you remember? How Rosina Vicente tried to take you?"

My head snapped up; my spine snapped back into place. Mamma tried to take Tizi. Mamma had tried to make it right. "Mamma came here."

"As you do now, full of stories of another world, a better life." Red dust spewed from the guaritrice's mouth, fouling the air in acrimony and coloring her words in venom. "Yet I'd given her everything. We traveled the world, saw places she'd never imagined. Then we came to the don's tiny village. It was no place, nowhere. Filled with donkeys and dogs and tiny closed-in houses, built one atop the other, like a giant hive. We went for one reason, the don's curtain. Your mother, she was so talented. Flick of a finger, twitch of a wrist. And we were there. Traveling as we never had. But your mother saw more than she told."

Guaritrice nudged the satchel at me. "Put the curtain in there, you ungrateful fool. Go back to your old man, back to your mundane world. Be a good girl and do what everybody tells you to do. I offered you a healthy baby. Take that baby and get out of here. The curtain is mine."

A curtain that was now dead, threadbare and void. A curtain that chose its window, chose its burden, chose its master. A curtain, I sensed, that had fulfilled its duty, found a way to live up to the old lady's bargain, and now wanted me to let it go. "You want the curtain to make a world where you can feed without ceasing. A world where sickness never fades, where war always continues. You needed my mother, you need Tizi, and you hoped to tempt me. We are what the don calls *vectors*, a means to your end. Because you cannot work the curtain on your own. You cannot even touch it. You can't do anything on your own because you need a host to help you."

I stepped toward the guaritrice, fingers curled, thinking I'd grab her by the collar, maybe wrap my fingers around her neck. "I didn't kill my mother. You did. Tizi gave her your tea. You wanted my mother to forget her failures, let go her fears, go on with her day like she'd never met you."

I pulled back, went to Tizi, wanting to put my arms around her, to apologize. "Your real mother made a bargain. My mother broke it." I put out my arms. "Please, Tizi, give me the baby. Take the curtain. Do what you want with it, then let's get out of here."

Everything collapses, every rough-hewn edge wears smooth. I was one girl, regretful of my past, afraid to face my future, overwhelmed by my present. I could not fix every broken thing. I could not fix most of them. But maybe this one thing, I could fix.

Tizi handed me the baby. She picked up the satchel, pulled out the curtain, shook it out like a tablecloth. She turned to me, head tilted, expression triumphant. "Only modern thinking?"

Then Tizi turned around, and flung the curtain over the guaritrice.

Twenty-Nine

The curtain landed on the guaritrice with the little hiss the burner made when I turned on the gas. The fabric covered her head, her shoulders, all the way to her waist, then shrunk into her, fitted to her form, like batter sears to a hot pan.

She screeched. The sound shot to the star-painted ceiling and ricocheted from every corner. The curtain sparked, the air grew tingly, and the stenches of singed hair, burnt rubber, automobile exhaust, and vomit knitted into a miasma. A choking, impossible miasma.

The guaritrice shrank to the floor. She got smaller, melted, like Dorothy's witch in the Oz book.

I wanted to run. Wanted to hold the baby close and just . . . run. I got as far as the beaded doorway.

The guaritrice whimpered.

I stopped. The old man knew where the curtain was. He knew what the curtain was doing. He knew the exchange had been made. And he knew I had a choice.

I handed the baby to Tizi. Benedetta's baby. "Hold her. Keep her safe."

"No. Don't help her. Let the curtain destroy her." Tizi transfixed on the guaritrice, her expression impassive. "Don't you understand? She's not human."

I didn't. Still, even then. All I saw was a struggling bundle of misery, alive, and suffering.

I scuttled in close, held my nose, held my breath, got hold of the curtain's edge, and yanked.

The guaritrice was gone, replaced by a spindly creature with a bulbous center. Horrible, misshapen, making grunty little huffing noises. It glared up at me, then skittered into the shadows, moving like a spider. Slime trailed in its wake.

I dropped the curtain.

From behind me came a creak, like that of new shoe leather. Another creaked to my left, more like a lugnut loosening around a rusty screw. A third followed, and a fourth, the sounds growing staccato and stressed.

The walls shook. The floor shimmied. The flower-wrapped bower swayed. A fake tree pillar, then another, toppled onto the carpet's scarlet poppies. Thunder clapped across the painted sky. I looked up. The ceiling cracked.

Tizi grabbed hold of my arm, she dragged me back, all the way to the strings of beads covering the doorway behind the guaritrice's counter. She hefted Benedetta's baby, and shoved me into the darkening passage. "Fiora. Stop daydreaming. Let's go."

Go. Of course.

Plaster fell from the edges in great strips, raising dust thick enough to bury us. The guaritrice's world was crumbling by chunks and my one defense against the darkness splayed across a poppy-woven carpet in a room held together with malfeasance and bad intentions. The curtain was my way back, my trail of yarn, the map that could negotiate the guaritrice's web of passages leading back to the alley behind the pharmacy. "Tizi, stop. We need that curtain."

"We can't go back." Tizi's panic, raw and real, reached out to slap me. "What's done is done."

Everything collapses, every petty thought laid bare. Every well-meaning act is tested.

And every good thing I needed in order to be what I was to become was already provided, alive, within me. Forever, for always. All I had to do was find it.

The curtain formed in my mind, the velvet fresh, the spare areas patched, the embroidery chain-stitching a path through the chaos.

The passage behind us fell to ruin; the floor beneath gave way. The ceiling shifted; the supports wobbled.

I stopped Tizi, took Benedetta's baby from her, and turned us down the path the curtain intended, a short walk down a hall, then out an everyday exit into an alley filled with smoke and the fire brigade.

The white-masked men arced around us, a half dozen in all. One pulled down his mask, talked to somebody I couldn't see who it was. "Are these the people you were talking about?" Then he turned to me. "Are you all right, miss?"

Equipment crowded the alley, buckets and hoses. A crowd gathered in the street at the end.

The druggist broke through, relief rising over the edges of his white mask. "I'm so glad you're safe. I was in my workroom when the fire broke out. I couldn't find the don's prescription. I didn't know if you were safe, didn't know if you were still back there." He gazed at Tizi, young and beautiful in the light of a half dozen lanterns. He pulled off his mask, revealing a man still in his prime, serious and reserved. "Ah. You must be Don Sebastiano's daughter. He told me to expect you."

One of the fire brigade approached the druggist. "The damage in the back room is bad, but repairable. It looks like an electrical switch sparked. We found this." He held up Mamma's curtain.

Whatever I believed had happened, a cover story had already been conveyed. I put out my hand. "That's mine."

Tizi scooted in front of me. "No. I believe that is mine."

Only one person could decide this dilemma. And whatever he decided, the curtain would make it come out all right. I turned to Tizi. "Let's go see your father."

We found the don in Benedetta's apartment, seated beside the cradle. Milk already warmed on the stove; fresh diapers waited on the bed. He stood when we entered, his calm neutrality gone. "Tizi?"

He stepped toward her. "Tizi."

She closed the space between them. "Poppa. I'm here."

The old man picked a packet off the table. His pills. He slipped the packet into his shirt pocket, close to his heart. From then on they'd always be there, because from then on, the old man had a reason to live.

Thirty

My mother was the neighborhood fortune-teller. People came to see her, asked their questions. Mamma would disappear into her bedroom, and when she emerged, Mamma told them not to worry, to be strong. Sometimes she warned there would be a change, but assured, in the end, everything would work out.

I sat at the old man's table and poured a little more milk into my espresso, and another heaping spoonful of sugar. Babyish, yes. For children, yes. But I didn't like the taste of it without. I still don't. "Her fortune-telling was all for show. Mamma didn't really know anything. She just knew people wanted to have hope."

The old man measured a piece of leather flattened out before him. He marked it, then measured it one more time. "Belief is powerful."

"You despised her."

"I didn't despise her." The old man picked a knife from the collection at his elbow. He made one cut, then another. "I despised myself. For not recognizing the danger, not being there when I was needed, for not rescuing your mother myself. I knew something was wrong, but was not brave enough to fix it. The curtain offered no guidance, and I did not trust myself to figure it out."

"The curtain is a fraud. A five-minute-forward-looking fraud."

The old man looked to the ceiling. Maybe he thought he'd find his next words there. "You are not like me, Fiora Vicente. You are so much better. You did not wait on Benedetta's baby. You went right to rescue her, then found the compassion to rescue my daughter. You are being shortsighted. You do not understand. The curtain is powerful and profound, but it only possesses the power you give it."

"What's that supposed to mean?"

"Maybe you can only look forward for five minutes because that is all you need. Maybe you can only look forward for five minutes because you are afraid to look further. Or maybe you only look for five minutes because telling fortunes doesn't really interest you all that much." He returned to his work. "Where is Tizi?"

Finally, a bit of conversation I could engage in without feeling like my brain were doing backflips. "She's with the baby. She says we should give her a name. She doesn't know."

It was Thursday. The day I was supposed to meet Benedetta's aunt at the train station. The day I had to say goodbye to Benedetta's baby. "Have you . . . heard anything?"

"You mean from the Children's Bureau." He slid an envelope across to me. "They will not let us have the boys. You're not married, a child yourself in the eyes of the law. I'm an old man. Benedetta's aunt will have enough responsibility with her own child and Benedetta's baby. The Bureau says they will revisit the situation in a few months, once the sickness dies down, after Nicco returns. In the meantime, the boys may be adopted. They said they will let us know what happens."

I didn't feel young. I felt old. Really, really old. "What about Tizi? She's not married, but she's old enough. All we have to do is find a place for her on Benedetta's illustration, the one that shows how we are all related."

"Tizi would not be a good choice. In many ways she is younger than you."

"The druggist doesn't seem to think so." He'd already been to visit. Several times. Tizi enjoyed his company and did pretty well at hiding that she'd been within steps of him for weeks. The druggist didn't remember Tizi, appeared to know nothing of the guaritrice. Nobody did.

Still, the old man looked worried, the lines of his face going deeper and more drawn down. "We shall see how that works out. I do not know how anything will go. Tizi has no papers. I have her birth certificate, but that does not prove much beyond that she is my child. I don't even know how Tizi arrived in this country."

"She arrived by boat, like the rest of us."

"So we all presume, but without an immigration record, Tizi may as well have arrived by broomstick. Or magic carpet." He drove a nail, then drove another. "Without records. Without proof the guaritrice emigrated with her from Italy to this country, as far as the authorities, as far as anybody who cares about paperwork, is concerned, Tizi does not exist."

I hadn't thought about that. "You knew this. You knew all of it. You knew the guaritrice was at the pharmacy. You knew Tizi was also. My mother was there. She would have told you."

The old man's face smoothed out at that last bit. "Your mother didn't tell me. Did she drink the guaritrice's tea?"

She had. I leaned toward him. "Then you didn't know. But you sent me to the pharmacy, said you were sending me because Carlo forgot to go."

"Carlo would forget his own name if we didn't keep using it to remind him."

"You're making up stories. Carlo didn't forget to go. Carlo was there. I ran into him. One door down from the pharmacy. You sent me instead of Carlo because you knew the guaritrice would be there. You sent me hoping someday, somehow, I'd return your daughter. I'll bet that's why you took me in that first night. You looked in my eyes. And you knew."

The old man waved an awl in my direction, pointing it at me like the nuns did when they were trying to make me hear more than their words. "I sent you to pick up my pills."

I threw my hands in the air. "So that's it? That's all the explanation I get?"

"Fine, signorina. Maybe I sent you because I planned to send Carlo, also. Because I wanted him to get a look at you. Because . . ." He clasped his hands together, then threw them wide. "Because even if you and Carlo are not the best fit, you may find you're perfectly suited to one another."

The old man wanted me to expand my expectations, consider alternatives I normally wouldn't. I felt old, wiser than I should have had to have felt, but I was still only sixteen years old, and I wasn't going to think about anything just because somebody wanted me to.

I tossed the letter from the Children's Bureau to the tabletop. "The guaritrice is gone. You tell me the curtain only possesses the power I give it." I stood, took a big breath of air, still moist and lazy, and far too heavy. "Yet the bubble persists."

The old man returned the awl to its proper place. "That, Fiora Vicente, is a mystery you alone can uncover."

Benedetta's baby made a tiny little sucking sound, halfway between a coo and a complaint. I adjusted the sling I'd fashioned from my scarf. I adjusted her bottle. "Go back to sleep, baby. Soon you'll be with your *zia*, with your cousin. Soon your poppa will be home."

I felt ridiculous talking to a baby like she were a grown person, but I didn't know what else to do. I felt more ridiculous talking to her with baby talk. And I wanted to talk to her. Wanted to look into her eyes, eyes quickly darkening to the color of Benedetta's, and tell Benedetta's baby all the worlds I'd imagined, the dreams I'd let go, the hopes that no longer seemed all that important.

Like typewriting school. "I was looking for something different from sewing, something interesting. Something . . . acceptable that my parents would agree to. Mostly I wanted something that wasn't something *here*. I wanted to see the real world." I waved my arm to show the baby what I meant. "The world beyond this neighborhood. I wanted to see the way life was." I dropped my arm back to my side. "Instead, I created this."

I touched the bubble's edge, not quite so tense as it had been, the border a little crinkly, dried out and tired. Like day-old bread. "I needed the old man. Needed him for meals, for shelter. I went to the guaritrice because nobody would hire me. The old man made me care for the Lattanzis, made me care for the boys. The guaritrice always offered me the easy way. To make money fast. To make the landlord suffer for being mean to me. To help you be born."

I looked to my side, kept my gaze to the cobbles, ashamed to confess what I needed and relieved Benedetta's baby couldn't understand any of it. "I used them both. The guaritrice *and* the old man. Tried to, anyway. People got hurt. The Lattanzis, the neighbors, the old man. Even your mother. And when things didn't work out, I blamed the Lattanzis. I blamed the neighbors. I blamed the old man. I blamed your mother. I even blamed that stupid curtain." I gave the baby a little bounce. "Yes, me, Fiora Vicente, Rosina Vicente's daughter. My life was not going the way I wanted, so I blamed a piece of fabric."

Mamma hadn't taught me how to use the curtain because she hadn't wanted to pass on that burden. She never meant that I should know. She hadn't wanted to chain me to any tradition other than the ones I chose to take on. Mamma had loved me. Had wanted the best for me. She'd wanted me to choose my own way. And I'd been too centered on myself to see.

I straightened my shoulders. "I have to accept. The old man has his daughter. Carlo's off pursuing his own ambitions." And I was alone. Uncertain. Afraid to move forward, unable to look back.

And due at the train station in less than an hour.

Misery, deeper than any well, threatened to swallow me whole.

I didn't want to go. I didn't want to do anything without Benedetta. I wanted to keep her baby. Not because I had any great desire to raise a baby, even hers. I wanted Benedetta's baby as a reminder. That Benedetta had lived, that she'd been my friend, that she'd trusted me and I her and we'd meant something to each other.

I wanted Fipo and Etti for the same reason. Because they represented a last link to Benedetta, to a short span of time when I'd belonged to somebody other than my family, been involved in something other than my own small concerns. When I gave up Benedetta's baby, the cord would be cut. I'd be the woman I'd always wanted. On my own, able to take care of myself. Needing no one.

And hating it.

Benedetta's baby began to fuss. I got my arms under her and hefted her to my chest, close to my heart. "The Lattanzis are dead, your mamma is gone, the boys have left, and soon you will follow. I tried to hold it all in, but life has moved on, and now the only thing collapsing under the weight of this stupid bubble is me."

The tears started. "I need to tell you something, something my mamma told me, something you won't understand this minute, but maybe someday will remember. Things have purpose, not people. People exist to be respected, to be enjoyed. Use things. Love people. You'll be all right."

I had nothing. No curtain. No money. No tuition for typewriting school. But like Signora Lattanzi's little silver box, the one that held the photo of the boys, all that was most important was in my arms. Benedetta's baby, and the knowledge I'd kept her safe for the day her father could take her in his.

I'd told myself I wanted to give people time. I made up plenty of stories why the bubble persisted. The curtain wouldn't release it; the guaritrice was making it worse; I didn't know how to collapse it, decided it was better that I didn't. I came up with one excuse then the other, hiding from the one thing I'd always least liked to face—the truth.

Carlo joined me, in cap and coat and stepping right to the bubble's edge like it wasn't there. He ran a finger over the baby's forehead. "You've been standing here for ten minutes, talking to yourself. I know because I've been standing there watching you." He pointed behind him, to a lamppost halfway up the block.

"I've been talking to the baby." I settled her back into the sling. "About things I knew I knew before I knew I knew it. But I was frightened, so I chose belief and called it truth. But really this is all so simple."

I moved my hands toward my middle, fingers splayed, like Benedetta did the first day I met her, the day she gathered the pieces. I meant to encompass Carlo in my gesture. I meant to encompass Benedetta's baby. I meant to encompass the old man and the Lattanzis,

Fipo and Etti, Mamma and Poppa, my brothers and even Tizi. I meant to encompass the selfish, the selfless, the wise, the foolish, the faithless, the trustworthy, the frightened, the brave. I meant to encompass every bit of every piece of everybody who'd helped bring me here, to the bubble's edge. Me, Fiora Vicente, Rosina Vicente's daughter, meant to encompass all who'd shared my journey.

So I could explain to Carlo what all that traveling had taught me, the one truth I'd carry with me from then until the end of my days. "I didn't understand. I can't stop the future. It's always arriving, this day, this hour, this minute, this moment, an unlimited currency we're free to spend any way we choose. The future is present. Right where we stand."

I gestured to our feet, wrapped in shoes mended by the old man, then I moved my hand back and forth between us.

"The future is here. For me. For you. A beautiful, an expanding, an infinite Now."

Thirty-one

The old man told me the curtain might take me down a path I did not want to tread. He didn't tell me the curtain was about truth, about making the owner, the bearer of the burden, face their own truths. Mamma faced hers when the guaritrice returned, when Mamma saw her and Tizi in the pharmacy, and saw Tizi grown up and doing for the guaritrice what Mamma used to do.

I faced my truth in those last moments at the bubble's edge, the last moments before I had to continue on and take Benedetta's baby to the train station: I didn't need Mamma's curtain, didn't need it at all. I didn't need it to save Tizi or Benedetta's baby, didn't need it to vanquish the guaritrice, didn't need it to show me the future, elucidate my path, or enlighten my present. Mamma's curtain was a piece of fabric, a special piece of fabric that drew its power from people, from all our wants and wishes, from the beliefs we proclaimed, and those we kept out of sight.

The curtain hadn't created that bubble, I did. And I couldn't collapse it because I didn't want to, because I didn't want to face the future. The curtain had accentuated every minute, every second. Its release might be uncontrolled. Overwhelming.

Then again, it might not. I'd never know, unless I moved forward. So I took a breath. I took a step.

And the whole thing dissolved.

No fireworks. No explosion. No marching bands or fanfares. The bubble deflated, going *pfft* like one of Benedetta's balls of risen dough, descending in a gray haze over our shoulders, then landing at our feet. It was shimmery, a rainbow of color. All I had to do was step outside to see.

Carlo scratched at his neck. "Not very exciting, signorina."

No. Not very. "Life isn't very exciting. Not when it's going pretty much the way it's supposed to."

"Not what you thought it would be."

I shook my head. "Not at all."

"You can still go to Atlantic City."

I could, but even that didn't seem all that interesting if I were going by myself. "What are you doing here?"

"I thought you'd like some company on the way to the train station."

"You thought you'd make sure I actually went."

"No. I knew you'd go. When you decide to do something, you do it. Benedetta's baby will be fine with her aunt. We will see her when Nicco returns." Carlo put out his hands, palms up. "It's just as well, two boys are plenty of work. I know, I was one myself."

The old man must have told him about the letter from the Children's Bureau. "You don't have to marry me, Carlo. Even for the boys. If Tizi marries the druggist, things may work out. I've still got goals to pursue, other ways I can be useful." I headed up the street, like I was going to pursue one of those goals that instant.

Carlo caught up. "You are wrong, signorina. I'm afraid I do have to marry you."

I didn't understand. Carlo knew that. He got ahead of me and walked backward. "You see, when Benedetta and Nicco came to live at the house, the Lattanzis gave them a letter that they should buy the house and take care of the boys should anything happen to them. They also left a second letter, in case circumstances changed for Benedetta and Nicco. That the house should go into a trust and I should have the option to make the purchase, put the money in escrow for the boys, and collect rents if needed. Now Benedetta is gone and Nicco wrote to me and said if I can figure out something better, I should." Carlo stood in front of me, made me stop walking. "So I've exercised the option."

"You've purchased the house." I put my hands on my hips. "You're the landlord, not the boys."

"Yes. But I cannot collect rent from the boys. I'd never think to collect rent from the don. Nicco won't be home for weeks, maybe months. And with Tizi living there also . . ." He slipped his cap off his head. "Please, signorina. You must marry me. Or I will have to pitch a tent in the don's garden. Every penny I have is in the house. I don't even have the money for oatmeal."

Well. No wonder the signora went on about Carlo having a clean tablecloth. Not because she thought I was questionable goods, because she wanted to make sure her house was cared for after she was gone. "You want to marry me for oatmeal."

"I want to marry you because you are beautiful, because you are outspoken, because you have ambitions. I want to marry you because you believe in magic, because we've already made a solemn oath, because we will never fail each other, because we will always be there to help, no matter what the other needs. We are mourning together, signorina, yes, but when times are good, we will also celebrate." He went down on one knee, clasped his hands before his heart. "Although, it might be better if I do the cooking. You aren't very good with a stove."

There were lots of things I didn't think I'd be any good with. Some of them were attached to Carlo. "Listen, I appreciate the offer, but, as you so kindly pointed out, I'm not like other girls." I started walking again.

He scrambled up. Caught up with me again. "Of course you are not like other girls. You are better, more than I could ever have hoped." He took hold of my arm, turned me to face him. "Why won't you give me a chance?"

"Have you forgotten? Because I don't like boys."

"That's all right, signorina. It's perfect. You don't like boys, but I do."

"You do what?"

"I like boys. A lot. Enough for both of us." He took my hand, and something warm and welcoming took hold of my heart. "Don Sebastiano is very wise. Where is there in this world for two people such as us? I love you, Fiora Vicente." He touched his head, then his chest. "Here. And here. Whether you marry me or not, we are family. A piece of paper won't change that. Just we'd have a lot easier time convincing the Children's Bureau if we looked like every other couple in the neighborhood."

I thought of Benedetta, how she'd reddened over the topic of sheets, of beds. "That's all fine for adoption, Carlo, but there's more to marriage than oatmeal."

"Plenty more. Wonderful and intimate. Look at you. Look at me. We have all the proper tools for this job. With a little tinkering we can make them work." He put his hand on my cheek. "Can't we give it a try?"

Try. "You mean, right now?"

"When else?" He imitated the movements I'd made earlier, moving his hands toward him, fingers splayed. "Didn't you just make a speech about how it's all infinite?"

And beautiful. And expanding. Unyielding and inexorable and kind of sloppy and definitely awkward with the baby in her sling between us. Also funny and sweet, him leaning in to me, and me reaching up to him. His face stubble was rough, his muscles hard, his angles sharp, and sinewy.

But it was a kiss. Our first.

I wiped at my mouth.

Carlo slid his cap back over his head. "We're going to have to work on that."

Three days later, Carlo and I were married. Two days after that, I was starting to regret it. Two days later, so was he. Four days after *that*, it felt a little more like fun. After two weeks, we stopped pretending like we weren't doing anything after the lights went out, and by the end of our first month, he was forgetting to wipe the mud from his shoes before tracking across my clean floor.

Good thing the boys arrived. Fipo rushed right upstairs. Then he rushed right back down. "Where's the don?"

"He's walking with his daughter. He'll be so happy to see you."

"He better hurry. Etti and me aren't here to move back. We're here to get our things."

The tall, thin lady from the Children's Bureau pulled me and Carlo aside. "He's been . . . difficult. Visit for a while. It may take some time for everybody to get reacquainted." She turned to Fipo. "I'll wait outside."

"You won't have to wait long. We don't have very much." Fipo pointed an accusing finger at Carlo. "Not even our house. Not anymore." He slammed the door after the lady.

Etti waved his hands. He mumbled a few words. Carlo went to stand beside him. "What are you doing, little man?"

"I'm vanquishing the lady from the Bureau." He tapped under his eye. "Like the signorina did with the guaritrice." He spread his arms wide and turned to me. "You fixed everything. The air feels good. Everybody can breathe again."

Fipo came out of his room, clothes bundled under his arm. "She didn't fix anything. And she's not a signorina. She's a signora. I'll bet she still can't make hotcakes."

"She doesn't have to. I can." Carlo put out a hand to Etti. "Why don't we make some together? Fipo and Signora Lelii need to talk."

Signora Lelii. After sixteen years as Fiora Vicente, Signora Lelii sounded strange, foreign. Dropped on me the way the house dropped on the Wicked Witch of the West's evil sister.

Fipo shoved an envelope at me. "For you. From Mamma. She left it under my mattress."

The envelope was thick, bulky. My name was on the front, written in Signora Lattanzi's flowing script. I opened it. A pile of bills fell out. Money bills. More than I'd seen together ever up until then.

The envelope couldn't have been left under Fipo's mattress. Or Etti's. I'd turned them and turned them again, anticipating the day they would return. "Fipo. What is this?"

"There's a letter. Read it."

Dear Fiora,

Enclosed please find what I think is fair for all your excellent mending. We all have dreams. May you find yours. Until then, I leave mine with you and Carlo.

Thank you.

That was it. No remonstrations, no criticisms, no reminders of everything I hadn't gotten correct. Just a thank-you, and, from the thickness of the wad, more money for mending than I could have earned in a year, much less a month.

"Mamma said you could use it for typewriting school." Fipo looked out the window into the street. "And maybe use the leftover to take care of us. If you wanted."

I followed where he looked. The Children's Bureau lady waited on the sidewalk.

Etti poked his head out the door to the Lattanzis' apartment. "Carlo wants to know if we should make tea."

Yes, it was still the Lattanzis' door. I cooked at the Lattanzis' stove, and ate at the Lattanzis' table. Carlo set up his business in the Lattanzis' shop, and he and I made love in the Lattanzis' bed. I did change out the sheets for the ones I'd used in the old man's attic. And I moved all the Lattanzis' things to the boys' room. I was pretty sure what Carlo and I did was the same as every couple did; still, I didn't like the idea of the Lattanzis' spirits lingering to see what we were up to.

But, tea. I didn't remember any tea.

I went to check, my heart sinking to see the familiar bag, smell the familiar scent. Cinnamon and cloves. Like Benedetta's coffee.

I got woozy, my stomach got churny, my nerves caught fire. "Etti, where did your mamma get this?"

"The lady at the drugstore gave it to her. Signora Bruni liked it, too."

Because Signora Lattanzi told her the spice blend would help the baby grow. I had to sit down. I had to put my head between my knees and sob with relief.

I hadn't spread the sickness to Signora Lattanzi. I hadn't condemned

Benedetta when I took her out of the bubble. The guaritrice poisoned them. She gave her flavorings to Signora Lattanzi, who gave some to Benedetta, who mixed it with her coffee and gave her coffee to me. I didn't get sick because I was resistant. But they weren't. The signora was already sick. Benedetta already infected. Whether the bubble stayed, or went, Benedetta was doomed. Because she already had the sickness. Because the sickness was hard on pregnant women, because, because . . .

I didn't sit in the chair. I didn't put my head between my knees. I didn't cry, I didn't wail, I didn't carry on. I didn't even think all of that. Not all laid out like I've just said. I thought all of that later. At the time, I couldn't make a scene because Etti was smiling at me, and Fipo was watching, and Carlo was flipping hotcakes that were starting to smell like strawberries.

So I acted like everything was fine and I threw the tea into the dustbin. "This is stale. I'll find us some fresh in the market later."

Then I opened the envelope, the one with all the money. I made a big show of counting it. "You know, Fipo, there's enough here for ten typewriting schools, and classes don't begin for weeks. Plus, you and Etti are still so little, I doubt either of you can eat enough to make a difference. I'll put this money away, and when the time is right, Carlo and I will put it to good use for you."

Fipo didn't look like he believed me. "Can I learn to fly an airplane?"

The question made me uncomfortable, uncertain. Made me think of smoke and flame, exhilaration and regret. I thought of the day Fipo flew his toy airplane into my rising dough. I remembered the sensation of acceptance, that control was an illusion.

Whatever happened to Fipo wasn't up to me. And I had no right to decide his dreams for him. I slipped the envelope into my apron pocket. "You can learn to fly an airplane, if that is where your heart lies. You can learn anything you want."

The hotcakes were ready. It seemed rude to leave the Children's Bureau lady standing on the sidewalk, so I opened the door to invite her to join us. She wasn't there.

I stepped out on the stoop, rubbing my arms against the December cold. I looked up the street. I looked down.

She wasn't there. She definitely wasn't there.

Etti tugged on my skirt. "I told you. I vanquished her."

"Etti, do you even know what *vanquished* means?"

Fipo answered. "It means we get to live with you. The lady told us if we couldn't find her, that meant we were definitely home and we could stay here forever." He put his hand in mine. "Come on. I'm hungry."

Thirty-Two

Nicco never returned to live in his and Benedetta's cozy little apartment. He returned to pack up her things and to thank the don for caring for her while he was in the war. I offered my help, but he seemed more comfortable with Carlo. I kept Benedetta's illustration, the one where she'd noted all our pretend relations. I put it in a frame and hung it on the wall. Nicco didn't know about it, so I didn't think he'd mind. A few months later, he sent a letter. Benedetta's baby was growing well; they were settled with the aunt in Coatesville. He enclosed a photo of the baby, along with others he'd found when he finally developed the film on the Brownie.

Fipo, and Etti, and the photograph of the Three Musketeers, together in Benedetta's kitchen, our hands clasped joyously over our heads.

I never heard from him again.

Signora Lattanzi once told me to make myself useful and everything would work out. I passed plenty of sunrises in what remained of Benedetta's kitchen questioning her assertion.

Carlo didn't like it. One morning he found me there, espresso brewed, expression somber. He placed my cup on the table, then ran a finger over the shelf where Benedetta had kept her Brownie. "This room is too empty. We should stay here. This baby is coming and the boys are growing like trumpet vines. I'm tired of stuffing my mouth with sheets so I don't pervert their tender years."

Live there. "Shouldn't we rent it out? What will we do with the Lattanzis' bedroom?"

"We can put the boys there. If this baby's a boy, he can join them when he's old enough to be scarred by our behavior."

For a boy who liked boys, Carlo sure had adjusted.

I ran a palm along Benedetta's rolling pin. So had I. "Why are you always so happy?"

"Because life is easier that way." Carlo leaned against the jamb. "The past is a road that never changes course, Fiora Vicente. Don't mire yourself there."

No. Of course not. "If we move the boys to their parents' room, what do we do with the boys' room?"

"I thought you might like it for yourself. A place to work at your typewriting. Plenty of people in the neighborhood need letters done. Letters in English that look professional. And letters in Italian for business there. You can use your skills and who knows what other ambitions you may realize." He put out a finger and lifted my chin. "And on the days you want to take the trolley into center city . . . well, there's a stop right outside in the market. I know it's not the same as working in an office, but you also have my love, as well as my encouragement. Maybe it will be enough."

Carlo was right. His love and his encouragement were enough, enough to get me through the first throes of motherhood, enough to welcome our son two years after that. They were enough to get me through nurse's training, enough to help me open an office beside Carlo's shoe business, stitching and bandaging and doing the things the doctor was too busy, and too expensive, to treat. Carlo's love and encouragement were even enough to get us through the old man's final illness, and enough to get us through Carlo's own.

An ailment of the heart the doctor told us. Just like the old man.

I still find that ironic.

The day after I returned Benedetta's baby, the day after Carlo decided we were the perfect match, the day after I dissolved the bubble, two things happened.

First, Mamma's Big Ben *tick-tick-ticked* its way back to match the time and rhythm of the old man's. Since then and ever after, no matter when or how much I wind them, the Big Bens *tick-tick-tick* in sync.

Second, and more important, the sickness dropped away. Profoundly and without explanation. Health officials reported it had "run its course."

The school year restarted, public venues opened for business. War news, never far from the front pages, again became our sole concern. The influenza retreated, memory of our attempts to control it lost among the clamor of propaganda and the clash of spears. But in the dark places where the ancient things grow, superstition lingers, waiting the chance to spring forth, searching the spark to bring it life, and seeking any transport to further its survival.

That knowledge weighed on me.

Tizi married the druggist. She had five children. She kept the curtain until the old man died, then kept it in the two years after. She returned it to me a week after I lost Carlo.

"I thought you might like this to, you know . . . look back." She looked uncomfortable, already large with her sixth. She lay a hand over her belly, eyes downcast, shy, I suppose, to be suggesting how I should manage my grief. "I mean, if that's what you want to do. But I don't think you need the curtain to remember Carlo. I don't think you ever needed the curtain. I think you could have done all you did with any piece of fabric over any window. I think you could have done it without the fabric, just looked out the window, closed your eyes, and imagined. I think everything you ever needed is inside you, Fiora Vicente. So I think you're going to do fine without Carlo. And I think wherever he is, Carlo thinks so, too."

Maybe she was right, also. Her father certainly had been. Despite the old man's protests, despite his claims he was no more magical than me, he understood plenty, even if he wasn't always aware. He knew the curtain would lead me down a path I hadn't expected, and he did his best to teach me to respect the road. But the old man was gone. I was no longer a child. My further path was up to me.

I dried my tears, rolled up the curtain, placed it in the old man's wooden chest, and again returned to college. To finish my undergraduate degree, then on to medical school. Because I knew what I knew before I knew it.

The influenza was a sickness unlike any we might have expected, a virus in a world that still didn't know they existed. Atypical and very much like the bubble, the flu triggered our beautiful immune systems to overreact, caused a response so concentrated, our defenses turned rogue.

We killed ourselves. Our young and our vibrant. Our best and our brightest. In a world on a hair trigger, was it any surprise *this* was the flu we birthed?

How much we learned, how little we understood. Epidemiology was a new specialty in those days, and of the few women who studied medicine, fewer still chose it for further study. But I was determined, driven, dedicated to vanquishing the guaritrice's children.

The day I graduated, I pulled the curtain out of mothballs, the temptation to see Carlo again, too strong. I could observe, not interact. Remember, not change. The past is fixed, my sojourns limited. A smile, a nod, a wave of the hand. Scraps of life, like those my children's grandchildren send in ten-second snippets on their fancy phones, but silent scraps, except for the slap slap slap of the reel sprocketing at its end. "The past is a road which never changes course."

I didn't want to mire there. I closed the flap, kissed the place on the wall where his beautiful lips said those words, and left Carlo to his well-deserved peace.

Mamma's curtain stayed out of mothballs for a long time after, but I never used it to go back, and rarely to go forward. Instead, I used it much as I had the day the old man collapsed beside the lamppost, not to stagnate time, but to slow it, to give myself the luxury of enjoying some moments a little longer than others.

A day at the beach. The birth of a grandchild. Fipo's graduation. The day Etti got married. My daughter's acceptance into the University of Pennsylvania, Fipo's into flight school. The day he took me for my first ride in an airplane. And his last visit before shipping out to Europe.

Moments illuminated by love. And if some of those moments were stretched into days or even weeks, can I be blamed? It helped carry me through the sadder times, the moments upside-down and reversed. The day my son lost his first child. The day Tizi lost her last. The day we received notice we'd lost Fipo in a mission over Germany.

There is no room for hell in hope. My daughter left me last year, following on her brother the year before. It doesn't matter they were grandparents and great-grandparents. Doesn't matter they lived long and full lives, achieved more than most, and were for the most part, happy. Their loss is the final and worst grief I've had to bear. The final test.

I am old, my work is ongoing, my research continues, but I long ago passed the baton to a younger generation, brighter, better educated, more inspired than me. They don't need Mamma's curtain. It was the proper tool for the proper time, but its greatest power lay in its ability to remember, and the newer generations are making discoveries which make Mamma's curtain quaint.

Etti's great-grandson tells me all times happen at once, the past, the present, and the future. That somewhere on that continuum exists each moment, perfect and whole. He has his doctorate; he has a second. Universities give him grants; government people come to talk to him.

Because Etti's great-grandson is an explorer. He's building a device. A device with an aperture no greater than a pinhole. An aperture he'll be able to focus on any moment of his choosing, guided by the power of deep mathematics.

He tells me the applications are limitless. The ability to examine molecules, and history, and maybe get a glimpse of what is beyond our imaginings. Etti's great-grandson, with his deep, strong voice, his eyes the color of licorice, and the resolute determination of Great-Granduncle Fipo, is building a curtain for a new millennium. A curtain based on science.

I still have the Big Bens, tick-tick-ticking together in tandem. I'm the only one who winds them, the only one who uses them when I want to know the time. Everybody else checks their phone. The Big

Bens are slowing, sometimes in leaps, sometimes in the tiniest of hops, but the phenomena is inexorable, the process inevitable, the end in sight. I'm not scared. The old man once told me time finds a new path after a great upheaval. Once Mamma's clock stops here, it will start again in another place. And I'll be with it.

Not everything found can be kept. Not everything saved will remain. We can't decide who we'll lose, nor who we'll keep. What moments will stretch into a lifetime and which will be gone in a breath.

The infinite Now is limitless, it is unyielding. And it is not to be wasted.

I think Etti's great-grandson understands. I leave this life comforted in the hope maybe someday, someone will look through that pinhole and focus on finding a magical time, a wondrous time, a time of small victories and great defeats, of practical impossibilities and impossible practicalities. A time of hope, of despair, filled with the wise, the foolish, and everybody in between.

I hope their focus spirals into the kitchen on the second floor of a building on Ninth Street in Philadelphia. A building long ago torn down, then rebuilt, and built again. I hope they focus on a particular table, set with bean soup and biscotti, where a young man and two girls talk about laundry and scrubbing and how best to clean snot. One for all and all for one as they discuss opening a shoe repair shop, or a restaurant, or going to typewriting school.

And telling stories. Of yesterday and today, tomorrow and beyond. Stories not of if, but when, not how, but why. Stories of the heart, the soul, recounted in the mix of English and Italian common among people of that age at that time.

A trio of friends—the Three Musketeers—young and happy and alive in a world doing its damndest to kill itself and everyone in it.

A time formed in a shaft of light, then cast in darkness. A single moment. Enshrined forever.

Carlo.

Benedetta.

And me.

Historic Notes:

Originally and incorrectly referred to as the Spanish Flu, epidemi-
ologists have put forth several theories as to where the Influenza of
1918-1919 originated. I found the idea that the flu may have originated
on a hog farm in Haskell County, Kansas most intriguing, a home-
grown disease exported to Europe because of America's entrance and
involvement in the World War, then returned to us at the end of our
involvement, like some kind of awful parting gift.

What experts do not dispute is the devastation wrought by the
disease—approximately one-third of the population infected, and
mortality estimated between twenty and fifty million, two to three
percent of the world's population at the time. The Influenza of 1918-
1919 killed more in a few months than the war killed during the
entirety of its brutal and bloody four years, yet the pandemic was so
overshadowed by the war it is sometimes referred to as the "forgotten
pandemic".

Typical influenza targets those with weak immune systems, the
very young and the very old. The virus responsible for the Influenza
of 1918-1919 caused an overwhelming immune response, turning
the body's defenses on itself, and thus proved deadliest to those with
the strongest immune systems, people in the prime of their lives, the
young and the healthy, an ironic footnote during a war which was
already hard at work decimating that same population.

Of American cities, Philadelphia was particularly hard hit, perhaps
because the city fathers refused to cancel the Liberty Loan Parade,

despite recommendations to the contrary by health officials. The parade went forward as scheduled on September 28, 1918. The incidence of influenza in the city exploded several days after. The disease burned through the population in an October scourge, then dropped off suddenly, all but gone by the armistice of November 11.

The passage Fiora reads to the boys is from Frank L. Baum's children's classic, *The Wonderful Wizard of Oz*.

Acknowledgments

Holed up with a laptop and an idea, a writer's life can be lonely but for the voices in her head. I'd like to give a shout-out to those who broke through with critique and encouragement, good cheer, and a smack upside the head when warranted. Sharon, Kelly, K.C., Jenn, Sandra, Crystal, Morgan, Brooke, Lauren, Julie. An enormous shout out to Lisa Miller for her regularly offered and excellent Story Structure Safaris and Expeditions. Without Lisa's amazing course, *The Infinite Now* might still be a cluster of ill-formed ideas ping-ponging between my temples.

Last, but always first, my love and gratitude to my children and my husband, my never-ending wells of inspiration.

Book Club Questions

1. The old man claimed "Belief is powerful." The young shoemaker declared, "Belief is a house for which the mind provides the mortar." How real was the bubble to the various characters? Did it ever exist, or was it a manufacture of Fiora's mind?

2. In a world without internet, without television, almost without radio, the primary source of news for most people was word of mouth, letters, and newspapers. In the United States, newspapers were loosely controlled by the government-run Committee on Public Information which encouraged all media outlets to a voluntary censorship, a censorship which included keeping all news and attitudes which did not promote the war effort in the sidelines. How might the incidence of the Influenza of 1918 been curtailed by free and well-disbursed public health information? Might that advantage be offset by the rapid pace of travel in today's world?

3. What drove Fiora? Love or loneliness? At the story's end, Fiora is a wise and well-lived woman of great age, but how might her life have been different were she born today, instead of a hundred and fifteen years earlier?

4. In Fiora's world, the curtain was as magical as she cared to make it. What items do we depend on today that might serve somebody like Fiora in the same way?

5. Discuss the symbols and tropes of *The Infinite Now*, those items drawn from the various myths and fairytales touched on in the story, as well as the old world superstitions. How were they used to deepen the narrative?

6. Be the author. If you could change aspects of the story, create different endings, what would you change, and why?

About the Author

© Ian Cassell

Raised by traditional people in a modern world, Mindy Tarquini is a second-generation Italian American who grew up believing that dreams are prophecy, the devil steals lost objects, and an awkward glance can invite the evil eye. She is an assistant editor with the *Lascaux Review* and a member of the Perley Station Writers' Colony, as well as the author of the novel *Hindsight*. A native Philadelphian, Ms. Tarquini resides in Phoenix with her husband. She loves writing heroines with special powers. Alas, she has none herself.

Mindy loves the Internet. Check out her website at www.MindyTarquini.com and stop by her Facebook page at www.facebook.com/MindyTarquiniAuthor.

SELECTED TITLES FROM SPARKPRESS

SparkPress is an independent boutique publisher delivering high-quality, entertaining, and engaging content that enhances readers' lives, with a special focus on female-driven work. Visit us at www.gosparkpress.com

Ocean's Fire, Stacey Tucker
$16.95, 978-1-943006-28-1

Once the Greeks forced their male gods upon the world, the belief in the power of women was severed. For centuries it has been thought that the wisdom of the high priestesses perished at the hand of the patriarchs—but now the ancient Book of Sophia has surfaced. Its pages contain the truths hidden by history, and the sacred knowledge for the coming age. And it is looking for Skylar Southmartin.

The House of Bradbury, Nicole Meier
$17, 978-1-940716-38-1

After Mia Gladwell's debut novel bombs and her fiancé jumps ship, she purchases the estate of iconic author Ray Bradbury, hoping it will inspire her best work yet. But between mysterious sketches that show up on her door and taking in a pill-popping starlet as a tenant—a favor to her needy ex—life in the Bradbury house is not what she imagined.

The Undertaking of Tess, Lesley Kagen
$15, 978-1-94071-665-7

A heartbreaking, funny, nostalgic, and spiritually uplifting story, you'll cheer on two adorable sisters from the first page to the last of this charming novella that sets the stage for the accompanying novel, *The Resurrection of Tess Blessing*.

Hindsight, Mindy Tarquini
$16.95, 978-1943006014

A thirty-three-year-old Chaucer professor who remembers all her past lives is desperate to change her future—because if she doesn't, she will never live the life of her dreams.

About SparkPress

SparkPress is an independent, hybrid imprint focused on merging the best of the traditional publishing model with new and innovative strategies. We deliver high-quality, entertaining, and engaging content that enhances readers' lives. We are proud to bring to market a list of *New York Times* best-selling, award-winning, and debut authors who represent a wide array of genres, as well as our established, industry-wide reputation for creative, results-driven success in working with authors. SparkPress, a BookSparks imprint, is a division of SparkPoint Studio LLC.

Learn more at GoSparkPress.com